YELLOW WIFE

A NOVEL

SADEQA JOHNSON

Simon & Schuster

New York   London   Toronto   Sydney   New Delhi

Simon & Schuster, Inc.
1230 Avenue of the Americas
New York, NY 10020

Digital recreation of Robert Lumpkin's Compound (Jail, Residence, Hotel, and Kitchen) by Burchell F. Pinnock, FAIA, Baskervill.

First Simon & Schuster hardcover edition January 2021

SIMON & SCHUSTER and colophon are registered trademarks of Simon & Schuster, Inc.

For information about special discounts for bulk purchases, please contact Simon & Schuster Special Sales at 1-866-506-1949 or business@simonandschuster.com.

The Simon & Schuster Speakers Bureau can bring authors to your live event. For more information or to book an event, contact the Simon & Schuster Speakers Bureau at 1-866-248-3049 or visit our website at www.simonspeakers.com.

Interior design by Carly Loman

Manufactured in the United States of America

10 9 8 7 6 5 4 3 2 1

Library of Congress Cataloging-in-Publication Data is available.

ISBN 978-1-9821-4910-9
ISBN 978-1-9821-4912-3 (ebook)

For my beloved children, Miles, Zora, and Lena Johnson.
To know where you are going,
you must understand from whence we came.

To my husband, Glenn, you are my wind.

You may choose to look the other way,
but you can never say again that you didn't know

—*William Wilberforce*

PART ONE

Bell Plantation, Charles City, Virginia, 1850

———— ◆ ————

CHAPTER 1

The Bell Plantation

*M*ama believed that the full moon was the most fertile night of the month, and that everything she touched held God's power. Each full moon, she dragged me out in the middle of the night with her to hunt for roots, plants, seedlings, and rare blossoms to use for healing. I did not understand why God's power could not be found during daylight hours, and as I trudged behind her the March cold overwhelmed me. Even my thick wool shawl was no match against the country freeze.

Fear of the woods made my feet clumsy, and I tripped over fallen sticks, scratched my shins on the spiky brush, and bumped my head on low-hanging branches. Mama, on the other hand, moved with skill and confidence, like the earth parted a path and presented the way for her. Even in the dark, she knew where to stop for herbs and how to avoid the dangerous ones. We had only a small lantern to guide us, and when I asked how she knew where things grew she responded, "My gut be my light."

We slipped through the thicket, past the drafty cabins where the field hands slept on pallets stuffed with hay and husk. I heard dry coughs and a low whine from a hungry baby. Farther down toward the James River, we traveled through the clearing where we met on Sundays for church. Then over the hill along the side of the cemetery, peppered with sticks to honor our dead. As we traveled deeper into the woods of the plantation, the thick forest blocked the light of the moon. I could hear the growls and grunts of unseen animals, and fretted over running into hungry raccoons or red foxes, or stepping on a poisonous snake. I tried to clear the worry from my mind as the land flattened out, but then something pricked my ankle. Before I could call out, Mama stopped suddenly and reached for my hand.

"This here is a black walnut tree. Grow deep in the woods, so you gotta know where to look. Cure for most everything. Ever unsure, come seek this tree."

Mama handed me the lantern, then pulled a blade from her satchel and severed a piece of bark. She brought it to her nose, then ran her tongue along the inside of it.

"Husk stain anything it touch. After we make a tea for Rachel, rest we use to dye those sheets for the nursery. Just hoping we ain't too late to save that girl."

Mama reached into her bag and pulled out a red ribbon. "Go on and mark it, so be easy to find when you come without me."

I reached up and tied the ribbon on a skinny twig, knowing I had no intention of roaming these woods without my mama.

◆

We stopped at the sick house on our way back home. That morning, Rachel, the house servant, had been moved from the big house to the sickroom on account of her high fever. Even though Master Jacob's wife, Missus Delphina, knew Mama worked plants better than anybody, she refused to bring her up to the house to tend to Rachel when she got fevered with lockjaw. Rachel grew up on Missus Delphina's family's plantation, and came with her to Master Jacob's as a wedding gift from her mother. Since Missus Delphina looked down on Mama's medicine, she called in a white doctor for Rachel, which Mama said was a waste of good money. "He ain't know nothin' 'bout doctoring no field hands."

And Mama was right. Now that the white medicine had failed, Missus Delphina had no choice but to moved Rachel to the sick house. When we entered the room, even I could look at Rachel's pale body and see death coming for her.

"You ready the hot water?" Mama asked the sick nurse, who nodded her head and pointed to the boiling pot. Mama reached into her sack and pulled out the bark and leaves from the black walnut tree. Then she pinched off a sprig of snakeroot and crushed up the stems.

"Let it steep for 'bout an hour. Then make her sip every time she open her eyes. If she make it through the night, there be hope."

Mama removed a few balms and poultices from her medicine satchel for the other patients, then gently pressed Rachel's forehead with the palm of her hand and whispered, "Lawd, look on Rachel with eyes of mercy. Restore her to wholeness and strength. Thy will be done."

◆

Few hours later, Mama and I were snuggled in our cottony bed, draped in heavy linens, when we were awakened by the ringing of the plantation bell.

"Oh, Lawd, what is it now?" Mama kept her eyes on me.

There was cause for each chime of the bell, and on that morning the bell rang twice. Two rings meant that Master Jacob wanted to see us for an announcement on the side of the big house.

I burrowed deeper into the blankets and mumbled, "Hope it is not Rachel."

Mama's face went slack. "Come, Delores. Needin' to move directly." She always called me by my middle name. Her way of claiming me as her own, I guess.

The fire had died out in the middle of the night, so the cold bled right through my woolen socks as soon as they hit the floor. Mama tied the back of her skirt while slipping into her leather shoes. Even in haste, she did not leave the house without oiling her molasses-colored skin with palm oil and pinning her thick hair just right. I fumbled around in the covers but could not produce my headscarf. Mama cut her eyes up at me as she descended the ladder, so I moved on without it.

I followed, barely awake in the predawn cold, up the bluff to the big house. Even at first light, I could smell onions, garlic, and butter wafting up from the kitchen house. Mama strode several paces in front of me, and I almost tripped over my own feet trying to catch her.

A rustling of leaves sprang from the woods, and then out of the thicket came a long procession of scantily dressed field hands. Mothers had babies tied to their backs, old people leaned on makeshift canes, and strong men carried little children on their shoulders. I fell in step with Mama as we rounded the side of the house, hoping to catch sight of Essex coming out the stables. Just a glance from him could change up my whole day. As I scanned the crowd, Mama squeezed my hand and pulled me on up front where we, as seamstresses, belonged. Aunt Hope, the plantation cook, stood nearest to the steps, and next to her was Lovie, the keeper of the house. Next to Lovie was Parrott: butler, driver, and manservant to Master Jacob. Women and children of the fields stood behind them. The men always had to stand farthest back from the house. Snitch, the plantation overseer, stood to the side of us with a cowhide whip around his neck, and his bloodshot eyes watching all of us.

When I got still, a warm breath broke across the back of my neck. Only Essex would be so bold, and I reached my left hand back and grazed his fingertips. It had been days since we touched, and I pulled away quickly as little shock waves surged across my belly.

Missus Delphina appeared on the side porch with a black scarf draped over her shoulders. Before I could wonder after Master Jacob, he came through the door wearing a flared frock coat with a high stand-up collar. He drew himself up to his full six-foot height, and the sun caught the honey streaks in his eyes as he looked down on us. I watched his Adam's apple bob around in his neck as he spoke; a habit that helped me avoid looking him in the eye when other people were around.

"It pains me to announce that our sweet servant, Rachel, has gone to be with her maker. May she rest in peace."

Missus Delphina leaned into his solid mass as if he was a pillar, and without his strength she would faint. The crowd gasped and a few called on Jesus, but Mama just sucked air through her two front teeth. Not loud, but I heard, and knew that it meant Missus was a fool for not calling on her sooner.

"Keep us in your prayers as you return to work."

Sounds of compliance stirred through the crowd, as the field hands started back down the hill, taking with them the smell of wet soil and manure. Master grabbed two women and instructed them to take care of Rachel's body. Then he looked over at me.

"Pheby. Need you up at the house now that Rachel is gone."

"Pheby?" Missus Delphina smacked her lips like she had been fed something sour. "I have her sewing sheets for the nursery. She fares better in the loom house."

"The girl knows her way around and can fill in just fine." Master Jacob pulled her close, smothering away any fight.

I looked down at my feet. On the few occasions I'd helped in the big house the strenuous work had been taxing enough. Now, to be holed up with Missus Delphina while she mourned her dearest Rachel would be like having a noose around my neck. My head started to throb as I climbed the steps, then from the corner of my eye I found Essex brazenly staring at me.

He was leaning against the silver birch tree, a piece of straw hanging from the side of his mouth. He brushed his nose twice, which was code for *Meet me in the stables after dark*. I scratched my ear as an answer—*I will try*—then put an extra drop in my hips as I pushed open the side door of the house. The entrance led into a small prep area just before the dining room. I started hatching a plan on how to get out tonight without anyone asking too many questions when, out of nowhere, a heavy slap landed across my face. My sight went blurry. When I refocused, Missus Delphina flared her nostrils at me.

"Do not come in here running amok. You better take heed or you will find yourself in the fields."

"Yes, Missus." It took full concentration not to touch the spot she had slapped. I refused to give her the satisfaction of knowing how much she had hurt me.

"And where is your scarf? Think you too pretty to tie up that hair?" She flicked my pinned-up hair and knocked it free. Waves of soft spirals flowed down past my shoulders. Missus eyed me like she wanted to slap me again, and I hurried to twirl my hair back up and tuck it away.

Her mouth turned down and rested in her perpetual frown. Missus Delphina was more handsome than pretty—a box-shaped woman with big, broad shoulders and startling green eyes that could cut through skin. She tended to favor the color brown, though it made her look much older than her twenty-four years. I thought she would look prettier in a shade of peach or plum.

"Lovie," she called to the woman who was in charge up at the house, "see that this girl looks proper and get her started cleaning the bedrooms."

"Yes, Missus." Lovie curtseyed, and I forced my knees to do the same.

The back stairs were hidden behind the dining room, which made it easy for the house servants to move around undetected. The steps were narrow and steep, but Lovie moved up them fast and certain. Out in the hallway, the upstairs rooms were strung together in the shape of a horseshoe. At the lip of the formal stairs hung a portrait of Master's sister, Miss Sally. She had been my teacher before she died two years ago, and adored me as much as my own mama. I stopped and stared at her thin fingers resting calmly on her lap, remembering how graceful they were on the piano. Her doe eyes fell kindly on me. My swollen cheek burned as I traced the gold frame with my fingertips.

The portrait used to hang in the parlor, until Missus Delphina arrived and had it moved up here. She also ordered Miss Sally's clothing, favorite curtains, tea set, and anything else that belonged to her packed in boxes and donated to a church on the edge of town. Once Master Jacob became wise to his wife cleaning house, he prohibited her from removing his sister's book collection and piano from the parlor. Then, while he and Missus attended the white church on Sunday, he had four of the field hands bring Miss Sally's bed over to the loom house for me and Mama.

"Pheby." Lovie snapped her fingers, beckoning me out of my head, and into Missus's chambers. The bedroom had a musky smell, like Missus had sprayed too many potions and fragrances. Lovie drew back the heavy, rose-embellished curtains and pushed open the window. The fresh air made it easier to breathe.

"Needin' a thorough clean. Been let go since Rachel down."

Lovie moved next to me, grasped my chin, and tilted it up. Her eyes were deep-set and gentle. She had a heart-shaped face, and skin rich as coffee.

"Problem with being high yella. That handprint gonna be on your face all day long. I try to slip you some ice."

She smoothed the loose strands of my hair back into my ponytail and then covered my head with a dull, itchy scarf.

"Be in Massa's room if you needin' me," Lovie called over her shoulder, then closed the door.

Missus Delphina's room was as large as the loft in the loom house that I shared with Mama. High ceilings and wide-plank floors. Adjacent to the bed sat a rosewood vanity, and I ran my hands over the floral carvings around the mirror. I listened for footsteps in the hallway and then let myself down on the matching stool. The mirror confirmed Lovie's prediction. I had three fingerprints marking my cheekbone. Mama would be beside herself.

Before I thought it through, I undid the rag on my head, unraveled my hair, and absentmindedly picked up Missus Delphina's brush. I glided the strong bristles across my scalp and down to the end of my curls. Missus's brush worked much better than the wire comb Mama and I used. With a little rouge and a proper gown, I could fit in like a member of the family.

I remembered the time Miss Sally had taken me with her on a carriage ride to Williamsburg. She and Mama fawned over my dress and hair until I did not recognize myself in the looking glass. When we arrived at the first shop, the shoemaker referred to me as Miss Sally's beautiful daughter, and she did not correct him. Nor did she right the seamstress at the dress shop, or the woman who served us tea. The memory made me smile, as I missed my teacher dearly.

The sound of the bedroom door scraping the floor sent me scrambling to my feet so fast I knocked the silver-plated box filled with hairpins to the floor.

"You thick in the mind?" Lovie hissed at me. "What if I's the missus?"

"Sorry," I fumbled.

"At seventeen, I expects more from you, Pheby."

"Just lost my head."

"Finish in here, and no more foolishness." She disappeared back down the hall.

Having idled long enough, I retied my hair and figured it would be best to start with sweeping the ashes from the fireplace and work my way around from there. Then I picked up the broomstick and beat the mattress and pillows until I was satisfied that there were no dust mites or bugs hiding out. Missus kept a porcelain pitcher on a washstand in the back corner, which she used to freshen up between weekly baths. I slushed it clean and hung fresh white towels on the side rail for her convenience. My least favorite chore was emptying her chamber pot. Then there was the task of Missus's closet. Even though we did not have much company, she still changed three or four times a day, and a pile of discarded dresses both dirty and clean had accumulated on the chaise. I was holding her evening dress on a hanger when Lovie cracked the door and handed me a kerchief containing a block of ice. "When you through in here, Aunt Hope needin' you to help serve supper."

◆

The dining table was long enough to seat twelve. Master Jacob sat at one end and Missus Delphina the other. They were so far from each other that they had to speak up so that the other could hear what was being said. When Mama and I ate, we sat right next to each other with our elbows touching.

I spooned mutton stew into each of their bowls, served slices of cornbread, and then retreated from their line of sight. Kept my back close to the wall without touching it, my white-gloved hands folded in front of me, and pretended not to listen. Mama always said the way to keep peace with white folks was to be available and invisible at the same time.

Master ate with pleasure while Missus idly moved her spoon around the bowl.

"Delphina, you must eat something. Need to keep up your strength."

"What is the point? I lose everything that I love."

"We are expecting a new life. Doctor Wilks assured me that this time will be different." He picked up his wine and drank. "To God be the glory."

Missus lifted the spoon to her mouth.

"I am heading down to Charleston in a week's time."

Her spoon clanked against the bowl. "You went to Richmond not four weeks ago. Do you have to leave again so soon? And me in my condition?"

"Trading is picking up. Getting so people only want wheat from our farm. Bell wheat they calling it. Many deals to be made."

"So soon after losing my Rachel? Who am I going to get to replace her in the house? And who is going to run the business?" she gripped the table.

"Pheby is capable. And overseer Snitch knows this place almost better than I."

"Pheby is dim-witted," she spat, like I was not standing there.

"I do not think you have given her a chance. Sally taught Pheby a lot."

"Your sister spoiled that girl rotten. Got her thinking that she is better than a slave. For once, I wish you would take my side," she pouted.

"I am always on your side."

Missus removed her napkin, dabbing roughly at her mouth.

"Going to stop by your parents' farm along the way. Anything you want me to deliver them besides the good news?"

She frowned. "Me, Jacob. I cannot stand to be here alone again. I declare, these darkies are trying to craze me."

"Oh," he said sweetly, "you are with child, dear, and need your rest."

"I need to be around someone I can have a real conversation with. The isolation is deafening. Cannot remember the last time I saw a white woman."

"Your parents were just here for the winter feast."

"Feels like ages ago." She sighed. "I beg you."

"The whole house would fall apart without you here."

"Then let it crumble," she declared, but then when she saw the crinkled-up look on Master's face, she shoved her spoon in her mouth.

He signaled to me for more stew.

"Who are you taking with you?"

"Parrott and Ruth."

"Ruth." She spat out Mama's name. "That nigger woman needs to stay here and work. We are already short hands and we need to prepare the house for spring. Not to mention the planting."

"All your worrying will make you sick. Now, I will send for someone from the fields to help. With thirty-nine slaves, I am sure we can make it work."

"Thirty-nine personalities for me to manage alone."

"Snitch is a good overseer. He'll keep everyone in line. Besides, it will only be about two or three weeks."

"You said that the last time you went south and you stayed away three months."

I could tell by the way Master chewed the inside of his jaw that his patience had waned. Missus must have noticed too, because she dropped her eyes and reached for her lemonade.

"Please let Lovie know to begin preparing my things for departure."

Missus pushed her bowl away from her.

"Pheby," Master Jacob called to me. I stepped from the shadows. His eyes registered the damage to my cheek and then he swallowed. "I will have tea and plum pudding in the parlor."

"Yes, sir."

"'Yes, master!'" Missus Delphina roared. "See, the girl has no manners."

"Yes, master." I backed out of the dining room before Missus could raise any more Cain.

The kitchen sat at the back of the property. The stone building had a wooden door, and a cloud of smoke bellowed from the chimney. Aunt Hope, the plantation cook, stood bent over her cast-iron pot. I guessed she was stirring up sweet potatoes from the smell of sugar, cinnamon, and nutmeg that peppered the air. Soon as I entered the room my body temperature climbed.

"What they needin'?" She shuffled from the pot to the ovens to the bowl of green beans on the center worktable. Sweat rolled down her neck and settled in a puddle in her ample cleavage. I fanned myself with the edge of my blouse and delivered Master's message.

"Ain't had nothin' on your stomach today." She reached into the wire-rimmed basket and handed me a piece of bread that I quickly stuffed between my teeth, and a boiled egg that I inhaled in the time it took her to prepare Master's dish.

Missus Delphina did not look up at me as I passed through the dining room with the dessert tray. The parlor sat off to the side of the carriage hall, enclosed by two grained pocket doors. It was my favorite room in the house, and where I'd spent countless hours with Miss Sally sitting by the fireplace, reading in the inglenook, learning arithmetic and geography, and playing the piano. Miss Sally's mahogany piano had a tapestry front, and legs that mirrored animal limbs, with feet and claws. As a child, I used to make up ridiculous stories about the animal carvings just to make Miss Sally laugh. I liked to see her happy.

She never married on account of her illness. No one bothered to tell me what ailed her, just that she suffered from woman problems and there was nothing Mama or the white doctor could do. Near her end, she was so frail that Master Jacob would carry her to the parlor and prop her up with pillows so that I could play for her. When she became too weak to clap, she mouthed, "Brava."

I found Master sitting in his wingback chair, smoking his pipe and reading the newspaper.

"Anything else I can do for you, sir? I mean master?"

As I placed the tray on the table next to him, he motioned for me to lean closer. Taking my face in his big hands, he turned it from side to side, surmising the damage.

"Hurt much?"

I shook my head.

"Tell Hope I said to give you a good bit of that mutton stew. Cure-all for everything and I know how you like it."

I smiled the best I could with the inflamed cheek.

"Play something nice for me?"

"On the piano?" I gasped. Missus Delphina had forbid me to play unless company needed to be impressed, which had not happened in a long while.

"Something Sally would want to hear. This month would have been her birthday."

"Her favorite song was 'Pretty Dreamer.'"

He nodded and picked up his tea. I sank into the plush stool and poised my fingers to play. My heart raced as I stumbled through the first section, but then the dust fell away and the notes glided off my fingertips. A calm came over me. I lost myself between the sound until I was so high it felt like I had the power to do anything. When I rose from the piano and gave Master a curtsey, he clapped his hands and whispered, "Brava."

I could not help but glow under his appreciation until I saw the back of Missus Delphina's skirt whip around her ankles as she moved away from the door.

CHAPTER 2

—— •── ——

Master's Promise

*M*y afternoon in the big house proved to be as backbreaking as my morning work. I dusted all the window curtains and wall hangings on the main living floor, and then swept the halls and formal stairs. Just when I thought I would pass out from fatigue, Lovie called me out back and handed me the jar of shoe blackening—a mixture of soot, sugar, syrup, molasses, and water to polish Master's dress shoes for his trip. By the time I finished, the sun's sketch traced the sky. Missus would be ready to retire soon, and if I wanted any semblance of harmony, her room needed to be warmed and ready. I could hear Aunt Hope humming a spiritual as I washed up in the basin on the side of the kitchen house. I scrubbed my hands with lye soap, then took the back stairs two at a time up to Missus's bedroom. I would have bumped into Lovie in the hall if she had not held up the lantern to light my way.

"Needin' to set up your pallet."

"Where?"

Lovie opened the door to a little closet off the entrance of Missus Delphina's bedroom. When my eyes adjusted, I sucked my teeth.

She rolled her eyes. "Ain't what you use to but it what Missus want."

The floor in the closet was narrow and short. I would have to bring my knees waist high just to fit all the way in. I longed to protest, tell Lovie that I would sleep with Mama and return before the sun came up, but I knew Lovie did not make the rules of the house. Only enforced them.

"Light the fire and turn back the bed. Once she down, go see 'bout your mama. I will cover for you, but be quick about it. Sometime she wake for water."

I was at the hearth kindling the fire when Missus trod heavily across the floor.

"Lovie, help me undress."

Once the flames licked up the logs, I turned back the bed linen and fluffed the pillows.

Missus tied her robe over her dressing gown, then took a seat at her vanity and dismissed me with a flick of her wrist. "Go help Hope shut down the kitchen for the night."

I bowed my head and exited the room. Once I got through the side door, I sprang across the grass to the loom house. Mama was sitting at the kitchen table bent over her needlework. Her cheeks rose into a smile.

"Thought Missus wanted you up at the house?"

"She down for the night. Lovie sent me to see about you." I moved in to peck her forehead, but she took hold of my face and frowned.

"I don't like that woman's hands on you."

"Not as bad as it looks."

Mama dropped her needle and walked to the back of the room to her medicine shelves. There were three rows: one for herbs and teas, the second with balms and ointments, and the bottom row held liquids, potion, wine, and whiskey. She reached for a green jar that smelled of frankincense and slathered it on my cheek. Satisfied with her work, she said, "Go on and get a bowl. Plenty stew for you here."

We had three mismatched chairs, and I put her needlework in the basket under the high-backed chair that she favored. As I reached for two bowls, I heard the door to the loom house slide open.

I looked at Mama.

"Ruthy?"

"I's here." She nodded to me.

I pulled down a third bowl. Mama moved to the fire and gave the pot a stir with one hand and slipped one of her chewing sticks into her mouth to freshen her breath with the other. Then she ran her hand over her hair and pinned it in place. I did the same.

Master Jacob entered our room and seemed to take it over with his presence. Mama placed herself on the edge of the bed with her ankles crossed and waited for him to address us.

"Evening." He smiled.

"A fine one it is," Mama answered back. "Care for something to eat?"

"Would not mind one bit." Master removed his jacket and I reached out my hand to take it, folding it carefully on the back of his chair. Mama kept a jug of wine for his visits on the lower back shelf. She wiped his glass with a cloth, then poured until the red liquid was half full. She served Master first and then brought our food, a stew of boiled potatoes, onions, and carrots, to the table. Once we were all seated, Master reached for our hands and prayed over the meal.

My stomach rumbled and I dropped my head into my stew. Now that Master had come to visit, I could cut my time short with Mama and stop in on Essex.

"I don't like her being handled that way." Mama gestured to my cheek. "Ain't fair. Pheby a good worker."

"I will talk to her."

"That's why we need to get her ways from here." Mama swallowed. "How much longer it gon' take?"

"Working on it, Ruthy. Pheby's birthday is still two seasons away."

"Wantin' her far up north. Where her freedom matters."

Master slurped up his stew. "Ruthy, this is delicious." He moved the bread around in his bowl for the last drop, then pushed back his seat, satisfied. "Taking you down to Charleston with me in a few days. Make sure you tie up loose ends."

Mama nodded her head. "But what is the plan for Delores?"

"There is a school in Massachusetts that I have been in contact with. She will be older than the other girls, but with all that Sally taught her, she will do fine."

"A real school?" Mama showed her teeth.

"Our Pheby will have a good life. Now, you quit worrying me, gal, and bring me some more wine."

Mama rose and did as she was told. Master reached into his pocket and held out a square piece of chocolate wrapped in shiny gold paper.

"Thanks for the song today." He winked.

I stood and curtsied.

"Delores, get on back to the Big House now before you missed."

I kissed Mama on the cheek and shoved the chocolate into my skirt pocket. It was not until I had started on the path to the stables that I realized I had forgotten my shawl. The wind stirred up, causing goose pimples to sprout across my arms, such that I considered roaming back. But then I remembered the one time I interrupted one of Master's visits to the loom house and caught Mama laid across the bed with her dress up, while Master's pants were gathered around his feet. His pale white hind parts moved back and forth, and he groaned like a wounded animal—the sound that lingered in my head for months. Mama caught me standing frozen at the top of the ladder. She made her eyes large and mouthed for me to go, so I did. When I finally returned to the loom house later that night, Mama waited with a bowl of split pea soup.

"Ain't many choices for a slave woman. Just know everything I do is for you. I'ma die a slave. I knows that. But you, baby, you are meant to see freedom. I's makin' sure."

After that night, we came up with a signal. Candle in the window meant clear to come up. No candle, keep walking.

◆

When I reached the stables, nightfall swallowed me in darkness. I coughed three times and then Essex opened the side door and drew me in. He smelled like a mix of soap and cedar, and I pressed into his skin.

"Hey, beautiful. Thought you weren't coming." He kissed me until I felt warm and sticky, and I placed my hands on his chest to restore my breathing.

"Mama held me up."

I followed him up the ladder to his flatbed loft over the haystacks. A single candle burned but did not mask the odor of damp animals and droppings.

"How do you sleep up here with these smelly horses?" I pinched my nose.

"Sleeping with the animals is how I become Massa to them." He untied my headscarf and released my curls. "Got something for you."

"What is it?" I sat cross-legged with my skirt pulled down over my feet.

"Close your eyes and no peeking."

I could hear him rummaging around. "Now, open them."

My lids blinked open to see Essex holding up two leather strips. Hanging from each was a wooden carving of a half of a heart.

"This one for you." He took one of the necklaces and tied it around my neck. "Just a little something to hold us over till I can marry you properly and get us 'ways from here."

I touched the heart to my lips. Then he gave me the other necklace and I tied it around his neck.

"I love it." I nuzzled my nose against his chin stubble until I felt him blush. "Thank you kindly."

"Anything for you."

Essex made a pillow out of hay and wrapped it in a piece of cloth. We settled back into the nook of the loft until our bodies were flush against each other. His strong arms around me made me feel safe. Essex nosed my hair, trailed his lips in sweet kisses down the side of my face until he found my mouth.

"You taste like sugarcane." He undid the buttons to my top, fondling away my chemise until he cupped my breasts with both hands. I arched and groaned as he massaged my nipples. Heat rose between us. I could sense desire taking over my reason and logic, so I kissed him one last time and then elbowed him away.

"What's the matter? Don't you want me?" he panted.

I fastened my buttons. "More than words can say."

"Then what is it?"

"Mama said not to catch no babies till I am free. Only a few more months, then we can leave this place and have as many babies as we want."

"You believe Massa's promise?"

I nodded. "Tonight he told Mama he was sending me to a school in Massachusetts. How much you save up for your freedom?"

"Round one hundred dollars since Massa been letting me hire myself out. But Parrott said a good stable boy like me worth two, three times more."

"What are we going to do?"

Essex leaned in real close and made his eyes big. "I aims to run if I have to."

"Hush that talk."

He put his mouth on my ear. "I have been testing how far I can get when I's working the horses on other plantations. Making a plan."

"You talking foolish, Essex Henry."

"I ain't letting you leave here without me."

"There has to be another way."

"You mine, Pheby. If I gotta run to be with you, then so be it."

"Dangerous talk and you know it."

He looked me deep in the eyes and fondled my cheek. "She did this?"

I nodded.

"Woman ain't no good." His mood soured.

"And I better get back up to the house before she starts wearing out my name." I stood, smoothing down my skirts.

"When will I see you again?"

"Soon as I can get to you. Please do not do anything foolish before then."

"We are going to be together, Pheby. That's a promise." He walked me to the door and kissed me long and hard; I bid him good night.

CHAPTER 3

Mistress of the House

*E*very morning Missus Delphina rose before first light. Up even before the overseer, Snitch, blew "de risin' horn." She liked to take what she called her constitutional—a stroll down to the garden, over to the dairy house, and then out to the fields. By the time Master woke up, she had already gotten a report on the crops from Snitch and written it all down in Master's ledger. Those who worked up at the house had to be up before she was, of course. Rachel, now dead, would stand at the ready with her work dress, while Lovie clutched a tray of morning tea. Aunt Hope toiled away in the kitchen, with smoke blowing high from the chimney carrying the promise of the day's meal. Essex groomed the horses, and even Mama and I sat at the loom spinning diligently in case Missus popped in on her way to the garden. Now that I slept in the big house, I tossed uncomfortably all night. Without Mama to wake me, I overslept my first morning.

"Come on, gal, make haste." Lovie nudged me in the middle of blackness. When I opened my eyes, it took me a moment to gather my wits. Sometime in the middle of the night I had turned my mattress sideways and slept with my feet in the hallway.

"She be up soon. You needin' to be ready to dress her."

"Why me?" I yawned.

"Was Rachel's job, girl. Now it's yours."

I wiped the sleep from my eyes, shoved my pallet back in the closet, and changed from my nightgown to my house dress in the dark. My tongue smacked with thirst. I was wishing I had a sip of some water when Missus started shouting my name.

I rushed to her door. "Yes, Missus."

"Do not stand there idle. Take down my walking dress. The day is wasting."

I hurried to her wardrobe and pulled out a mauve dress.

"That one is for dinner, you ninny. The plaid one." Missus stood tapping her foot with her arms crossed at the bosom. She looked ghostly by the candlelight in her bloomers and chemise.

"Where is my corset?"

"I have it right here." I held it up. She turned her back to me and held out her arms so that I could fit the corset over her belly bump. Not sure why she bothered with the corset to walk the plantation. 'Less she was trying to impress old Snitch.

None of us cared if her belly was in or out.

"Do not have all morning, girl."

I tried not to touch her skin as I stretched one long lace through the corset, then fastened each end so the string pulled through the eyelet. Through the mirror, I watched her face to see where the corset fit comfortably.

"Missus Delphina, can you take a long breath in?"

When she did I settled the corset a pinch lower, fitting it under her waist flab.

"Rachel would have been finished by now."

I fastened the front elastic and pulled sharply at the strings to make it even tighter. Missus gulped.

"Tight enough?"

She did not respond so I kept pulling until the corset was anchored and she looked strained in the face. The price of beauty for a white woman. Even when with child.

"Fine."

I held out her basic petticoat and then helped her into her walking dress.

"When you finish in here, Lovie will get you started on the laundry."

She left me in the bedroom. I went through all the chores I had performed the morning before: wiped down the four-poster bed frame, footboard, and headboard with a mixture of olive oil and vinegar until they gleamed. Tied back the curtains, made the bed, sorted her dresses, swept the ashes from the fireplace, scoured the hearth with soap and sand, then stacked in fresh wood that I would light before dinner. Afterward, Lovie led me down a short flight of steps and down a hall to the scullery, tucked away at the back end of the house. In this room, we prepped the big meals, washed dishes, and laundered the clothes. Lovie had soaked a batch of whites overnight in rainwater and ash lye.

"Know how to use the dolly stick?"

I nodded, a half-truth. I had seen it done before. I lifted the dolly, which resembled a milking stool attached to the bottom of a broomstick, and heaved it into the metal pot. Plunging it into the water, I twisted and turned the bedsheet, Master's white shirts, undergarments, and towels. Within a few minutes my forearms blazed and my shoulders ached from the repetitive movement.

"All 'ight in here?" Aunt Hope stood at the back door.

"Yes," I said despite my fatigue. Did not want Aunt Hope to think that I could not handle my share of the load.

"Bet you hungry. I snuck an egg and piece a bread." She took the dolly from me and twisted it into the pot. Aunt Hope was stronger than me even though she was an older woman. I tore through the food while she kneaded the clothing.

"Needin' to hurry wit' this. Missus on a rant 'cause your mama leavin' wit Massa and you don't want her to find fuss wit' you." I took the dolly from her and beat the laundry, adding a little fury to my work. Before long I wrung out the pieces and hung them out back. As I smoothed down the last sheet on the line, Missus appeared suddenly by my side, clutching Master's coat.

"Reinforce the buttons. Make sure they are evenly spaced and tight. Do not want him catching his death in South Carolina on account of your incompetence."

"Yes, Missus." I reached for the coat.

"Tell your mama that I aims to have the summer drapes for the sitting room measured and sewn before Master Jacob leaves here day after tomorrow."

I wanted to ask why on earth she would choose to worry over summer drapes in the middle of March, but kept my eyes low and mouth shut.

"And tell her no lazing. I will get as much work out of her as possible before she goes."

When I crashed through the door of the loom house, Mama was bent over a roll of material with a pin in her mouth.

"Slow down, gal, 'fore you hurt somethin'."

I delivered Missus's message and Mama just huffed air through her nostrils.

The first floor of the loom house had one long table, a bench, and two chairs. I worked on the coat, straining to keep my eyes steady but still needled my skin.

"Ouch." I sucked on my finger.

Mama stopped the loom and took the coat from me. I slumped back in the chair, arms, legs, and shoulders burning with exhaustion.

"Gon' have to get use to more work. I ain't always gon' be round to protect you. 'Specially now you in the house." She easily threaded the needle through the buttons.

"I am just so tired, Mama." I put my good cheek down on the table and closed my eyes.

"I knows it. But you got to get stronger, Delores, or you ain't gon' survive the Missus."

I sighed deeply.

"Ain't no white woman ever goin' treat you well as Miss Sally, so get that out of your head and do as Missus say, 'fore she says it. Me and Master be away only a short while. Best to stay out of her wrath with us gone."

As Mama worked on the button, I drifted to sleep. I did not know how much time had passed when she murmured my name.

"Up, Delores. Need you to pay attention."

I opened my eyes and saw Mama clutching a small sack. She took a jar of ointment from the bag and placed it in my hand.

"Rub down Rachel's pallet with this. Keep her spirit from haunting you in your sleep."

She then handed me a mixture of dried leaves, small seeds, and her fingernail clippings, tucked into a scrap of lace. "Sew this into the hem of your skirt. For your pro'tection while I's gone from here."

I took the needle from her and followed her directions.

"'Member now, even in the big house you's still Pheby Delores Brown, born on Christmas Day. You the gran-daudder of Vinnie Brown, who was the gran-daudder of a Mandara queen. You a slave in name, but never in your mind, chile."

Her face inched closer to mine until we sat eye to eye. "You a woman born to see freedom. No matter what Missus say or do, you ain't nobody's property. Hear?"

"Yes, Mama."

She yanked me to her bosom and I inhaled her sweet scent.

Mama handed me the coat. "Now get."

◆

On the morning that Master was due to leave, Missus Delphina threw up in her water basin. I took it out, soaped it clean, and brought it back so that she could wash her face and hands before her last breakfast with Master Jacob. She had soiled her first dress, so I helped her change into a blue dress with a fan-front bodice and close-fitted cap sleeves. I brushed her hair and twisted it into a neat bun at the nape of her neck. When I finished, she stood in front of the mirror, touching the dark circles around her eyes.

"Running this plantation has robbed me of my beauty."

"You look nice, ma'am," I offered.

"I look weathered." She pinched her cheeks to make them appear rosier. "No wonder Jacob does not want to take me with him. What have I given him?"

"You are carrying his child."

She turned on me with blazing red eyes. "How dare you? No one asked for your wretched opinion. Out!"

I fled the room as the book she flung at my head narrowly missed. Aunt Hope waited for me at the bottom of the steps.

"Just her nerves got her out of sorts." She handed me a pair of white gloves and ushered me to help serve breakfast.

SADEQA JOHNSON

Master sat with his ledger open on the table. Missus arrived moments later, and he stood and pecked her on her cheek.

"How are you feeling today, dear?"

"Ill."

"Dr. Wilks said it is important to get your rest."

She sipped her tea. "I need more than rest."

"Anything I can do for you?"

She shook her head. They ate the meal in silence.

When Master raised his finger, I cleared the table, carried the dishes back to the scullery, and washed, dried, and put them away. By the time I had swept the dining room floor and restored the table, I could hear the others from the house gathering out front for the farewell. Parrott had secured the last piece of luggage onto the carriage when I came down the path. Essex stood with the horses, talking to them, rubbing them down, but his eyes kept finding me. It had been an excruciating three days since we had been alone, and while my chest ached over Mama's departure, I longed for his touch.

Not twenty minutes later, the wide front doors were slung open by Lovie, and Master Jacob walked through with Missus Delphina at his elbow. When they reached the edge of the porch, Missus put her head on Master's chest. Whatever he whispered into her ear, I did not hear.

Just then, Mama walked into the courtyard, and the sight of her halted all conversation. She floated in a red calico dress with covered buttons, a loose-fitting bodice, and bishop sleeves. Her hair was rolled back and shining with palm oil. She looked better than this place—regal, even. Certainly not like someone's property. No one would ever have guessed that the dress she was wearing had been repurposed from Miss Sally's old petticoat, stiffened with hominy and water, with a hoopskirt made out of grapevine.

Parrott reached for Mama's hand and helped her into the front carriage. Aunt Hope emerged from the kitchen house with a packed lunch and handed it to me to carry over to Mama. When I offered the basket up to her she rubbed my hands and squeezed my fingers.

"Lovie, carry the mistress inside and accompany her to her room so that she can rest." Master Jacob let go of Missus's hand. She held her mouth open, no doubt to protest, but then pursed her lips. When Master passed me on the step he patted me on my shoulder. "Be good, Pheby. I am counting on you."

"Yes, sir."

Parrott opened the carriage door and then closed it behind Master before climbing up front next to Mama. I worried about her riding up front in the open elements, but she had confessed to me that a few miles down the road, she would always enter the carriage to keep Master Jacob company.

Parrott lifted the reins. "Step," he said to the horses, and the carriage moved on. Mama turned to me and we locked eyes until she was too far and the dust too high for me to see her.

Essex stood by my side. "She be back soon."

"Does not make me feel any better."

"I can." He brushed his arm against mine. His touch charged right through me.

"Guess we can meet in the loom house now instead of with the smelly horses." I smiled up at him through my lashes.

"Pheby," Missus shouted at me. "You do not have time for foolery. Fetch my coffee."

"Yes, Missus. Right away." I did not risk looking back at Essex, but I could feel his eyes on my hips as I slipped away.

CHAPTER 4

Evil Women Do

*T*he heavy April showers made May a breeding ground for mosquitoes, and the pesky bugs showed me no mercy. Mama's balm had stopped working, and red bite marks peppered my arms and legs. It did not help that Aunt Hope had relegated me to caring for Missus's garden. Since Master left, she had neglected her vegetation something terrible. So it became my job to prune, weed, and plant the beets, carrots, tomatoes, lettuce, and cabbage.

The leisure time I had hoped for with Essex proved nonexistent. Missus kept me bottled up in the house at her beck and call. Between catering to her whims, gardening, fetching, serving, and doing dead Rachel's work, I never stopped feeling weary in my bones. Essex also stayed busy mucking out the stables, watering, feeding, and exercising the horses. Then, every Saturday before the roosters crowed, he hired himself out to neighboring plantations to work with their horses. Most times, he did not make it back until late Sunday night. A few times I tried to sneak out to see him, but Missus heard me moving through the hall. One time, I had made it out of the house but then did a turnaround when I spotted the overseer, old Snitch, sitting in front of the stables drinking from his flask.

After Master had been away for two months, a letter arrived from him informing Missus that he needed to extend his trip by an additional few weeks or so. Missus relayed the news to Aunt Hope and then crushed the letter in her palm before tossing it in the fire. Later that afternoon, I could tell the news had fermented her mood by the way she stood over me nitpicking. The windows were streaked, the floor harbored dirt, and the table felt sticky. When I went outside to tend to the laundry, she followed behind me.

"Honestly, Ninny, a blind man could see that this sheet is covered in filth."

She had taken to calling me Ninny ever since Master and Mama left. The name burned me up, and I straightened my back so that my agitation would not show as I took the sheet down and carried it back to the ash water and scrubbed it again with lye. As soon as I had hung up all the laundry, Lovie brought me a basket filled with odd clothing that needed mending.

"Make time for the sewing after you serve dinner. Missus getting so thick in the waist, you need to let out a few of her dresses."

I wanted to shout to Lovie that my fingers were too stiff from pounding the dolly stick to sew, but then I realized that being sent to the loom house could provide an opportunity to see Essex. I nodded and held my tongue.

On my way to collect Missus's evening meal from the kitchen house, I sauntered past the stables. Essex was crouched down changing a horse's shoe, his white shirt pasted to his back with sweat. When he looked up at me, I pointed toward the loom house and tugged on my ear. He flashed all his teeth and brushed his nose twice. The secret meeting was set, and it gave me an extra spring in my step.

During most meals, Missus only ate half of what I put on her plate. I was not sure if her appetite had waned, or if she did not want to put on too much weight. Either way, Aunt Hope saved her scraps from the day and passed them down to the field hands at the end of the night.

"More pudding, Missus?" I held out the silver bowl, but she shook her head and stood to retire.

Her ankles had swole so much that it became my nightly job to soak her feet in white willow bark and massage her legs until she seemed satisfied. Once I patted them dry and propped her on the bed with pillows, Lovie entered the room to brush her hair.

I had left the mending in a basket on the porch and grabbed it up on my way to the loom house.

Outside, the evening was damp and moisture hung in the air. I could smell the sweet scent of oncoming rain. A patch of bellflowers grew along the side of the house, and I pinched one off and tucked it behind my ear. I felt both nervous and excited over what I planned to do. Tonight, my yearning for Essex was going to outweigh Mama's repeated caution. We had fevered for each other long enough, and I had lost the ability to contain my fire for him. No one had cherished me like Essex, and I was ready to give him my all. I climbed the ladder in the loom house, and when I saw Essex sitting in my chair, goose pimples prickled my arms.

"Glad you came." I tugged on his lip.

My thirst for him burned the back of my throat, and I lifted my skirt and straddled his lap. He seemed startled by my boldness, which fueled me to press my hips into him while undoing the buttons on his shirt. Essex removed his mouth from mine and stopped my hands.

"What is wrong?"

"I's something to tell you."

"Can it wait till after?"

My insides were all worked up, but he lifted me off his lap by the waist. The bellflower fell from my ear, the pink petal already wilted. I had come on too strong. Maybe he thought I was unladylike. My nerves were suddenly on edge, so I reached under the seat for Mama's needlework to focus my hands.

"I thought you wanted me."

"Oh, beautiful, it ain't you."

"Then what?"

He stood, buttoning his shirt. I looked up at him, trying to read his expression, but could not.

"I done something terrible."

"You are scaring me, Essex." I inserted the knitting needle under the front loop of yarn, but the movement did not comfort me.

He hesitated then said, "Missus Delphina. She been . . . forcing herself on me."

"Forcing? Forcing how?"

"To lay down with her. Like she should wit' her husband."

The room started swirling, and my head felt too heavy for my neck. The needlework slid from my lap onto the floor. "What are you saying?"

"I ain't want to. You gotta believe me."

"A white woman? Master's wife?"

"She made me, Pheby. Said Massa spent so much time with his nigger woman, she needed a nigger too."

I grabbed his arm and dug my nails into his skin. "All this time I have been saving myself for you and you laying with the missus?" I slapped him across the face so hard my palm stung.

"You know I ain't have no choice."

"Ain't you a man?"

Essex glared at me. "In this place, I's a slave first."

I stood with my fist balled, ready to hit him again, but he pinned my arms down by my sides.

"Calm down."

"How! When you stomping all over my heart!"

"I's so sorry. She said if I ain't do what she said, she would tell Massa I forced her with a knife. Said he have me strung up."

I wriggled but he held me tighter.

"Baby, you know I don't want that woman. All I wants is you."

The betrayal made me choke on my own saliva. I broke into a fit of coughs until my lungs finally made way for air to flow. Not wanting to stand so close to Essex, I tried to push past him, but he held me in his arms. Over and over again, I banged my fist into his chest. All my life, Miss Sally had me thinking things would always go my way. Mama had me thinking I was more than a slave. But nothing was working in my favor. Not even my man was mine. Essex stood tall, taking every punch until I crumpled in my chair from exhaustion. When I settled down, he passed me his canteen of water. I drank and then held the cold metal to my forehead, trying to get my thoughts right.

"When did this happen?"

He sat across from me. "During her morning walks she come get me from the stables."

"Why are you telling me now?"

"I cain't be wit' you like man and woman with that secret wearing a hole in my heart. I hated keeping it from you but I ain't want to hurt you either."

The silence between us grew like a presence in the room. Then a bigger worry weighed down on me. "When did this thing between you start?"

Essex's face flashed pain. "'Fore the winter festival."

I counted the months by my fingers, then counted again to be sure.

"What you doin'?"

"Missus could be carrying your baby."

He winced. "What you mean?"

"Enough moons have passed to line up with how long you been . . . together."

Essex grabbed his ears and started pacing the floor. "I don't want this trouble on my head."

"If Missus have a dark baby, she still gon' accuse you of rape. Be her word against yours. You be hanging from the tree fast as Snitch could get to you."

"I have dishonored you, Pheby, to survive, and you telling me my circumstance is gettin' worst?" He stopped walking.

"We have to get you off this plantation before that baby is born. You have to run."

I could see the degrees of emotion as they passed through his eyes; then he clenched his jaw tight. "Ain't leaving here without you. Got to come with me, Pheby."

I swayed unsteadily on my feet, smoothed back my hair, and tried to regain my bearings. "I better get back to the house 'fore I am missed."

"Pheby." He reached for me but I slid away.

"You have dumped a lot on me tonight. Wrecked me in my core. Just give me a little time to sort things." I let myself down the ladder.

When I got outside, it had started to rain. I trampled through the wet grass feeling a heaviness in my soul. It made me more tired than all my work combined.

CHAPTER 5

———— • ————

Betrayal

I tried to focus on my morning chores, but pain dragged behind me like a weight chained to my ankle. I could not stop picturing Missus all over Essex. Kissing him, touching him, finding pleasure with him. The vision of them together made me sick to my stomach. Even though I knew Essex had no choice, my heart hurt no less. Last night was supposed to be special, and Missus Delphina took that opportunity away from me.

When she called me to dress her that morning, I wanted to wrap my hands around her neck until her eyes popped out of the sockets. She had everything. Why did she have to take what was mine too? As I yanked her corset over her belly, all I kept thinking was that her baby could be Essex's. Essex could be killed over the child she carried, and I knew it fell on me to help him escape.

All my agony made me terrible at my responsibilities. Lovie caught me staring off several times and cautioned me to get my head right, but not even her chastising fixed my concentration on my work. In the two days that followed Essex's confession, I broke two bowls, skinned my knee, spilled Missus's coffee in her lap, and uprooted radishes that were not ripe. Aunt Hope sent me to the henhouse for a basket of fresh eggs and I wasted three on the floor. Down on my knees, mopping up the spill, was where Essex finally found me.

"We needin' to talk."

I wiped the sticky yolk on the front of my apron. It was the first time I had seen him since we talked, and as much as I wanted to stand in anger, I still loved him. Still wanted him.

"Aunt Hope is waiting on these eggs."

"Meet me in the stables in ten minutes," he whispered.

I left the eggs with Aunt Hope and mentioned that I would be in the loom house letting out Missus's petticoat. She nodded, humming one of her Jesus songs while mixing a wet batter for the fried flounder we would eat later. I ducked around to the back of the stables, and before I could cough, Essex opened the side door and pulled me in. He led me to the stall, tucking us behind a horse named Thunder.

"Best place for us to talk during the day."

I held my breath so as not to breathe in the stink of horse manure. Essex put his mouth to my ear and spoke so soft that I struggled to hear him.

"Been thinking about my escape route."

I reached into my hidden skirt pocket and pulled out a folded piece of paper.

"What's that?"

"It is a map I stole from one of Miss Sally's books. Part of my geography lessons with her." I opened it up and pushed it against the wall so that we could both see.

"I traced the route north for you last night. Traveling by dark and hiding during the day would be your best defense against the slave catchers."

His hand grazed mine, sending a familiar spark up my spine, as he took the map from me. I watched as he dug a hole in a bale of hay and stuffed the map deep inside.

"You brilliant, Pheby."

I searched the dark space for his eyes. "You are not afraid?"

"Been thinkin' about running when you set free for a long time. Guess I's just getting a head start."

I shuddered in my skin, scared for him. It seemed such a long way to freedom. "It is dangerous, Essex."

"Come with me." He grabbed my hands. "Two heads better than one. We can stand back-to-back and fight off the enemy together. At night, keep each other warm."

"But Mama—"

"We can make it."

I dropped his hands. "Mama has worked hard on securing my freedom. Seems like before I was even born. I owe it to her to see her plan through."

"You trust Massa that much?"

"I do."

Essex bit down on his bottom lip.

"I think we had better bring Aunt Hope in on the plan. Jasper was her son, and the only slave who made it off this plantation."

He nodded. "But I want you to come, Pheby. Cain't picture my life without you."

I put my finger to his lips. "Everything happening so fast now."

"You forgive me?" He pulled me to him so tight, it was hard to see where one of us began and the other ended.

I knew our time together was limited. No sense wasting it carrying a grudge. "Past is in the past. Got to move forward."

"Ain't leaving here without you."

I touched his face with the back of my hand, kissed his cheek, and then turned for the big house.

◆

The next morning, I went down to the kitchen house to fetch Missus's breakfast tray. Aunt Hope had just poured the coffee and covered the pot with tin. I stood next to her and whispered in her ear. "Essex in trouble."

"Kind?"

"Big kind."

Aunt Hope dropped her head under the table like she searched for something in case Missus snuck up on us with those hawk eyes and dog ears.

"Meet you t'night. Once she go down."

That evening, I ground up some magnolia bark and stirred it into Missus's evening cup of tea. It made her so sleepy that she waved off her nightly read of *Godey's Lady's Book*. When I heard her snoring, I tiptoed out. I listened for odd noises and footsteps near the kitchen house before tapping the door three times like Aunt Hope and I planned. Under the cover of night, she and I headed to the stables. I coughed and Essex opened the side door.

"Two days in a row." He smiled at me, then greeted Aunt Hope by taking her hand. Essex led us into the back of the stables in the same small space behind the horse, Thunder. If anyone came in, we could crouch low and not be seen. Aunt Hope sat down on a haystack and then unwrapped fish and biscuits from a handkerchief and handed a bit to each of us. We ate in silence.

Essex's eyes were on me.

"Now your belly full, what is it?"

I opened my mouth and recalled Essex's confession. When I finished, he balled up his fist, but Aunt Hope did not look surprised.

"Whites always want to lay wit' us and leave us wit' they problems."

"Then get rid of us to hide their indiscretions," I added.

Essex started pacing the small space of floor.

"Ya mama teach you how to mix herbs to lose a baby?"

"No." I felt embarrassed that I had not asked Mama more questions about her medicine. "Anyway, Missus too far along for herbs."

"What you goin' do?" Aunt Hope looked up at Essex.

"He has to run. I tore him a map from one of Miss Sally's books."

"Timing is everything," Aunt Hope said. "How soon?"

"Soon as I can," replied Essex.

"Got to be before the baby is born," I pushed. "Aunt Hope, Jasper the only one made it off this plantation."

"And they drag him back here like a mangy dog."

"We thought you could tell us his plan." I tried jogging any memories she might recall.

"Jasper's plan was to make it up to Balt'more, find work at the docks, and then save money to get to New York." She turned to me. "Best for Essex if you write him a pass from the Missus. Give him some protection out there."

"I can try in the morning, while she walking the plantation."

"I pack you provisions and one of my good knives." Aunt Hope moved to stand. "Pheby, you goin' too?"

"Master promised me papers when I turn eighteen. He promised Mama."

Aunt Hope let out a bitter laugh. "White folks' promises ain't but dust. 'Specially the white folks called Massa." She stood up and hissed over her shoulder, "The blood ones hurt you most."

She closed the door behind her, but I suddenly felt cold. Something took hold of my body, and even wrapped in my shawl, I could not shake it.

"Come here." Essex held my hand and led me up to the loft above the horses. When we kissed, I felt like a dying woman and his lips my only antidote. This raw, desperate hunger for him dulled my sense of logic and reason, and I considered running with him.

"I love you, Essex Henry," I breathed, and he swallowed my words down in his throat. I saw them when I sucked on the spot. His hands fevered me everywhere, and our clothes melted away from our skin as we clumsily found the straw bed. My need for him grew more impatient with each inhalation. I sought for him to reach my cold spots and make them fiery again. We rocked and clung until our circumstance drifted away. A quiver rolled through me as his sweaty body convulsed against mine, and I wrapped my legs around his waist, absorbing all his fears and worries.

The fluids between us dried, but we were too exhausted to dress. My fingers caressed Essex's chest while I contemplated. Lovemaking must be equivalent to the feeling of freedom. No ties to time or space, hindrance or restraints.

"Come with me, Pheby. I will protect you. You heard Aunt Hope. We cain't trust any of them. You all I got."

I grabbed his face and kissed him long and hard, until his desire for me stirred and I could offer him more.

CHAPTER 6

Homecoming

$\mathcal{M}$ aster's promise of freedom had lived inside of me for so long, I found it hard to let it go. Mama talked of it as often as she did her recipes for healing, weaving it into the fabric of my life. All Essex talked about was me running with him, and the conversations filled me with dread. I wanted to speak to Mama, needed her wisdom to help me make sense of it all.

A few weeks passed, then a letter from Master Jacob arrived. Missus left it on her writing desk, so I waited for her to take her evening walk around the plantation before I read it in secret. It said that Master would be home by the sixth of July, and for her to let Aunt Hope know that he wanted her to slaughter a hog to celebrate his good fortune in his business affairs and his return. Our preparations to receive him began right away; the entire house had to be deep cleaned including the windows inside and out, his favorite foods prepared, and the lawns and bushes manicured. Missus Delphina worked us from dawn to dark for nearly a week. We were all relieved when she gave us a rare half day's rest on the Sabbath.

Aunt Hope sent me to the smokehouse to fetch the pork drippings, right after I had finished bathing and washing my own clothes. Now I would have the smell of smoke in my hair. I had just placed a small sample of meat between my lips when I heard the plantation bell. One. Two.

I lifted the left side of my skirt while balancing the meat in my right palm, walking swiftly past the garden and over to the side of the house to hear the announcement. When I got there, I saw that Lovie had rung the bell. She beckoned me over and whispered.

"Pheby, Missus needin' you directly. Massa's carriage been spotted. He on his way home." She beamed.

I tucked the meat under a cloth and dropped it off in the scullery. My heart thudded against my chest as I bounded quickly up the narrow steps, then took three seconds at Missus's bedroom door to steady my breath before entering. When I walked in, she threw a fork at me and it hit me in the arm. I bit my lip so as to not yell out.

"Why are you always moving to your own time? Get down my green dress now."

"I do not think that one still fits." I gestured to her protruding belly. According to Lovie's calculation, Missus had about another month and a half to go before the baby would arrive.

That did not leave Essex much time.

"Did I ask for your wretched opinion?" She moved to slap me but I sidestepped it, then dropped down to the floor as if I were searching for her shoes. Bruises already paraded up and down my arms from her constant hits and pinches. Gave me a mind to push her down the stairs to help get rid of the baby, and all of Essex's problems with it.

Lovie appeared in the doorway. "Missus."

"Maybe you can help me change, since Ninny does not know her head from a doorknob." She pursed her lips.

"Somethin' wrong . . ."

"What is it?"

"There been an accident. Parrott had to leave Massa at the doctor's house nearin' your parents' farm."

"Is Jacob all right?" Missus stood wringing her hands like she did not know what to do next. Lovie took Missus by the elbow and ushered her down into a chair, then started fanning her. I poured a glass of water from the pitcher, but Missus would not take it. If Master suffered an injury, then what about Mama?

"Go ask Aunt Hope to make Missus a cuppa strong tea." Lovie made her eyes big at me and mouthed, "It's Ruth."

On my toes was the best way to run through the house without producing a sound that would further wreck Missus's nerves. I flew from the front door and down the stairs. When I got to the carriage, Parrott had Mama in his arms and was carrying her across the lawn toward the loom house.

"Mama?"

"She hurt," Parrott called over his shoulder. He heaved Mama up the ladder and placed her on the bed.

"Tell me what happened," I urged Parrott. He looked like the trip had aged him. A fistful of gray had sprouted in his beard. He lowered himself down in Mama's chair.

"We were coming through Jamestown and out of nowhere came two wild horses. Spook't our horses and they took off runnin'. We hit a ditch and the wheel pop off. Massa and Ruth thrown from the carriage. I held on by the streng't a God. Happened so fast."

"Tell me what to do." I leaned down to Mama, her face twisted in pain.

"Give me a sip from the brown jar."

The brown jar was Mama's strongest medicine. The thought of giving it to her scared me, but then I noticed the smell. The scent of infected flesh burned through my nose and turned my stomach over. Mama's right leg was cut from the top of her thigh to below her knee. I covered my mouth to keep from choking.

"How long she been like this?"

"Two days. Rode as fast I could after fixin' the wagon."

"Feel like gangrene," Mama breathed. "Get camphor from the shelf." I left Mama's side long enough to locate the bottle.

"Pour till it bubble."

Once the wound was cleaned, I remembered what I needed to wrap it with.

"Be back directly."

There was yarrow growing alongside the stone fence in Missus's garden. Mama had told me the plant worked wonders in drawing out infection. I stuffed as many as I could in my pocket and had two fistfuls in my hands when I heard Lovie shouting my name. I looked up, and she had pushed her head through Missus's bedroom window.

"Make haste!"

I dropped the yarrow that did not fit in my pockets and sprinted up to Missus Delphina's bedroom. Lovie stood over Missus with a cloth to her head as she squirmed in the bed.

"Baby coming early. Needin' you to help deliver it."

"What about the doctor?"

"Missus said she ain't want a doctor. Gotta be you," Lovie said, and narrowed her eyes in a way that let me know she was aware of the trouble.

I had attended many births with Mama but had never delivered one alone without her help. I tried to ease the panic growing in my chest. If I stayed here delivering Missus's baby, then who would care for Mama? Her wound was wide open. Missus moaned, and I had no choice but to wash my hands and feel for the baby. I shoved my fingers and then my arm inside of her but did not touch the head.

She groaned louder. "Get it out."

"Soon, Missus," I assured her.

Lovie rubbed Missus Delphina's forehead with a damp cloth and forced her to drink a little wine to dull the pain. I had never seen Missus so helpless, and would have felt sorry for her if not for Mama lying in the loom house equally distraught. Aunt Hope appeared in the doorway with a bowl.

"Brought soup, ma'am."

But Missus could only stomach a few spoonfuls before she threw it all up.

"Got to get something down in her stomach for streng't," Aunt Hope said, and then tried a little more. "Missus, you wantin' to write Essex a pass to ride out to the doctor's house and get a word on Massa's condition?"

Missus Delphina clenched her teeth as pain ripped through her.

"Hand me my stationery." Sweat dampened her forehead as she scribbled a note that she gave to Aunt Hope.

"Pheby, come get clean water and towels." Aunt Hope gestured for me to follow her out.

When we reached the bottom of the stairs, I asked, "You see about Mama?"

"She sleepin' now."

I handed her the yarrow. "Pack this loosely over her wounds. She getting any better?"

"I's doin' what I can." She looked at me, and her eyes told me what her mouth would not. My head started spinning on what herbs and remedies I could mix up for her, but all the chatter stopped when I opened the kitchen door and saw Essex standing with a bag tossed over his shoulders. He moved toward me and grabbed my face. Even though I had planned his run, I could not believe it was really happening. My lips parted but the words did not follow.

Aunt Hope closed the door firmly behind her. "Time is now with all the commotion."

"Come on, beautiful. We gotta go."

My heart sank. "Essex . . . I cannot leave. Mama is in bad shape and Missus expecting me to deliver her baby."

Aunt Hope poured hot water in a basin. "Now be best. You have to take what God gives."

"Please, Pheby." Essex's eyes darkened.

It was not supposed to be like this. To have to choose between Essex and Mama.

My lips trembled, and tears clouded my eyes. I pulled Essex to my chest and squeezed my love into him. I tried memorizing everything; the curve of his back, the way his stubble felt when he brushed it across my cheek, the hardness of his muscles, his calloused hands.

"We will meet up in Massachusetts. I will find you."

He shook his head.

"You must go on. You are the one in danger." I caressed his hand.

"Gotta hurry 'fore Snitch get wind of Missus in labor." Aunt Hope gave Essex the pass that Missus Delphina wrote. "Give him the travel satchel," she said to me.

Under one of the bricks of the stove, I had hidden a small bag for Essex. I removed the piece of paper on top.

"This is a pass to Baltimore. Says you are going to work for Missus's uncle."

"You rippin' out my heart."

"This is harder on me than you know."

I kept my face brave as I explained the other items in the bag. "Rub this red onion on the soles of your feet and the horses' hooves every few hours. Whenever you see pine or spruce, rub it on your hands, face, and clothes. It is how you keep the hounds from picking up your scent."

A tear welled in the corner of his eye and I kissed it away. "Look for the all-girls school in Massachusetts. Be there sometime 'round the first of the year." I touched my heart necklace to his lips and gave him my sweetest smile. "Go now. Promise, we will be together soon."

"You have my heart, Pheby." He pulled at his necklace and clutched the wooden piece in his hand.

"And you have mine."

He kissed me hard on the lips for the last time and then walked out the door. I did not follow to watch him ride off. I busied myself with gathering the towels and basin of water, trying to put my concentration anywhere but on my brokenness.

Aunt Hope whispered, "Soon as you can, burn everythin' with his smell."

I covered my mouth with my hand, forcing my cry to stay quiet.

She patted my back. "Go on now, Essex needin' you to be strong 'round the Missus. 'Member, you is the distraction."

Straightening my back and pursing my lips, I told Aunt Hope that I would take care of it all. As I crossed the grass, I strained for the sound of Essex's horse, but he was gone. Lovie shouted again from the window.

"Make haste, girl!"

I made my way into the big house holding the basin of water, towels bulging from my arms. When I entered Missus's chambers, I did my best to keep my emotions from reddening my skin.

"What took you so long? Where do you keep running off to?"

"The towels, ma'am." I held them out in front of me.

"Does not take that long to get towels."

I hesitated. "My mama was hurt in the carriage accident too. Her leg is infected. I think she needs to see the doctor."

Missus *tsk*ed her teeth. "Lovie, go tell Hope to give Ruth some soup and blankets."

"Ma'am, her flesh is open and the wound is festering. Please." My voice cracked. "She needs the doctor."

"Your mama work roots, she will figure it out."

"Never seen an infection this bad before. She might not . . . This is different than the work she does. It smells like her skin is already decaying."

She clapped her hands to silence me. "That's enough out of you. Now, do not leave this house again until I give you permission. I will not die in this bed." She gripped the covers as another contraction rolled through her. "Deliver me from this baby. After that, we will see about Ruth."

I got down between her legs, hoping that Mama would hold on.

CHAPTER 7

─────────── • ◆ • ───────────

Delivery

*I*t took two risings of the moon before the baby crowned and another full hour before I caught it. Missus gave birth to a tan baby boy with ears that promised more pigment. I cut the cord and handed the baby to Lovie for cleaning. Missus moaned in an exhausted delirium. The infant had started a light cry, and Lovie rocked it while I helped Missus deliver the afterbirth.

"Shall I fetch a wet nurse from the fields?" Lovie held the baby toward Missus Delphina.

"No one else," Missus murmured as the child's cries grew louder. She looked at the baby and, after taking in his skin, turned on her side like she did not hear, refusing him. The boy cried and cried as I mopped up the mess from the birth. Finally, Missus reached for the baby and gave it her breast.

I packed Missus with towels to catch the bleeding. When the boy had his fill, she handed him over to me like it pained her to touch him. The child had almond eyes like Essex's with rounded cheeks and a fuzzy patch of hair. Just looking at him made me mushy, and I knew I would do whatever it took to take care of Essex's son. I swaddled the baby in a blanket and hummed in his ear while Lovie spooned more soup into Missus's mouth. After she ate, she fell into an exhausted sleep. Lovie steered me out of the bedroom. Once I closed Missus's bedroom door, she muttered, "Go see 'bout Ruth."

She carried the baby to the nursery and shut the door behind her. Outside the air did not move. I could not remember the last time I'd had more than an hour of sleep. Essex had a two-day start, and thus far he had not been missed. Still, I worried over his safety. When I climbed the ladder to the loom house, I heard Aunt Hope singing softly:

There is a balm in Gilead
To make the wounded whole
There is a balm in Gilead
To cure a sin-sick soul

The odor of Mama greeted me before I even laid eyes on her. Aunt Hope had a rag and cool water beside her bed, and I knelt, then swabbed the sweat from Mama's forehead.

"How is she doing?" I asked, though Mama's dull skin, hollowed-out cheeks, and swollen thigh conveyed it all.

"Ain't good. Lord have mercy." She grabbed my hand.

We both watched over Mama in silence. Then Aunt Hope asked about Missus.

"Had a boy."

"And?"

I nodded my head in a way that conveyed our suspicions.

Aunt Hope wiped her hands on her apron. "Trouble ahead. I's best get on up to the big house."

"See if you can convince Missus to send for the doctor. Tell her how bad Mama is suffering," I said hoarsely.

She nodded her head and let herself down the ladder.

I slipped in and out of sleep as I sat next to Mama. She moaned and seemed to have small fits in her slumber. The sun had dipped behind the house by the time she opened her cloudy eyes.

"Mama." I caressed her face as our eyes locked on each other's. The intensity of her gaze took me by surprise. I felt the depth of her love, though no words passed between us. For a moment, my mind went empty of everything but her. Then she motioned with a bent finger to the brown jar. I held it to her lips and she swallowed. She lifted her mouth and breathed into my ear.

"'Member who you are Pheby . . . Delores Brown."

"Mama, save your strength."

"You ain't nobody's prop—" She drooled saliva and then her face went limp.

"Mama!" I shrieked.

But she was gone.

First came shock. Then the wail rumbled deep down in my gut until the grief gurgled up in my throat. Agony poured from my lips as if I were being decimated like a hog. Felt that way, too. Into her warm chest, I sobbed. How was I meant to go on without my mama? I slipped to my knees, held my head in my hands, and wept.

I knew I should get back up to the big house, but I could not make myself move toward the ladder. I did not know how much time had passed when Aunt Hope came for me. When she took in the scene she swooped me up in her arms and held me tight.

"I's sorry 'bout this," she said, as she patted my back. "Ruth ain't deserve to go like this."

I could hear flies already flitting around, and Aunt Hope moved to cover Mama's body with a white sheet.

"Know it's hard, but you got to keep goin'. I didn't know my mama at all. Thank God you had her long as you did." In that moment, I did not feel like the lucky one.

She wiped the dampness from her eyes with the back of her hand. "We need our heads right now. Snitch sniffin' 'round the kitchen asking me questions about Essex. Think he might make his way to the house for a word with Missus."

It took a few moments for me to comprehend.

"Needin' your smarts, gal, to get him off the trail."

I rose, feeling crippled; kissed Mama's forehead; and pressed my hands against my cheeks, hoping they would arrange me into some sort of order.

The temperature outside had dropped to a chill, and there was no sign of the moon. Snitch stood at the foot of the back steps, with his whip hanging around his neck like a snake hungry to strike. His left cheek was puffed up with tobacco and he smelled like whiskey.

"Where is the stable boy?"

"Missus sent him to see about Master Jacob," I answered.

"I ain't seen the mistress taking her walks. Where is she?"

"Under the weather, sir."

"Gon' need confirmation of that. Let me in."

Aunt Hope and I blocked the path to the door.

"Missus Delphina is too weak to take the stairs," I replied.

"Ain't proper for a man ain't her husband enter her bedchamber this late at night."

Snitch's dark eyes forced fear in every slave he came across. I was no different, and it took careful concentration for me not to fidget and show our lie.

"I'll be back in the morning. Tell her I needs to see her." He spit on the ground in front of us, then mounted his horse. Once he'd disappeared through the thicket, I exhaled.

"What are we going to do?"

"They gon' know sooner or later. You get rid of his things?"

"Not yet, been with Mama." Her name on my lips made me choke, and then my knees trembled.

Aunt Hope grabbed me up with her strong arms. I sniffed and forced my lungs to breathe in the air to keep from feeling light-headed. Aunt Hope pulled a handkerchief from her apron and wiped the fresh wetness from my eyes. "Burn her things, too, so infection don't spread."

I nodded and watched her walk to the kitchen house. If Snitch planned to see Missus first light, under the cover of the moonless night seemed the best time to burn Essex's things. I could not bring myself to disrupt Mama—her stuff would wait—but I made my way over to the stables. Parrott stood on a stool brushing one of the horses, a corn pipe dangling from between his lips.

"Snitch looking for Essex, so be careful."

"Just saw him. Came to burn up Essex's things."

I climbed up into the loft area where Essex slept and grabbed everything he'd left behind. An old work shirt, a worn-out straw hat, and a threadbare blanket. I gathered them along with the straw pallet he slept on and lugged them down the path that led deeper into the woods. It was not until I passed the cemetery that I realized I was headed to the black walnut tree. Instinctively I knew that to protect Essex, I needed to burn his belongings on the grounds of Mama's tree.

The red ribbon I had tied flapped against the wind, welcoming me. I could feel Mama's presence as I prayed for Essex's safe passage to freedom. Then I placed everything in a pile and created fire with a flint and steel. Once the spark caught on the char cloth, I tossed it onto the pile and watched the flames lick through his things. Now that Mama had crossed over, I wondered if I would have fared better running with Essex. With them both gone, Master Jacob was all I had left. That thought settled in my belly like a heavy stone.

The fire had all but died when I saw movement down by the river. I expected it was a white-tailed deer. Mama always warned me that they tended to be more active at night. But then I heard a faint cry. Curiosity made me walk toward the sound, and when I reached the river's edge, I spotted Missus Delphina wading out into the water past her knees. I heard another high-pitched cry, and then she plunged down to her chest in the water. I took off running.

"Missus," I called, but she did not answer me. When she emerged from the water, I saw the infant boy. It laid limp and naked in her arms. Missus stepped out the water and then threw the lifeless body into my arms.

"Bury it."

She turned for the big house while my tears ran like an open spigot. How could she be so cruel as to kill her own flesh and blood? She could have given him to a field woman to raise. No one in Lowtown would have asked questions, just accepted him as their own. His poor little body felt cold, so I untied my headscarf and covered him with it. Two beautiful souls lost on the same day. I carried the boy up to the storehouse, removed a shovel, and then went back to the spot where I had burned Essex's clothes and started digging a grave for his son.

CHAPTER 8

Snitch

I woke up the next morning haunted by the infant boy's face; then I remembered Mama's body under the white sheet and hot tears stung my eyes. Soon as I got dressed, I found Lovie heading into the nursery and told her what Missus had done to the baby. Her bottom lip quivered, and she rocked on her heels, looking as if she might faint. Snitch, yelling from the side door, pulled her from her stupor.

"I will take care of him." I handed her a towel for her face, then sprinted downstairs to the door.

"Needs to talk to the mistress now. Go tell her I am here."

Missus Delphina had not emerged from her bedroom, nor had she beckoned me to bring her anything. While I stood there trying to figure out my next move, Snitch shoved me aside and entered the house.

"Mistress Delphina," he called out. "I needs to speak with you!"

He moved through the service room and out into the entrance hall, trying to decide which way to go; then he grabbed my arm.

"Show me to her room. Now."

Lovie appeared just as I was beginning to discolor. "Mr. Snitch, what can we do for you?"

He pushed past her, took the front steps three at a time to the second floor, and shouted for the missus. The upstairs bedrooms fanned in a U shape, and he started knocking on doors until he came upon hers.

"Yes," she croaked. "What calls for so much racket?"

"It's Snitch and I needs to talk to you. Are you all right in there?"

We followed him, and Lovie moved to speak through the door.

"Missus, are you proper?"

Snitch knocked again. "I needs a word now."

"Come in."

Lovie and I went after Snitch into Missus's chambers. She had the covers pulled up to her chin and her hair could have used a comb.

"What is the meaning of this unplanned visit?" she barked.

Snitch removed his hat and explained that he had not seen Essex in a few days. "The yella girl said you sent him on an errand and I want confirmation."

Missus sat up in her bed. "That was a few days ago."

"I did not know you wrote the pass."

"My husband pays you finely to make everything that happens with our property your business."

"No sighting of him is why I am here, ma'am. Thinking he might of gon' astray."

Missus looked at Lovie and then me. "Ninny, where is Essex?"

"It is like you said, Missus, he rode out to check on Master Jacob at the doctor's house. Perhaps Master asked Essex to stay with him until he felt well enough to travel home."

She threw back her covers, then thought better of it and pulled them back over her. "You make it your immediate duty to alert the patroller," she barked at Snitch. "He is my best nigger and I want him back here."

Lovie showed Snitch out, and Missus fixed her eyes on me. "My mama died last night."

Missus Delphina brought her hands to her mouth. I did not know if she hid a smile or shock. "Lord have mercy on this plantation. How much more can a mistress take in one day?"

She pushed back her blankets. "Tell Hope to get the men to dig a grave. A small service can be held Saturday night after the work is done."

"Yes, Missus."

She looked at me. "Ninny, I cannot imagine how you feel, but there is work to be done. So stop moping and help me dress so that I can get this place back under control."

Missus had me pull her corset extra tight, but I could still see the puffiness around her middle. It made me remember the tan baby boy and what she had done to him, and to Mama by not calling for the doctor. Disdain for her settled in my fingers, and I yanked on her hair as I brushed it.

"Ow!" She tried to grab the brush, but I held it tightly in my fist.

"Sorry, it got tangled."

"Watch it, girl." She bumped me with her shoulder.

I removed the brush and swept her hair into a simple twist. Once she felt satisfied with her appearance, I walked after her downstairs. Outside she located Snitch and ordered him to ring the bell.

One. Two. Three. Four. Five. Five rings meant a slave had escaped the plantation. In a matter of minutes, the ones from Lowtown hustled up the hill while thick pillowy clouds hovered overhead. Standing at the edge of the porch, Missus Delphina clasped her hands together and looked down at all who had gathered. Thirty-six of us now since Rachel, Mama, and Essex were gone.

"Essex Henry has gone astray. If you know anything about his disappearance, please step forward."

Parrott removed his hat. "Missus, he prob'ly on his way. Got held up by them patrollers. Gave me a hard time when I was carryin' back Ruth."

Just her name on his lips made me hug my waist.

"Anyone else?"

Snitch clutched the whip that hung down to his hip. "That yella gal know something 'bout it. Them two was quite close. Let me take her to Lowtown for a bit. Sure I get some information out of her. More than she say?"

"You well know that Master Jacob forbids this child to be whipped."

"Got other ways to make her talk 'sides whipping," he snorted.

"Thank you, Mister Snitch. Anyone else?" No one else spoke.

"Fine." She gripped the railing with both hands. "No more rations will be given out until Essex is returned. You want to keep secrets, then you will starve." She turned on her heels and slammed the door behind her.

The lot of the field hands looked stunned. Cutting off their rations served as a cruel punishment. Even with the scraps that Aunt Hope sent down at night, it was not enough to feed everyone. I watched as folks headed back down the hill, many with sloped backs and shuffling feet.

When I finished my morning chores in the house, Lovie sent me to can fruit and vegetables for the winter.

Ordinarily it was not my job, but it was a mindless task. There were strawberries, blueberries, peas, green beans, and cucumbers. I washed then soaked each fruit in a barrel with brine. Then I lugged the heavy barrels down to the root cellar, where they would stay until we needed them. The cellar was cold and dark, and once the door closed behind me, my knees sank into the dirt floor. Hurt rose up in my throat and my lungs did not want to breathe. My mouth opened and I grunted out my pain. I cried and howled and groaned until there was nothing left inside of me. Then I opened the door and threw up.

On my pallet that night, I felt three times my age. For the first time in a while, I fell into an immediate sleep. Then I heard Mama. Her husky voice addressed me, but I could not understand her words. I shifted my body in her direction, fighting hard to take her in. As I was on the cusp of connecting, a splash of wetness drenched my hair and gown. My eyes fluttered opened, and Missus Delphina stood over me, her empty chamber pot on her hip. My eyes burned with shock and disbelief.

"You did this. You helped him escape." She kicked me as I lay frozen, covered in her urine. "Do not play dumb with me. Jacob is always bragging about how smart you are. How Sally taught you this and Sally taught you that. You think you are special because Sally used you as a little pet?"

I could not speak, so I shook my head no.

"I am so tired of living in everyone's shadow." She dropped the pot, and the meager contents that were left dripped onto the wooden floor.

I battled with her smelly piss streaming down my face while she ranted and raved. I tried not to breathe. *Don't open your mouth else her piss will make its way inside of you.*

I forced myself up and off the floor of my closet room. Missus berated me for so long that I began sinking under the heaviness of it all.

"You are a poor excuse for a slave. You are a wretched whore, just like your mother was," Missus Delphina shouted, and then moved to slap me, but I caught her hand in the air and tried to crush her fingers. She looked aghast, and that gave me courage.

"Do not speak on my mother. She would be alive if you had only sent for the doctor. Her blood is on your hands," I declared, sounding so steady, it frightened even me. "You will not put your hands on me ever again."

Lovie appeared. "Come, Missus. Let me get you in the bed."

"Did you see that wench touch me? I will have you whipped until you are begging me for mercy. I do not care what Jacob says. You will be sorry."

Lovie took her by the elbow and escorted her across the hall to her bedroom, closing the door behind them. I marched outside and over to the kitchen house.

"What happened?" Aunt Hope lit a candle and then dragged over a bucket of water.

I explained, while washing away Missus Delphina's waste.

"Why does she hate me so much? I have never done anything to her."

"You are Massa's child. She knowin' that why he favor you."

"My lineage is not my fault."

"White women too wrapped up in they own head to figure out we ain't ask for this life. We take what's given and makes the best out it. That what your mama did. What you has to do."

Aunt Hope gave me a clean dress that hung big. I slipped it on and took a seat next to the fire. She cut me a piece of leftover pie and the sugar helped.

"Shame what she done to that innocent baby." Aunt Hope raked the coals hard. "Big sin she gon' have to deal wit' when she meet her maker."

We watched the flames crackle in the fire.

"I cannot go back up there tonight. All right if I sleep here?"

"Course, chile."

I made a bed for myself in the corner out of rags, and Aunt Hope blew out the candle.

CHAPTER 9

---·---

The Funeral

*A*unt Hope woke me at first light and sent me back up to the house to do my morning chores. Lovie assigned me tasks away from Missus Delphina's eyesight, which included washing sheets in the scullery, beating the rugs behind the house, and polishing the silver in the service nook. Halfway through the polishing, the sky let loose and seemed to cry heavy tears for Mama. Fat raindrops beat against the outside shutters, and the roof shingles clapped with the gusty wind. Whenever it rained during the middle of the day, Missus Delphina favored a nap. The moment she took to her bed, I slipped out the side door and over to the loom house to retrieve some of our treasured items before the loom house was assigned to someone else, now that Mama was gone.

Since my birthday was on Christmas Day, Miss Sally had taken to giving me a birthday gift in the morning when I arrived, and a Christmas gift in the evening before I retired with Mama. On my twelfth birthday, Miss Sally had given me a leather-bound diary. The book was a little bigger than my palm. Brown leather, with a thin strap to tie around the middle to keep it closed. The rag pages were a faint beige, with scalloped edges. Miss Sally had said the book was imported from England and showed me where that was on her world map. On the inside flap of the diary she'd inscribed:

Dearest Pheby,

Hold fast to your dreams, whilst they come true.

With affection,
Miss Sally

That evening she gave me a bottle of ink and a metal pen point. Mama fretted the moment I brought my gifts into the loom house and constantly cautioned me. "Slave got they fingers chop't off and eyes burn't wit' lye for readin' and writin'."

Now, a film of dust had collected over Mama's jars. My fingers grazed the bottles, and in that moment Mama's recipes and lessons came alive in my head. I had to get them down. From the underside of our mattress, I retrieved my diary. With it in my hand, I could almost conjure up the feel of Miss Sally's bony fingers. Then I walked the shelves in the back of the room until I located the yellow jar that contained my ink bottle, deep below the hempseeds, and the pen I had hidden in my pillow, wrapped in tin and stuffed between the straw.

At the kitchen table that Mama and I had shared, I opened my diary and began to write. Mama's husky voice steadied my thoughts as my hand glided across the page. Healing herbs, powerful teas, where things grew, the right time to pick them, what leaves need to be crushed, steeped, and left whole. The amount of mint to mix with cow manure to make tea "fur consumption." Where to find the jimsonweed for muscle pain and the chestnut leaf for better breathing. Which herbs to place in the bath to help with dropsy, and how much sassafras root to use for searching the blood, and healing all that ailed.

The sun had moved to the other side of the plantation, so I knew I would be missed up at the house, but I could not stop. Mama's roots and recipes were all I had left, and I scribbled until I'd exhausted my memory.

Mama had always sewn secret pockets on the inside of my skirt so that I could move goods around without being detected. I decided to start carrying the diary with me tucked in the hidden pocket of my petticoat. I wrapped the book inside of Mama's mauve headscarf; that way I could smell her like she was in the room with me. Not wanting to leave all of Mama's hard work behind, I loaded up the containers and made several trips to the sick house, where her herbs and tinctures would be of use, then carried the mixtures Aunt Hope would appreciate to the kitchen.

Back up at the big house, the lanterns were out, and Missus Delphina had gone down for the night. The next morning, she did not utter one single word to me. All my instructions came through Lovie. I was not sure if the encounter between us had spooked her or not, and I did not have room in my thoughts to care much. Mama's funeral was only two days away, and with my workload I had no time or material to pull together a proper mourning dress. Aunt Hope sent me with a basket of scraps down to Lowtown, and on my way back I stopped in the loom house to see if I could find anything to wear.

When I climbed the ladder, the room smelled like lemons and vinegar, and I suspected that Aunt Hope had come over and tidied up the way Mama would have. Draped on the hook behind the door hung the red calico dress that Mama had worn on the day she left with Master Jacob for Charleston. I had not noticed it when I recorded her recipes, but it jumped out at me now. The red was rich and bright. I brought it to my nose, then held it at arm's length. It was the finest piece that Mama owned, and the perfect way to honor her memory.

For the next two nights, I snuck over to the loom house and worked on Mama's dress, taking it in to fit my slimmer size and repairing the lace on the bodice. When Saturday morning arrived, I had one last piece to hem to complete the transformation of the dress, but I still felt anxious that I would not finish. Lovie must have sensed my angst, because when she noticed me struggling with waxing the floor, she offered to take over so that I could prepare.

I stripped out of my house clothes, splashed down with water, and then tied a piece of material around my waist to suffice as a corset. My diary I hid in the pocket of my petticoat. Next, I put on Mama's hoopskirt, being careful with the grapevine. When I buttoned the bodice of the red calico dress and caught sight of myself in the small hanging mirror, I clutched my chest. Looking back at me was the spitting image of Mama. Just younger, with fairer skin. I wrapped my arms around myself and exhaled my grief. She had been meant to see my freedom and now it would never happen.

A piece of silk bobbin lace was left over from a tablecloth, and I used that as my mourning veil. At sunset, I met Lovie and Aunt Hope in front of the kitchen house.

"You look so beautiful." Aunt Hope teared up.

Lovie squeezed my hand. "Your mama be proud."

The three of us walked to the clearing in Lowtown where the service would be held. The clearing served as the slaves' meeting place for Sunday church services, jumping-the-broom ceremonies, and general time-off gatherings. Farther down, behind the old barn house, was the cemetery where Mama would be laid to rest.

People arrived in pairs and groups to pay their respects. The field hands cleaned their faces, but most did not own a second set of clothes in which to honor Mama. A few girls picked rosebuds and put them in their hair, and the men tied bows made of plant stems around their necks. Once everyone arrived, we stood around the fire holding hands. Aunt Hope and Lovie stood on either side of me. Johnnie White, our preacher, gave the word.

"Peace I leave with you; my peace I give you. I do not give to you as the world gives. Don't let your heart be troubled and be not afraid."

I took Mama's needlework and placed it over the rough, homemade coffin for her to use in the afterlife. Aunt Hope put down a cup and saucer, Parrott a medicine bottle filled with her favorite herbs, and Lovie woolen socks to keep her warm. I then removed the white orchid from my hair and tossed it over the coffin. All the women and children followed. Then the men picked up their shovels and started layering the box with dirt. The smell of soil reminded me of burying Missus's infant boy and covering up her lie. A woman started to sing a hymn.

Voice by voice, more singers joined in, and soon I was enclosed by song. The kids clapped their hands to the beat. All of us swayed, sang, and prayed until Mama's coffin was buried.

Missus had lifted her constraints on the food rations and allowed a feast to be prepared for the occasion. Aunt Hope ushered everyone to the long wooden table; it was covered with stewed chicken, sweet potatoes, dumplings, spinach, corn, and sweet bread. The field hands brought their bowls, and I watched as Aunt Hope made sure they were filled to the brim. I did not have an appetite for food, so I dished out the applesauce for dessert. Once people's bellies were content, the music started up and the dancing began. The griots had brought with them homemade instruments; the banjo, a drum, tambourines, a balafo, and panpipes.

A new wave of sadness came over me. I usually danced with Essex at our parties, but now Parrott lifted me to my feet and we moved together. I closed my eyes and pretended he was Essex, the necklace he had given me pressing against my neck. Everyone clapped and I stirred my hips, trying to shake all the pain from my body. My feet stomped and the movement rinsed and released my heart. I had not felt so free in weeks. As I curtsied to Parrott I heard horses up the hill. With the wine being passed around it seemed that most were too relaxed to notice. Aunt Hope looked in the direction of Hightown and I knew she heard it too. I scooted over to her, wondering if the patrollers had come with news on Essex.

Aunt Hope and I kept looking up the hill, but the darkness made it hard to see past the thickness of the bushes and trees.

I heard a rustling of branches being crushed and pushed aside. Then Snitch appeared through the thicket. His dark eyes fell upon me. Before my mind could tell me to run, he had me in his arms so tight that I could not smell anything except the whiskey seeping through his pores. I kicked and screamed but he held me tighter.

"What's the cause of you 'rupting the funeral like this?" Aunt Hope demanded. "Ain't you no respect?"

"Mind your bizness, old lady. I am in charge here."

"Not of Pheby. She works the big house. Missus know you down here causin' trouble?"

"Shut up."

"Poor child just buried her mama. Ain't you got no manners?"

Snitch turned around and with one hand slapped Aunt Hope hard across her face. She stumbled but did not fall. Then he dragged me by the arm up toward Hightown. I was terrified of what I would find up there. Remembering Aunt Hope's son, Jasper, and how swollen and bloody he looked when he got hauled back from running away, I tried to prepare myself to see Essex that way. Snitch pulled me past the loom house. I looked up at the window, recalling Mama's sign of the lit candle. Wished it was there now, telling me to come on home.

When we reached the front of the big house, Missus Delphina stood in the light of the porch. There was a rickety wagon parked in the lane with three men in irons and two women, sparsely clothed and tied in ropes, but I did not see Essex. If he had not been caught, then what were the slave traders doing on the plantation? Before I could figure out the puzzle, Snitch heaved me by the waist and carried me toward the wagon. I kicked him, screamed, pounded my fist into his chest. When he put me down, I tried to run, but he grabbed me by the hair. Then I felt a knock in the back of my head. Static flooded my eyelids as I felt myself being scooped into the air. That was when I realized: the wagon had come for me.

I looked up at the big house. Missus was standing on the edge of the porch, hawk eyes blazing.

"You dare put your hands on me." Her mouth turned into a snarl.

"Master Jacob would not approve of you selling me," I shouted, staring her squarely in the face.

"You telling me what to do with my property, girl?"

"I am not property. Now let me go."

She threw back her head and laughed. "You have a lot to learn, child. Take her to the Lapier jail, where she will be punished properly for helping my best nigger escape. Then have her sold as a fancy girl to live out the life she deserves, as a whore."

Missus twirled her finger to the burly trader behind the carriage. On her command, he reached for me. I struggled to get free, but the trader's hands were coarse and quick as he tied me to the other women in the wagon. One of the women had knotted hair, and she reeked like Mama had when she lay dying. Blood stained the front of her dress and her gaze was unfocused.

The field hands who just a few minutes before had been celebrating my mother's life had gathered to watch the scene. Some reached their hands out toward me. I could hear Lovie calling my name, and then Aunt Hope dropped down on her knees, raised her hands up to the sky, and crooned:

In my sorrows, Lord walk with me
In my sorrows, Lord walk with me
When my heart is aching, Lord walk with me.

Folks followed Aunt Hope's cry and sang too. I had never felt so powerless in my life. Even still, I refused to give Missus Delphina the satisfaction of seeing one tear leak from my eyes, or one plea of mercy fall from my lips. Instead I turned my terror into fury and glared at her.

"I curse you and all of your unborn children in the name of my grandmother, Queen Vinnie Brown. May all your worst fears come to pass, and all the evil you do come back on you tenfold. This plantation will be your living hell. Mark my words." I spat on the ground, bracing myself for her to march down the stairs and slap me. But she stood as if stunned.

All eyes were on me as the wagon pulled away from the house, so I kept my back straight and my sight on the road ahead. Once Master recovered from his injury, he would come for me and send me to that school in Massachusetts where Essex and I would be reunited. He had been a good master, and when he found out that Missus had let Mama die and sold me to traders like I was a common slave, he would be outraged. With Miss Sally gone, I was the only blood family he had left.

"Neigh," called the driver to the horses.

The old carriage picked up speed, rocking me against the bloodstained woman. I ducked my head under some low brush and then closed my eyes to the rising dust.

PART TWO

The Devil's Half Acre

CHAPTER 10

Marched

Before Snitch drove the Bell plantation, the job belonged to a driver named Reade, a thickset man with meaty hands so large folks said he crushed men's skulls for sport and boiled children in the middle of the night for his supper. One day, while I was out chasing a white-tailed rabbit, I accidentally ventured past the clearing on the Lowtown side of the river, and found myself behind the overseer's white clapboard house. My stomach sank at my mistake. Before I could run, Reade walked out of his side door dragging a teenage girl behind him. The girl cried, clawed, and screamed, but Reade tossed her over his shoulders like she was a rag doll. I hid behind the nearest oak tree and tried not to breathe. When I braved another look, Reade had tossed the girl against the whipping post and tied her wrists and ankles until she could not move. Her voice begged and apologized but Reade reached into her mouth and pulled out her tongue.

The girl's guttural screams sounded like glass exploding in my ears. It was a sound that haunted me for months. I never told Mama what I had seen, and thought I would never experience such terror, until I found myself sitting in the back of the rickety wagon, tied to unfamiliar bodies and headed to a jail for punishment. Would I be burned at the stake like the witches in Miss Sally's stories? Stretched out and whipped like a runaway, or sold farther down south as a field hand? Mama always said the deeper south you went, the harder life proved for a slave. Wherever we were headed I would need all my strength and fortitude. I put on a brave face and prayed that the whites of my eyes did not betray my horror.

The woman with the bloodied dress and knotted hair wept loudly. I looked to the woman in the green scarf who sat across from us for an explanation. Blood smeared her hands too.

"What happened?"

She looked to the front of the wagon, then spoke out the side of her lips. "I delivered her baby in this wagon few miles 'fore we pick't you up. Baby come out with the cord 'round 'em neck." Her breath was hot against my ear. "Trader take the dead thing from her arms and throw it in the ditch. Don't bury 'em or nuttin'."

The woman kept staring at me. "You real pretty."

I looked down and saw that I still wore Mama's red dress. Suddenly, I felt ashamed. "I was at my mama's funeral when they came for me. My name is Pheby."

"I's Alice."

The wagon rumbled along. The bloody woman's head bounced from side to side like she had no control over her neck. The men in the wagon were clustered in one corner, we women in the other, and the three drivers rode up front. I felt the lump swelling in my head from where Snitch hit me, but it did not compare to the sense of dread that swam in my stomach. I was wishing that I had eaten something at Mama's gathering, when the bloody woman doubled over with her hands on her belly. She groaned and seemed to bear down like she was defecating. Then the afterbirth oozed out from between her legs. She shrieked and then fell back, her face withered in pain.

"Shut up back there," the trader driving the wagon called over his shoulder.

The blue glob with bloody streaks sat between us, wiggling with every bump of the wagon. We smelled the foul metallic odor the whole way up the road. I closed my eyes to shut it all out, but could not find stillness. Sometime in the middle of the night, we stopped at a little roadside shack.

"Up," the driver shouted at us. He had a long beard that reached the top of his shirt collar.

When we stepped down out of the wagon, I concentrated on walking close to the bloody woman, holding her up like a crutch. Inside the dank, windowless cabin, people were crammed together, leaving no room for even a pill to fall. But still we were shoved in too. The heavy air smelled rancid and our captors left us to go outside. I imagined they chewed to-bacco, passed whiskey, and discussed their profit shares.

The bloody woman leaned into me. "I's Matilda."

"Pheby Delores Brown."

"That's a lotta names." She placed her head on my shoulder, and just that quick, I heard her snoring.

I did not sleep. I focused on supporting Matilda. We were packed in-side the hot, tiny house for a while. Had I been home, I would have col-lected the eggs from the chicken coop, waited on Aunt Hope to fry them, and served breakfast. But I was not home; I had been stolen from my family. To survive this, I could not let my mind succumb to the misery that threatened to strangle me.

Just before daylight, a clean-cut man walked through the door. He car-ried himself like he was the man in charge.

"Move out," he barked at us.

His accent had more twang to it than I was accustomed to hearing. He probably came from farther down south. Maybe New Orleans or someplace like that. My gang lined up, and as we moved outside, the man in charge counted us off. Altogether we made sixty-one. Forty men and twenty-one women. All of us women from the wagon were untied and then retied to the other women from the shack. The ropes around our wrist made our hands jut forward, and a halter was slipped over our necks. I continued to stay close to Matilda through the sorting process and she was tied behind me. Alice stood way at the other end of the line. When our captors completed our bondage, they told us to sit on the damp ground and went on to ironing the men.

"Boys, get in two straight lines."

One hefty man paused to figure out the instruction and earned a whack over his back with the club. "Move it, nigger. Ain't got time to waste."

After that, the men hurried to make the lines. The whites with clubs moved through the men slaves, fixing a thick iron collar around each of their necks and then securing it with a padlock. A thick chain of metal was threaded through the clasp of each lock, securing the row together. Their hands were then cuffed tightly in front of them. I had never seen a coffle before and felt sickened by the sight. Despite Miss Sally's piano lessons and pampering, and Mama's protection from the hardships of Lowtown, I stood ill prepared to be tied up and driven like an animal. Here I was just like everyone else. Handled like goods to be sold.

"Get up," called the man in charge. "March out."

We obeyed, and began our procession to God knows where. I walked as one of the few people wearing proper shoes. I could not envision what it felt like to trek through the woods barefoot with the constant pricks of stones, pine cones, and needles. The first few hours tired me like doing my morning chores, but they passed in relative silence. Then, after a while, Matilda resumed her whimpering.

The white men were on horseback: one at the front, one in the middle of the line, and one bringing up the rear. Matilda's moans got so loud that the man in charge slowed his horse next to her and put his club in her face.

"If I hear one more thing from you, I'll shoot you in the head." He rode up and shouted for all to hear. "Keep your mouths shut and your feet moving forward."

Matilda stayed quiet after that, and no one else in the coffle made a peep. While we traveled down the road, deeper into the night, the temperature dropped and the clouds rolled in. My dress was made well, but some wore threadbare scraps that barely covered their private areas. The sky gave way and it drizzled off and on but that did not halt our journey. When the sun came up, we stopped for a small break. They passed around a few buckets with drops of water, but it did not quench my thirst. Hunger pains stung my belly, and the rope cut welts into my wrists.

We marched again until nightfall, and stopped when we reached an open field. Two women were released from the front of the line and instructed to make a fire. The rest of us were told to sit on the ground. Even though the dirt was cold and hard, it felt good to stop and stretch. My feet ached, and my ankles had puffed up like dough rising. As much as I wanted to remove my shoes, I feared not being able to get them back on. Plus our hands were still tied.

Cakes made of cornmeal and boiled herring were passed around. We were given water to wipe the journey from our fingers, but the dirt remained mucked into my palms. Somehow, I managed to get my food into my mouth. The meal did not taste good, but I sensed it would be a stretch before we were given more, so I forced it all down. When the canteen came to me, I drank with desperation. It was the first time in my life that I did not care if the water ran clean or held contamination.

"Lie back and get some sleep," commanded the man in charge.

Matilda fell asleep before I made peace with the earth. I had never slept outside on the ground before and could not find respite. The night sounds frightened me. Crickets rubbed their legs together, birds squawked, a coyote howled in the distance. I tossed and turned, worrying over snakes sneaking up to strangle me. Even the crackle of the fire made me uneasy.

Since rest would not come, I passed the time conjuring up my memory of lying with Essex. I replayed his hard body moving against mine in the stables until I could smell him in front of me. Pretending to be in his arms proved to be the only thing that eased my anxiety and allowed me a little peace.

Before sunrise we were roused and then were at it again. We repeated the march schedule for days. We walked until my feet had blisters on soft, tender skin. We trekked past the time that the raw skin on my feet opened and my socks were soiled with blood. No matter how terrible I felt, we had to keep stepping or else be clubbed. Some in my gang sang to keep the rhythm but I did not. I kept my despair quiet, close to my heart.

◆

On the eighth day of walking, we reached a quaint town near the mouth of the river. The sun smiled brightly from the sky while the wind cooled my face. I had never seen so many boats in my life. Big steamboats, flatboats, small fishing boats.

Along the water's edge sat a string of homes built close together, two and three stories high, multicolored, narrow, on tiny patches of land. As we got closer, the air smelled sour, like a combination of old fish and forgotten fowl, killed but never fried. That, mixed with the smell of those of us in shackles, made my stomach swirl like a spinning top. I held my breath and tried to keep up with the line. Then one of the men told us to stop.

"Sit where you are. Wait for my command."

The man in charge chatted with a round-faced man standing near a boat with steam drifting from long pipes. The boat had two stories with a paddle wheel in the back. A flask moved back and forth between the two and they shared a laugh.

Not knowing what came next simply unnerved me. On the plantation, there was always order. In the amount of time we waited in the grass I could have weeded and watered Missus Delphina's entire garden, had I been back home. The horseflies showed no pity, and I moved my roped hands up and down to shoo them. Finally, the two men appeared and ushered us up from the ground.

"Go up the ramp to the boat. Move to the front of the vessel and lie down in a straight row."

The women went first. The wooden ramp felt unsteady under our weight but we shuffled across. We were packed tightly at the point of the front of the deck, with our backs on the floor and our heads toward the sky. A crew of men stood above us on the second level with a clear view of us below. I longed for a bath and clean clothing.

The men's voices strung together in quick conversation. One said, "Cain't wait to get to Richmond. Got me a fine piece waitin' on me."

"You ain't got no woman nowhere," said a man with a high-pitched voice.

"Jest jealous 'cause I get luckier than you."

"Dream on, sailor. Better get that paddle wheel going if you want to keep this job. Capt'n coming."

I looked around the boat deck wondering on the possibility of escape, but could barely move my body because we were so tightly knitted together. A few minutes later the boat pulled away from the dock. As we drifted, I wondered if we were on the James River. What would Richmond be like, and would it be our final stop? How would Missus Delphina's call for punishment play out?

There were four white men on board, including the captain. The youngest of the group had long black hair tied back and a hook nose. Whenever I looked up to the top deck, he stared down at me. I must have been a sight in my filthy red dress among the others wearing browns and burlap. He tried catching my eye but I turned the other way.

The boat sailed through the water, and the dipping over the waves made me nauseous. We were not offered any food or blankets. As the night grew long, the crew got louder from the upper deck. No doubt a bottle of spirits passed between them. I closed my eyes and tried to forget my suffering. I was unsure how much time had passed when I awakened to cold fingers on my knees, traveling higher up my thigh. My eyes flew open as the man with the hook nose climbed on top of me.

"Stop." I crossed my ankles.

Not only did I want to protect my virtue, but my diary was hidden a few inches from his hands. I shook my leg so he would not detect it. Several teeth were missing from his mouth, and he reeked of tobacco. I scrambled to get out of his grasp, but there was no place to go. Not enough air to breathe.

"Stay still," he mumbled and fumbled with his pants, "or I'll make it hurt real bad."

The people around me could not help me. Panic tightened in my chest. When he leaned over me, forcing my ankles apart, everything I had shot up from my belly. I threw up on him.

"Bitch." He slapped me across the face. I called out to get the attention of the captain. He glanced down from the upper deck.

"Jack, leave the goods alone."

"Come on, Captain."

"Don't want you messing with the money. Get back up here."

Jack wore my waste on his shirt. He kicked my foot as he stood up, but to my relief, he followed orders. Matilda turned her matted head and linked her sad eyes with mine.

"Overseer put the baby in me."

We comforted each other by letting our feet touch. The boat wafted along. A man in our row coughed and hacked all through the night, making sleep impossible. When morning came, Jack and another man passed out mush for breakfast. He handed me a bowl. When I looked down, my portion swam with phlegm. While the others ate, I closed my eyes and pretended to be in Aunt Hope's kitchen. I must have fallen asleep again, because Matilda yanked at my rope and brought me to attention.

"What?"

She pointed with her chin. That's when I saw it. The rise of tall buildings. The outline of a city the same way it looked in the newspaper. Beautiful, with the sun at its back and the sky pink and blue. It had to be Richmond. Our boat pulled along the river's edge and the men dropped the anchor. A few canteens of water went around to revive us, and I drank heartily.

"They don't like us parading the niggers 'round during the day. We will wait for nightfall!" the captain shouted to the crew.

Jack walked alongside me. "Got time to turn one of them loose for a little fun?" he shouted.

"Last time I turned one loose to you she lost her teeth. Cain't afford to lose money on this deal."

Once again, we were told to sit down on the grass. I still had the bug bites on my legs and arms from the last time. The water from the river was murky, but given the chance, I would still have bathed in it. We all sat quietly as the breeze whispered through the trees. I drummed my fingers on my thigh like I was playing the piano. It soothed me some. Then I hummed under my breath. At dusk, they passed around some cornbread and bacon. The small ration was not enough and I wished for more. When we finished eating, we were instructed to stand. Night had shaded the sky, and a handful of stars winked down at us.

"I don't want to hear a sound from you. No talking, crying, singing. Now move along."

The captain need not have admonished us; stories of hopelessness oozed from our sweat. I could see the despair of my fellow prisoners in the slump of their necks. We walked through the brush until I spotted a bridge up ahead. The post sign read MAYO BRIDGE. As we crossed it, the lights from the building in front of us twinkled like sparkly buttons. We marched past a big white building with pediments and columns. Then we were taken down streets with signs. I read CARY STREET. MAIN STREET. We made a right onto Franklin Street. I tried to record the direction in my head in case the opportunity came for me to run. Then our coffle turned into a smaller alley. It was chilly and stank of the most offensive odor I had encountered so far. Like the sweaty stench of death. The sign scripted on the wall read LAPIER'S ALLEY.

When I looked up, I saw a twelve-foot-high fence that was thickly set with iron spikes and stretched around the buildings. So this was the jail that Missus Delphina had sent me to. I had the keen sense to know that once I was inside it would be impossible for me to escape or even communicate with the outside world. I would be a prisoner. I tried to continue forward but stumbled over my misfortune. Before I could fall to my knees, I was yanked up by the rope connecting me to Matilda.

CHAPTER 11

———— ◆ ————

The Lapier Jail

I took in every sight and sound as we were paraded through the court-yard. There were six wooden buildings on the small plot of land. Two of the structures were large, about two stories high. One looked to be the main house. The other four buildings appeared similar to those on the Bell plantation: the kitchen, laundry, office, and maybe a supply shed. I could hear dogs barking not far away. The stank I smelled in the alley intensified. Sickeningly pungent. A new crew of white men stood waiting for us. Five in total, clutching knives and rifles.

"Boys to the right. Girls to the left."

The crew started unraveling the rope cords from our necks and cutting away at the ones binding our hands. The wounds on my wrists had crusted into scabs. Free for the first time in ten days, I stretched and arched like a newly awakened cat. Chains and metal padlocks clanked against the cob-blestone as the men were unhooked from their restraints. Before any of us could enjoy this small sense of freedom, we were steered toward the cen-ter brick building. The wooden door was unlocked and the men shouted, "Move into the jail."

We were crammed into the already overcrowded holding cell, forced against the sweaty flesh of unknown bodies. The door quickly locked behind us. There must have been hundreds of people already packed in the room when we were added. Heat and funk surrounded me. The combination of feces, blood, and vomit made breathing impossible. I could taste the rotten air settling in my throat. When I walked, my feet trod through a runny, sticky substance on the floor. How could Missus Delphina send me to hell? This place that was completely unfit for human habitation? My head started to spin and I felt myself descending. Before I reached the floor, Matilda grabbed my arm and held me up.

"You okay?"

I could hardly make out her face in the dark, so I rested my head on her breast.

"This be the jail. We stay in here till they get us ready for auction."

"How do you know?"

"Been here 'fore I's sold to my last massa."

"Do they ever clean it?" I hacked.

Matilda patted me like Mama would have. "You get use't it."

But I knew I would not. I had entered the bowels of slavery. My stomach contracted again, and I dry heaved until the sensation passed. I was alone and scared; sweat dripped all over me. Once our eyes adjusted to the blackness, people started moving around, looking for lost relatives and friends, seeking news of their whereabouts. Then Matilda gave a shout and scuffled away from me. She threw her arms around a tall man with broad shoulders. They hugged, kissed, and hugged again. I stood watching until she looked my way.

"This be my husband," she explained with tears in her eyes. "He sold 'way from me three years ago."

"Sam."

"Pheby Delores Brown."

"Ain't that a lotta names?" Matilda laughed, and even in the dark her true beauty shined through. Watching them together made me long for Essex. "Nice to meet you."

I walked on to give them time. After what Matilda had gone through, she deserved this slice of happiness, if only for one night. I turned sideways, stepping over bodies and into piles of crap as I made my way back to the front of the room. Mama often said that her mind was most clear after she had a bit of rest. I covered my nose and mouth with my sleeve and leaned my head against the grimy wall.

◆

I did not know that the sun had risen until the door creaked open. The men shielded their noses and mouths behind white cloths as they belted out orders.

"Girls, move out."

Matilda found me. "We goin' to the block now. Some ain't so lucky. Runaways be sent here for the whippin'."

A fresh terror came over me. I whispered that my missus had wanted me punished for raising a hand to her.

"Pretty gal like you worth more unharmed. Copy me and don't worry none."

I followed her into the light. The air blew a little fresher and I breathed deeply.

"Over here." The men handled us roughly, the same way they would push and prod hogs. We were divided into packs of five and then led into the yard where there were four water pumps.

"Clean up well."

Two of us used one pump at a time, and while I waited my turn I noticed that some had small bags with them. I only had my diary stowed in my secret pocket, along with the necklace Essex had given me. Nothing to change into. When I stepped up to the spigot, I could only splash my face and hands and dampen my hair in the few minutes allotted. Next, we were directed into a small back room where a few servants handed out tin pans containing cabbage, Indian peas, and cornbread. I felt so relieved to have real food that for a split second I forgot my circumstances.

"May I have a spoon?" I asked.

The woman standing before me was dressed well, with her hair pinned up in an elaborate bun. "A spoon? You ain't in the big house no mo'." Her eyes chastised me, and she clucked her tongue before moving on.

Embarrassed by my mistake, I buried my face in my food. Using my fingers, I dipped the cabbage and Indian peas between my teeth. The dish could have used a bit of salt but besides that, it was indeed the best meal I had had since leaving the plantation. Once everyone in my group had eaten, the same servants returned with things for our hair. Wire cards, like the ones we used on the plantation for wool, flax, and hemp.

Some of the women tied red scarves on their heads. I combed my hair simply because it felt good to groom myself, and then twisted it away from my face. My dress contained stains from my journey, and my shoes were mucked in waste, but I did not plan to doll myself up to please anyone. If Parrott brought Master Jacob to Richmond by carriage, he would get here fast enough to stop all of this foolishness. I just prayed that his injuries would not delay him further. After my many days of torture, I was ready to return home, even if it meant dealing with Missus Delphina.

The men barked more orders, and we were led toward the back door to one of the smaller buildings on the lot. A red flag hung over the entranceway. I could smell smoking pipes and hear men talking loudly, laughing, from inside. I was with five other women including Matilda, and four men followed closely behind. One of the women clutched a young girl to her chest, her eyes blazing with worry. Must have been her daughter. I prayed these men would be kind and keep them together.

The room we entered was small and stuffy. White men sat in tight rows; some stood along the back wall. All were wearing the latest fashions akin to the pictures in Missus Delphina's magazines: highly starched cravats, silk vests. Some wore frock coats, even though it was hot as the dickens. A wooden platform shaped like a block sat in the center of the room. We walked in a row and stood in front of it. The first man on line was ushered up on the block. A robust white man with ruddy cheeks stood at the podium, cleared his throat, and began to read.

"Full Negro called Arthur. He comes from the Madagascar tribe. A skilled blacksmith and carpenter. He can also work the fields. Perfect health." As the presenter spoke, a potential buyer stuck his hand in Arthur's mouth. Another pinched his limbs and asked him to bend over. I did not understand if the men were looking for something specific, or just wanted to humiliate him further. As if being under the foot of their dominance did not demean him enough.

"Drop you pants. Turn around and squat."

When Arthur turned, I could see the anguish in his eyes, but he did his best to keep his face pleasant.

"There is no lameness or weakness. He had been examined by one of our best doctors. His price starts at one hundred and fifty dollars."

The bidding for Arthur ended up being a battle between two men. Arthur's eyes dashed between them, probably praying under his breath that he would leave with the kinder master. In the end, he fetched seven hundred and fifty dollars.

Next up, Matilda. She whispered to me that she had hoped to stay with her husband, who was in the group behind ours.

"Disrobe." Matilda's upper lip trembled but she gave no resistance. She slid her arms out of her burlap sack dress and let it fall to her knees. She wore nothing underneath. Her hands flew to her full breasts to hide the milk that leaked. I turned my head, ashamed by the scene.

"Face back and squat."

When Matilda obeyed, a trickle of blood ran down her thigh.

"I would like to see her up close," a large man called from the back.

"Very well. Step down and follow the gentleman."

Matilda stepped off the platform with her dress still in her hand. She caught my eye before following the man into the side room. My heart sank. She had just lost a baby, reconnected with her husband, and was now being taken advantage of by a stranger, for no other reason than that it was his right, and she had none.

"Next!" the ruddy-cheeked man called to me.

My dress got snagged on my shoe and I almost tripped up the steps to the top of the block. I wished for something to hold onto. Somewhere to rest my hands.

The presenter read from his slip. "Mulatto girl from Charles City named Pheby. This here is a house nigra. Excellent at sewing and knows how to work the loom. She is prime age for breeding and would also make a fine fancy girl." He made his tone deep and melodic, like he was describing a prized possession.

"Disrobe in order that we might see how formed and sound you are." He looked at me.

I did not budge.

"Disrobe now."

Wringing my hands, I responded. "I will not."

The room gasped and murmured while the presenter's cheeks deepened even darker. He looked like a lobster ready to claw my eyes out.

"Disrobe, wench, or we will have you struck with one hundred lashes!"

Something shifted inside of me. I had never been whipped in my life, but I had been snatched from my home, lost my mama and my truest love, traveled on foot in ropes for days, starved, slept in the equivalent of a hog pen with feces up to my ankles. Nothing else scared me. I would not take off my dress in front of these men. I would not follow Matilda into that back room. I would not sink further into degradation than I already had. They would have to kill me first, and I stood with my feet grounded, preparing to put up a good fight.

"I plead to be exempt from this exposure. My credentials shall suffice." I stared the presenter square in his pig eyes.

He signaled to two armed men standing by the door. "Remove her dress, now."

When they came for me, I braced myself to bite, kick, scream, fight to the death, but before they reached me a voice called out.

"Stop."

The men froze and we all turned toward the speaker. He stood tall, outfitted finely with a tie at his neck. His snuff-colored hair fell long over his ears with the front swept back in a wave. He moved through the crowd like a man who only had to say things once. When he got to the block he reached for my hand. The men in the room huffed.

"Get down."

His skin felt soft, and besides Master Jacob it was the first time I had touched a white man.

"I will take her."

"But . . ." The presenter stumbled. "We have to bid."

A hush fell over the entire room, and I felt my stomach give way.

"I said she is mine." The man's eyes dared the speaker to question him again, and he did not. There was a servant boy at the back of the room, and when the man lifted his hand, the child appeared by our side.

"Take her to Elsie, and see that she is fed well and dressed properly."

He let my hand go, and I had no choice but to follow the lad. We walked across the courtyard and over to the kitchen house. I knew that this was not the end of things. If anything, it felt like the beginning, and I did not know if I should be relieved by the gentleman's kindness or frightened to death.

CHAPTER 12

Elsie

O n our short walk through the courtyard, I learned that the boy went by
the name Tommy. Born at the jail, he had no memory of his mother
and had grown up running errands for the master. Tommy was dark and
skinny, with slits for eyes, and a head that seemed impossibly large on his
little neck. He led me up three short steps to the kitchen house, a wooden
A-frame building with smoke puffing from the chimney. When we entered, the heat rose just like in Aunt Hope's kitchen and something in the
air caused me to sneeze.

"God bless you," said the thick-hipped woman who appeared to be the
cook. When she turned my way, I saw that she was the lady from whom
I had earlier requested the spoon. She sat at the table and began to shuck
corn. She did not seem surprised to see me. I could tell by the way her lip
twitched that she knew something that I did not.

"Marse Rubin said to feed her and give her a dress."

The woman put an apple in Tommy's hand. "Go 'n fetch some water
for the bath."

Tommy skipped off.

"What's your name?" She appeared to be my senior by about ten years,
like Lovie. Round in the cheeks, with a gap between her two front teeth.
Her face arranged itself unkindly.

"Pheby, ma'am." I hoped addressing her formally would make up for
our rough start.

"Elsie." She stood and turned her back while fixing something on the
cookstove. "We don't have to like each other. Just needs to get along."

The tin bowl she handed me was filled with steaming salted pork, cabbage, and rice. Then she made a show of handing me a spoon. I sat atop a stool and ate quickly. "This is delicious."

"You wantin' more?"

"Yes, if that is okay. It has been a long journey."

"Where you come from? Talk like them white women."

"Charles City."

She gave me another serving and I devoured it, then washed it down with a sweet, lemony drink.

Elsie wiped down the stove. "Done here. You can go up in my quarters and take a bath. Tommy should have it ready by now." I offered to help clean the dishes but she sent me on.

Clearly the kitchen was her domain. I took the narrow wooden stairs. The heat from below ascended to the second floor, making it airless. The upper room did not seem as large as where I lived with Mama, but would serve me better than being roped to a gang, with nothing at my back but the whine of wind and wolves.

The tub was a big silver bucket, filled with hot, steamy water, that sat in the middle of the floor. I peeled out of my soiled layers of clothing. The man who had rescued me from the auction block expected something from me. Elsie knew it. Mama often said, no kind deed from a white person went without a return. I squeezed the rag of dripping water over my shoulders, then dunked my head back until my hair sopped with wetness. As soon as I submerged my body in the water, the tears fell. The hurt in my gut clamped down unbearably. I told myself I could only cry for one minute; that was all Mama made way for. One minute of sorrow and then back to a straight face, a stiff back, and work. But that one minute of sadness melted into ten minutes, and before I knew it, I had cooled off the water with my steady stream of grief.

A swift knock shook the door, and then Elsie breezed in with two dresses in her arms. "This one you can sleep in. Other one for work. Marse asked that you join in servin' him."

"Marse?" I repeated. Did she mean Master?

Elsie looked appalled. "Yes, Marse Rubin Lapier. The one who own this jail. Ain't they got marses where you from?" She reached for the calico dress. "This we'll take out to burn."

"No, wait." I held my hand out. "Please, that was my mama's."

"Smells bad, but up to you." Elsie bunched the dress in her arms. As she moved to put it down, her fingers touched my diary. I stayed still, remembering Mama's warning about slaves who could read and write getting their fingers chopped off and eyes washed with lye. She made no eye contact as she draped the dress neatly across the chair. I hoped to God that meant we had an understanding.

"Get dressed. Then take a rest. I will wake you in 'nough time to prep for servin'."

Elsie shut the door behind her. The room had little furniture. Three pallets for sleeping, two chairs and hooks fastened to the wall where skirts were hanging. In the far corner, there was a table with a lantern. I dropped down on one of the pallets like a lump of coal. There were windows on two of the walls, which let in a cross breeze. I heard the depressing sounds of the prisoners. Suffering as I had just one night ago, trapped in the bowels of that hellhole. The scratchy blanket became too much and I pushed it off, but then I felt cold. Back and forth I went until I drifted. When I opened my eyes, Elsie stood over me.

"The matter wit' you?"

I tried to speak, but no words pushed past my lips. She tipped the canteen to my mouth and I drank, then fell back on my pillow. I woke, slept, drank, shivered, threw up, cried out. But the fever would not turn me loose. On the third day, Elsie brought me a stew but I could not stomach more than two or three bites.

"You must not want to get betta." She sounded offended, so I held my head up and took down a few more sips. As I leaned in for more, my stomach bubbled, and all the food came back out and onto the floor.

"Why the hell you got me cleanin' up after you? You ain't the missus, and this sure ain't the big house."

I felt terrible for making Elsie so mad, so I forced myself up, took the towel from her, and started wiping at my waste. I only lasted a minute; then my head got light and I fell back on the pallet. The only thing that brought me comfort was sleep, so I coasted off again and could not only see Mama, I could also smell her. We were curled next to each other in our old bed and I felt at peace. She brushed back my hair and whispered in my ear.

"*Have her make you a tea with white willow or meadowsweet. Drink that three to four times a day. Slice a piece of onion and leave it in a dish next to your bed. That should break the fever.*"

I wanted to hold Mama, but just like that she disappeared. When I asked Elsie for the tea, she grumbled about having to go find the herbs. "If Marse wasn't worryin' me sick 'bout you."

A young girl appeared the next morning with the tea and onion.

"I's July. Marse told me to sit wit' you till you feelin' well."

"Thank you."

Her kind smile soothed me. She was a pretty girl with strong hair woven together into two long braids. Her skin brought to mind gingerbread, and her eyes were like two chocolate drops. She served me tea four times that day and stayed while I slept. As I dozed, she swept and sang a song that Lovie used to hum while she worked. By night, I felt well enough to sit up a little and eat the stew. The tea drew the fever out and had me feeling myself again by the next morning.

Elsie lifted the curtain. "Most sleep you ever gon' get. I hears you can sew."

I nodded.

"Left a pile for you up front that need mendin'. No time for lazin' 'round here. Work to be done."

The sickness still clung to me, but I resolved to do something useful. Once I dressed, Elsie directed me out into the courtyard. The light of day took me by surprise and I had to pause to let my eyes adjust. A gang, much like mine, passed me by; chained, hungry, feet so worn they left footprints of blood trailing behind them. As I followed Elsie, the click-clack sounds of their iron confinements rang in my ears. The moaning from inside the jail cell cried steady and constant. I clutched my ears, wishing it would all stop.

"You will get use't it," Elsie huffed over her shoulder. "Just be glad it ain't you."

She showed me to a small spot in the supply shed. A tiny space in comparison to the loom house, but it gave me some breathing room from her. Overseer Snitch had snatched me up so fast I had left without my sewing tools. As if she'd read my mind, Elsie dropped a bag in front of me.

"See if'n this will work. Abbie, the house girl, goes to the market once a week. She can get what ain't there."

After sifting through the implements, I selected the best needle and started picking through cords. It eased my mind to do something familiar. Slipping the thread through the needle, the needle through the fabric, pulling, knotting, tying, looping. A little song popped into my head. I hummed to block out the memories of home, the sounds of the jail, and to push back the despair that seemed lurking at the door ready to choke me. I had just stitched the hem on a pair of men's trousers and bent for a shirt when a shadow appeared in the doorway. I glanced up and saw the white man who had removed me from the auction block. He had a protruding belly and wore spectacles perched on the edge of his thin nose.

"Nice to see you feeling better." He fingered his gold pocket watch, carrying with him the scent of bergamot and cigars.

"Yes, sir. Thank you."

Even though Elsie had told me he was my new master, I did not see him as such. I looked at his face to see if he objected to *sir*, but his expression did not change.

"I do not believe we made a proper acquaintance. I am Rubin Lapier."

"Pheby Delores Brown."

"Folks call you Pheby? Pheby Delores? Or Pheby Delores Brown?"

I could tell he was fooling with me by the way his dimples spread across his cheeks. If I guessed accurately and Elsie was ten years my senior, then he had to be twenty years more than me. Not as old as Master Jacob, but definitely older than Mama.

"Just Pheby is fine."

"Well, Pheby, I brought you something." He took the few steps toward me and held out his hand. Inside there was a thimble. Silver, shiny, and quite honestly the most beautiful thing anyone had ever given me.

"Thank you, sir."

"You are welcome," he said, and then turned out the door.

Once I felt sure that he had gone, I slipped on my new thimble, and for the first time in weeks, I smiled.

◆

In the days that followed, I quickly fell into a routine. After breakfast, I sewed in the supply room straight through to supper, so consumed with my task I did not have time to think about my situation. I learned from sweet-faced July that the jail cell that I had spent my first night in held folks waiting for auction, and others who were sent by their masters for harsh punishment. Rubin Lapier (who I simply thought of as the Jailer) was the master of it all. From what I could see from my little sewing shed, the Jailer ran his operation from the tavern. It housed the auction room and his office, and served as a place to entertain the men who came to make purchases. I watched him from a distance, but our paths had not crossed since he gave me the thimble.

I liked my sewing spot; it was nothing more than a little shed, but it felt all mine. I mostly hemmed and mended socks, pants, shirts, and a few drapes and blankets. Plenty of work to keep me busy and my mind from wandering off. Elsie sent food to the room with July, but whatever I chewed came right back up. Most dishes I pretended to eat and then gave the rest to July.

From my shed, I figured out that there were six people who tended the jail and lived on the property: Basil was the Jailer's manservant; Abbie worked in the house; July and the boy Tommy were children who did what they were told; Elsie was in the kitchen; and then there was me. I did not intend to get to know any of them too well. My only plan was to keep busy and be helpful until Master Jacob arrived for me. But that did not stop them from trying to get to know me. When that first Sunday rolled around, Elsie sent July to fetch me so that I could eat with the others behind the kitchen house.

"We do it every Sunday. Sort of like our time off."

The first thing that caught my eye when I joined the gathering was a vase of bright, cheerful daisies, which decorated a long table painted black. A whiff of mint and sage came from Elsie's little garden. Made me long for one of Mama's teas. She always made me a cup on Sundays just before bed. "To search the blood and keep things movin'."

"How do everybody?" I said, wiping my sweaty hands on my skirt.

I received nods and greetings of hello. Abbie from the house smiled at me. She was missing a tooth on the left side, and her small body made her appear childlike. I took a seat on one of the long benches that straddled the table, and July plopped down next to me.

"Basil, lead us in grace," commanded Elsie.

We dropped our heads and then in unison said, "Amen."

Elsie served us each a bowl of crispy chicken, sweet corn, and roasted carrots. The smell did not agree with me, so I paused.

"Ain't you goin' eat?" Elsie cocked her head at me.

Not wanting to offend, I started in on the dinner.

"Been told a man come through here from up north yapping 'bout freedom coming," chewed Basil.

"Betta hush that talk, less you find trouble." Elsie heaped a bit more chicken on his plate.

Basil leaned forward. "Marse ain't here."

"But he has ears everywhere," Abbie added.

It was my first encounter with Basil up close. A handsome man, dressed in a button-down shirt with his sleeves rolled up at the elbows, he had a crescent-shaped scar on his left cheek. He looked as if someone had branded him. He sat beside Abbie, who seemed to smile into her spoon. The conversation shifted toward talk of the weather, prepping the grounds for winter, and storing food. Then Basil stood from the table. I sensed a restlessness in him.

"Delicious as always, Elsie." He kissed her cheek.

"Yes, thank you kindly." Abbie rose and collected the empty plates, then made her way to the washbasin. I noticed that she limped when she walked, dragging her left foot slightly behind her, and I wondered if she'd been born like that or had an accident or worse.

July asked the boy Tommy, "Wantin' to play kickball?"

Tommy nodded, and the two of them scurried off, leaving me alone with Elsie. I forked another bite into my mouth despite the churning in my stomach. Then I felt the force of the food shooting up my throat. I pushed back from the table and stuck my head in a nearby bush. Everything came up. When I turned, wiping my mouth, Elsie stood over me with her hand on her hip.

"When the last time you bled?"

I had to think. "Before I left the plantation." Even before Missus had dumped her chamber pot on me. "I think around May."

"Chile, it's August. You is wit' child."

I panted. "A child?" How could this be?

"Guess n' that'll keep Marse from sniffin' after you for a while." Elsie bent down in her garden and picked at something.

"Here some ginger. Help wit' you stomach."

I walked toward my shed, stunned by her revelation. How could I be carrying a child? Essex's child? My hand dropped down to my belly. Mama had told me to watch myself. Not to bring no slave babies into the world. How could I let her down? I had stumbled and now I did not know how to feel.

When I reached the courtyard, there was a malnourished man in chains lying naked on the ground. Blood seeped through open wounds, and he looked at me with such anguish I wanted to help him. As soon as I moved toward him, the Jailer appeared at the tavern door.

"Run along, Pheby." He had a pipe to his lips and puffed on it. I hastened my steps and closed the door to the shed behind me. My nose started to run. How could I raise a child in this place of horror? I dug inside my hidden pocket and pulled out the necklace that Essex had given me. Just holding it between my fingers calmed me. We had made a baby. I pictured his eyes on me as I told him the news. The smoothness of his face, and the calloused skin around his hands as he embraced me. I was going to be a mother whether I liked it or not. But how? In this foreign place? Alone without my mama to guide me?

Same way I raised you.

CHAPTER 13

Favor

T he days had grown shorter. Red, orange, and purple leaves drifted to the ground as July and I bent down over the silver wash bin scrubbing the laundry. The motion of pounding the heavy, wet material against the wood-and-metal washboard was making me dizzy.

The lye soap stung my hands and the October air had stiffened my back. I must have looked on the brink of fainting, because when Elsie huffed by me she *tsk*ed her teeth.

"You's a weak gal. Don't know what Marse see 'n you."

I wanted to tell Elsie to shut her fat mouth. Did she not have enough business to tend to and people to feed around here without constantly studying me? Still, her comment lit a fire under me and made me more determined to finish the chore. I was scrubbing a resistant bloodstain out of a white shirtsleeve when a shadow crept over me. I looked up and saw the Jailer blocking my sun. Discomfort slid down my spine.

Elsie's hands were in the bowl of string beans. "Marse?" She made his name into a question.

"I want July to be with Pheby for the next few months."

"But July my best—"

"And move Pheby into the back room of the house."

"The big house?" Her mouth opened wide enough for me to see her tonsils.

The Jailer nodded and I shivered.

"Ain't show me no favor when I's carryin'."

"Mind your tongue."

"Worked me so hard, lost all three of my ninnys." Elsie parted her lips to sass some more, but then the Jailer raised his hand and slapped her concerns right back down her throat. The sound popped so loud, it stopped me from breathing. I watched as Elsie dropped her head and returned her eyes to the beans. She said nothing more, but I could feel the anger, embarrassment, and indignation radiating from her skin.

"Have it done before supper." He walked away. His boots left footprints behind in the sand.

"Best be movin' on," Elsie murmured toward me.

I left the wash and climbed the stairs to the upper room. I gathered the few things I owned: Mama's dress, a blanket, and the thimble. My diary stayed hidden in my pocket at all times, and I was already wearing the necklace and shoes. When I turned to leave, Elsie had filled the doorway with her wide hips. She looked older than she had just ten minutes before. Her jaw had started to swell something awful. I moved to pass, but Elsie seized me by the arm.

"He ain't what you think."

"Turn me loose."

Her fingernails dug into my skin. "You know what they call him? Bully. This place? Say it's the Devil's Half Acre. Now who you thinkin' the devil be?"

She released my arm and stepped aside. I hurried down the stairs with her words vibrating in my head. July met me outside. We moved from the kitchen house across the path that led to the big house. It was enclosed by a black wrought-iron gate, and was the building farthest away from the jail. I lifted the latch and crossed a small patch of grass. Abbie, the house girl, stood at the door to greet us. Her yellow dress hung like a sack from her lanky body. When I reached the front door, her smile, which seemed genuine, comforted me. It took strength not to collapse into her arms the way I would Mama's.

"Right this way." She hobbled, dragging her left foot behind her.

This was my first time inside the big house, and given that it was about half the size of Master Jacob's, my thought was that it did not appear to be big at all. Directly in front of me was a wide staircase with a dark wood banister. To my left, a dining room. On the right, a parlor. Both rooms had floor-to-ceiling windows with hardwood floors. July and I trailed Abbie down a long hallway and into a small bedroom behind the staircase.

"Here we are." Abbie gestured.

The room was quaint: big fluffy pillows on the bed, yellow curtains, and a shaggy throw rug. A side table held a pitcher of water and a clean glass. As I walked around touching everything, Elsie's warning quickly vanished from my thoughts. Tonight I would sleep in a real bed, and I reveled in the comfort of it.

"Thank you," I said to Abbie.

"Let me know if you needin' anything. July know her way 'round pretty good." She closed the door behind her.

I sat down. July came next to me, and I pulled the girl to my chest and hugged her.

As I became acquainted with my new living quarters, I decided to hide the diary Miss Sally had given me under a small chest in the back of my bedroom closet. Seemed safer than carrying it around with me, especially with my dress getting tight. I also moved the desk and chair farther into the corner to make more space for July in case she wanted to bring over some personal things.

The next night, Abbie came to my room. July had just finished brushing my hair and twisted it into a chignon. I had found a ball of pearl wool in the shed and was guiding July on knitting a scarf.

"Marse Rubin like to see you in the parlor."

"Why?" My heart raced at the thought of being alone with him.

"Best put on something from the closet."

July hopped up and pulled open the closet door. There hung three dresses. I'd seen them before but I had not known they were intended for me. There were beautifully fussy white-women dresses with embroidered edges and puffed sleeves. Finer than anything that Mama had ever made for me. But I sensed wearing them was a trap.

"What I am wearing will do."

"You sure?" Abbie made her eyes big.

"I am." My fingers shook as I smoothed down my linen work dress. It had grown snug over my belly in the past few days, and I noted that I could probably make it another week or two before needing to let the bodice go completely.

"Betta hurry, Marse hates to wait," said Abbie. I did not wish to go, but being without choice, I stretched my face into what I hoped was a pleasant expression and headed down the hall.

The Jailer sat in a high-back Victorian chair, with a nightcap on the table next to him and the newspaper in his lap. Logs burned away in the fireplace, and out the window I could see the sun setting over the buildings behind us. I pushed my knees together to steady my trembling.

"Please sit." He looked at me over his spectacles.

"I prefer to stand, sir."

He looked at me again. "Sit."

I gathered my skirts and sat on the edge of the chair farthest away from him.

"Do you find your new living quarters fit?"

"Yes. Thank you for your kindness."

"July will stay with you night and day. Attending to your needs."

I tried to keep my posture erect, but I was no longer comfortable in my body. I dropped my eyes, but not before they spotted the piano. It was even lovelier than the one on which Miss Sally had taught me. I recognized it to be a square grand piano made of rosewood with sparkling ivory keys. It had been so long since I had made music and experienced the release that playing gave me. I deepened my breathing, wishing I had brought the ball of pearl wool to keep my hands occupied.

"You look tired. Go get some rest."

"Thank you, sir." He stood when I did, and I could feel his eyes on me as I walked out of the room.

July was laying on her pallet next to the closet, practicing looping the wool. I had offered to share the bed with her, but she refused.

"What Marse want?"

"I have no idea."

"He scary," she whispered.

"What makes you say that?"

"He has two faces. One minute smiling, next you stretched on the whippin' post. Basil know betta than all of us." She turned over and got under her blanket. She fell asleep in the time it took for me to prepare for bed.

◆

After that, the Jailer called for me nightly while he had his whiskey, newspaper, and nibble of dessert. Each time Abbie suggested that I put on one of the white-women dresses from the closet, but I continued to refuse. I did not want to ignite additional interest in me beyond what was there. When I sat with him, I stayed mostly quiet, thinking about the piano, my baby, and Essex while he read the newspaper. Then, about a week into our evening meetings, he ordered Abbie to bring me a slice of apple pie. My mouth watered for the treat. It seemed that the baby had me constantly craving sweets, and in this place sugary snacks proved hard to come by. Like a kid, I wasted no time cutting into the crust with my fork and bringing the thick candied apples to my lips.

"Do not rush, now." His eyes twinkled. "I want to watch you enjoy it. Slowly."

His rate of breathing had increased, and his anticipation took the satisfaction of the pie from my mouth. The Jailer kept his eyes on me while I slid the pie off my fork, chewing each bite carefully and until there was nothing but mush in my mouth, then swallowed. He leaned toward me from his chair, his cheeks red, his eyes glistening.

"Go on, lick the spoon. Do not waste a drop."

I put the plate down on the table next to me and faked a smile I knew would not reach my eyes.

◆

As the days grew shorter and the weather grew colder, the Jailer started trading his reading in favor of talking to me. He told me things about his chattel business. I did not say much in response—just offered a nod or some sign that I'd heard him.

Over bread pudding he revealed, "I was born here in Richmond. Lived in a two-room shack just up the road. After my father died, I had to figure out a way to put food on the table. We did not have much to begin with and I was never good at starving. My mother and younger brother needed me to look after them, so I left home at sixteen in search of work."

He shared how he had gotten his start as an itinerant trader, much like the men who had brought me to the jail. Moving up and down the East Coast, knocking on the doors of tobacco and rice planters, inquiring whether they would sell.

"It took about four months to assemble a profitable coffle of about three hundred, and then we would march farther down south. I got good at trading and developed a reputation, but after a few years the travel wore on me. On a trip home, I saw this place for sale with all the buildings intact, and I knew it was time to settle down and expand my business endeavors."

He purchased the jail for six thousand dollars and quickly established himself as the proprietor. While he spoke, I kept my face pleasant and my eyes on his large hands. The more he drank, the more he waved them around to illustrate his point.

Not once on our nightly visits did he ask about my growing belly. I figured he spent his time with me because he was lonely, and often wondered why he did not have a wife. My fear of him never subsided and I remained on guard. But after a few weeks, I came to look forward to those moments of human kindness. He always spoke to me as if I had what Miss Sally would call good gumption, which made life at the Lapier jail bearable. While I waited on Master Jacob to come for me, I could temporarily endure his company for a few small comforts. Besides, sitting in the parlor provided an escape from the droning, depressing music of my confined circumstance.

"You are always looking at the piano. Can you play?"

I wrung my hands. "Yes, sir."

"I would be pleased." He motioned.

I could barely calm the eagerness that surged through my toes as I stood and moved toward the instrument. Sitting at the piano, I arched my back to make room for my front. The baby started kicking as soon as I poised my fingers to play, and I hoped the music would settle it.

The first song that came to mind was the last one I'd played for Master

Jacob, "Pretty Dreamer." I felt a bit off-center and my fingernails scratched the keys. But by the third stanza, I did not have to think about where my fingers traveled. I just walked across the keys and let the sound flow through me. I was no longer in the parlor, the jail, or Richmond. I floated high above this place. Dancing, feeling, recalling Essex, my mama, and all my family on the Bell plantation as if no one controlled me. Like I was free.

When I finished, the Jailer rose from his seat and offered me his hand. I got to my feet, and he caught me off-kilter by kissing me on the neck. I stood still as plywood.

"I have chosen well." He took a rose from the vase on the table and handed it to me. I did not look at him when I wrapped my fingers around the stem.

"May I go?"

"I am not trying to frighten you. You are special, Pheby Delores Brown."

I could not move, because he stood in my way.

"I am not feeling well, sir. May I go?"

He leaned down and kissed me on the cheek. The kiss was wetter than the first, and my skin burned with repulsion. No other man had touched me except for Essex. I clutched the rose stem tighter.

"Please, sir." I felt sweat gathering under my armpits.

"Yes, you may."

I hurried to my bedroom and closed the door behind me. When I opened my hand, my palm bled from where the thorn had pierced my flesh. I dipped a cloth into my water pitcher and scrubbed at each of the spots on my body that he'd touched, until my skin felt raw and bruised.

CHAPTER 14

Christmas 1850

*W*hen I lived on the Bell plantation, Christmastime was the season of the year we all looked forward to. Rules were relaxed, and Master Jacob permitted the field hands a whole week of rest and leisure between Christmas and New Year's Day. Aunt Hope would have Parrott slaughter the fattest hog and sometimes, if the season turned a good profit, a few chickens and a lamb, with the meat to be distributed evenly amongst the field hands. Most of Lowtown spent the free time repairing their cabins, tending to their gardens, hunting for game, and fishing. If they had family on a nearby plantation, Master Jacob wrote passes for them to visit.

Every night there was a party in Lowtown, and even those of us who lived in Hightown were permitted to attend once we were finished with our evening chores. Down in the clearing, the fire pit blazed, food was plentiful, men drank whiskey, women plum wine, and the children apple cider. After the feast, fiddlers and banjo players would start playing together, keeping the rhythm so that everyone could dance.

When we danced, we cast our worries to the wind. All our troubles and ailments forgotten. We seized life with both hands, crushing our tribulations with the sway of our hips and the stomp of our bare feet. On the eve of Christmas, a yearly allotment of goods and clothing was distributed. Men were given one new shirt and a pair of pants, women a burlap dress, and the kids new socks. Last year Missus Delphina had surprised everyone when she gave out ribbons to all the women and girls in the fields. Master took pleasure in lining up the children and handing out new balls, wooden instruments, and small dolls, but the kids mostly looked forward to the candy.

The next morning was my birthday. Most slaves did not know the date they were born. But Mama made sure I did. December 25, 1832. And for as long as I could remember, 1850 was to be the happiest celebration of my life. I would finally turn eighteen and receive my freedom papers.

Instead I opened my eyes on that agreed-upon morning, with child, confined to the back bedroom of the Jailer's house, and a rage opened up inside of me so hot I grabbed the glass water pitcher from the side of my bed and slammed it to the ground. I picked up the chair and flung it against the wall, and then tore the bed linen from the mattress until it fell into a tangled heap. I wanted my free papers like Master had pledged. How come he had not come for me yet? I had lived my life on that promise.

July knocked.

"Go away."

"Elsie prepared a Christmas breakfast."

"Not hungry."

I felt July hesitate at the door, but I urged her to go and enjoy the day without me. Not a soul at the jail knew that it was my eighteenth birthday, and I aimed to keep it that way. After hours of staring at the walls, I restored my room and then ate the cold biscuit that I found on the dining room table. I did not know where the Jailer had gone, but when July returned that evening, she told me that Elsie was mad with me for not coming to eat.

"Said you uppity." She folded her legs underneath her on the floor; her thick braid sat on her shoulder, tied with the pink ribbon I'd made for her. I bunched my covers over my lap.

Things had been like icicles between Elsie and me over the past month, since I'd moved into the big house. She took to saying only what was necessary, and mostly relied on messages sent through July. I had no problem keeping my distance. I passed my time in the supply room mending clothes, bundled in layers since it had gotten cold. I had moved a few things around, and Tommy carried old rubbish out so that it felt like my cozy little nook.

That is where July found me a week later, on New Year's Eve, when she burst through the door like her tail had caught fire.

"Girl, what is the matter?"

"Marse is back."

"That is no cause to near break your neck."

"I heard 'em talking while I served drinks in the tavern. Ya old marse? He dead."

"What?" I dropped down on my stool, gripping my belly.

"I heard 'em say so. Marse Jacob Bell died few weeks ago." The air left my body. Master Jacob, gone? It could not be. I opened my mouth and out came a bloodcurdling scream. July leaned over me, rubbing my back, but I could not stop shaking. I growled, shouted, pounded the table, pulled things from the shelves, and hollered over my bad luck until my throat was raw.

"It is goin' be okay." July rubbed my hair off my forehead. "There, there."

But I knew it would never be all right. With Master Jacob gone, I would be stuck in this place for the rest of my natural life.

I pulled myself together long enough to walk over to the big house and shut myself off in my room, hoping to retire early so that the awful day would end, but when evening fell the Jailer called me to the parlor. I told Abbie to tell him that I felt ill, but she refused to disappoint him. I lifted myself from the bed and let Abbie wipe my face with a damp cloth and July brush my hair.

"Cake?" he offered, once I sat down in my usual chair.

I shook my head, concentrating on keeping my emotions from clouding my eyes. The room felt stuffy. I moistened my lips and asked. "May I play something for you?"

The moment my fingers glided across the ivories I fell into a trance and played every fast, erratic-sounding song I knew. I played until the sweat poured down my bosom and I had exhausted myself with my own fury. I pounded out my angriest tunes, surrendering my whole body to the rhythm of the music until my fingers cramped and my back throbbed.

"Simply lovely." He clapped once I had depleted myself. "Think I might take to hiring you out."

I hoisted myself up from the bench, smashing my palms down on the piano. "I want to go home."

"This is your home." He crossed the room. Then, before I could move, his fingers ran the length of my sweaty spine and then started massaging my collarbone. I stiffened as his hands traveled downward and cupped my buttocks.

"Oh, Pheby." The longing in his sigh scared me.

"May I go?"

Every spot he touched on me flamed hot. Then he reached for my head and brought my face so close we breathed the same air.

"Do not be afraid of me, Pheby. I want to open up the world for you." He forced me to look at him. His eyes were emerald green.

"I . . . must lie down in my condition." I faked a cough.

He put his nose to my neck and inhaled my skin. "Good night, Pheby Delores Brown."

When he released me, I shuffled to my room and stood with my back against the door, tearing off my dress and rubbing away his touch from my skin. When I got in the bed, I tried to sleep but could not stop thinking of Elsie's warning.

They call this place the Devil's Half Acre. Who you thinkin' the devil be?

CHAPTER 15

Fancy

Six months after I arrived, I watched as the snow melted into slushy puddles, knowing that it was not the last fall for the season. I waddled now instead of walking, and worried that the weather conditions would cause me to slip and hurt the baby. Most days I felt fatigued. During the night, I could not find a comfortable position because of the heaviness of my belly. The nausea never subsided and I would hang my head over a pail, trying to decide if the rumbling I felt was hunger or sickness. When I moved, my feet ached as if I had stumbled on thorns and spikes. The baby's kicks felt as though I was being beaten from the inside. Most days tiredness followed me from sunup to sundown, but I knew my survival depended upon me proving useful.

I was in the middle of sewing a nightshirt for the baby from leftover scraps when the Jailer appeared in the doorway with a girl. She looked younger than me by a few years, and so fair that if she had not harbored ropes around her wrists, I would have believed him if he introduced her as kin.

"Fit her in the best dress you have. Make sure she is clean and fed. Need her at the tavern in one hour's time."

I nodded and he left the girl to me. Her cobalt eyes scanned the shed like those of a cornered sheep and I knew she was trying to make sense of her new situation. I remembered the feeling well, and as soon as the Jailer closed the door to the tavern, I untied her. The ropes were just obnoxious. She would never get out of the jail anyway, unless escorted or with a pass.

"What is your name?"

"Charlott."

"Where are you from?"

"'lizabeth City." Her eyes were red rimmed, signaling little sleep, and her dress bore a gaping hole in the waistline like someone had tried to rip it off. I thumbed through my small collection of dresses and found a blue one that appeared to be the right size. Charlott stared at the ceiling, and while I tightened it to fit her figure, her gloom was obvious. I tried shaking it off by make-believing that I was preparing the sweet child for a party. I hummed and sang, but no matter how hard I pretended, the image of Matilda on the auction block, naked for all to see, clouded my head. The deafening silence got to be so painful that I could not stand it, so I peppered her with questions until she told me her story.

"When I's three, I's given as a gift to Master's first wife, Miss Sarah. Life was happy till she fell from her horse and died. Massa took a second wife. Where 'n my troubles began."

She went on to tell me that from the moment her new mistress laid eyes on her, she seemed set on punishment. Charlott could not please her no matter how hard she tried. Her master was adamant about not wanting his slaves scarred by the whip, so after a few paddles and kicks, her mistress turned to the punishment of the pump.

While I had experience with a missus who did not like me no matter how hard I tried to please, I had no familiarity with a pump made to inflict pain, so while I fixed Charlott's hair, she explained that her mistress would have her stripped naked and then lowered by cable cord down into the well. The spout of the pump was elevated and angled on top of her. At the mistress's command, water would be released in full force.

"The water went ice cold in a blink of the eye. Felt like bein' struck wit' heavy sticks in all directions. Was a game to her. How long 'fore I cried out from the sting. Then how long 'fore I fell silent from the shock."

Charlott told me after her last time under the pump, she was fevered for over a week. No amount of blankets could make her warm. Once she got better, she tried to run but did not make it out the neighbor's woods before the bloodhounds caught her.

"Next day the wagon come for me. Then I's here."

I took her story in to digest later. Time ran short, so I finished by giving her my old shoes. "I am sorry for this. If there was anything that I could do for you I would. May God be with you through it all." I squeezed her cold hands and then walked her up to the tavern. When she reached the door, she squared her shoulders but did not look back.

I could not rid my thoughts of Charlott's story. The more I stuffed it down, the more it bubbled up. I needed to do something. Since I knew the Jailer would be at the tavern for a while, I left my post and went to the house. I called out but no one answered, so I made my way to the library. The Jailer's writing desk was pushed against the wall. I stood in the middle of the room, listening to make sure no one followed me. When I felt certain I occupied the house alone, I pulled on the gold handles and slid the drawer open. Inside there was a calendar, writing paper, and two dip pens. Farther back in the drawer sat a small bottle of ink. I took the pen and ink, shuffled down to my room, and retrieved the diary from my hiding space.

When I opened my diary, the pages smelled like Mama. I flipped past her recipes until I found a blank page. Right there on the floor, I dipped the pen and jotted down everything that Charlott had told me along with a description of her and approximate age. Something about preparing her for sale had touched a vulnerable place deep inside of me. Perhaps I recognized that it could have been me, dressed and marched off. Our backgrounds were not the same but were similar enough, and I needed to do something that felt like help.

I slipped the diary back into its hiding place and walked down the hall. When I moved into the library, the Jailer was standing next to his writing desk. I tried backing away but he turned at the sound of my footsteps.

"Pheby. I did not know you were here."

"Needed hairpins from my room, sir."

He peered at me thoughtfully. "Where are your shoes?"

I looked sheepishly at my feet tied with wood and linen, which I had used as makeshift shoes once my ankles swelled up.

"Too small."

"You should have told me."

I kept my eyes on the floor.

"There is work waiting for you. Run along."

I wobbled on. The ink and pen weighed heavily in my pocket.

◆

Two nights later, the Jailer called me to the parlor. Once I sat down, Abbie brought me a paper bag tied with a silver bow.

"What is this?"

"Open it." He leaned forward in his chair.

I unraveled the bag to find a pair of royal-blue silk slippers. They were stunning, covered on the outside with a finely woven straw.

"Thank you."

"Try them on."

Abbie knelt before me and slipped the slippers onto my feet. They fit beautifully.

"Better." He smiled. "Dessert, Abbie."

She got off the floor and limped off, returning with two plates of raspberry tart, then took her leave.

I held my plate in my lap. "May I ask a question, sir?"

"Of course."

"Who bought Charlott?"

He looked at me like he did not comprehend.

"The girl you brought to me two days ago. Blue dress?"

"An associate from Louisiana. Has a thriving business that he thought she would be perfect for."

"What was her sale?"

His lips crinkled like he tasted something sweet. "Eight hundred dollars."

"More than a male field hand?"

"Ah, so you have been paying attention to our talks." He pushed his spectacles up his nose. "She will pay back that money to him in dividends."

"Why so much?"

"Mulatto girls like her are a fancy breed." He eyed me up and down and then it hit me. Missus Delphina's last words. *Take her to the Lapier jail to be a fancy girl to live out her life as a whore.*

Dear Lord, I had fixed Charlott, a girl younger than me to lie with strange men. The thought turned to acid in my stomach. I fanned my face with my hand so that he could not see my distress.

"Play something for me. Soft on my ears."

Now that I knew the whole picture, I lost whatever guilt I had over stealing the ink and pen. Writing her story down, acknowledging that she had passed through, that she had a name and a history—it was all I could do.

◆

There were more girls after Charlott. Sometimes up to four a day. It was the same routine: fit, feed, bathe, oil, and get them dressed. When the house grew quiet at night, I wrote down their names in my diary, where they were from, their ages, descriptions of what they looked like, things they said to me during our brief time together. As I prepared each girl, it did not escape me that it could be me for sale. The poor people housed in the derelict jail were never far from my thoughts either.

I had just released a girl named Eliza to be marched across the court-yard to the white man who would be in control of her fate, when I felt a sharp pain in my belly. It came so sudden that I held the table so that I would not collapse.

July noticed me leaning into the door. "What's the matter?"

"The baby. I think it is . . ." I hunched over as the pain rippled through my stomach and up my spine. Then it shot like daggers and made my whole body burn as if ignited.

"I get Elsie." She led me to the chair, and before I could sit water gushed down my legs and onto my feet. The pain hit again so fast I bit my tongue.

Elsie appeared and put her hand on my shoulder. "Come on, gal." She held one arm and July took the other as they led me into the house. The sharp pain came again and I had to stop at the gate and wait for it to pass. My vision went blurry as we walked down the hall to my room. I wanted to flop down but Elsie held me up while July padded my bed with rags. The discomfort hit again, harder this time, and I wailed. Elsie dropped between my legs and I could feel her hands inside of me.

"It's right here. Just gimme a little push."

I pushed.

"One more."

I bore down again and then I heard a loud cry, powerful and strong.

"Got a boy." Elsie held the baby up for me to see. "Let me clean him for you."

"What you gon' name him?" July wiped my brow with a cool rag.

I dared not take the chance and name him Essex. I had always been fond of Miss Sally's lessons on the Founding Fathers of the country. Particularly of James Monroe. She said that he was so honest that if you turned his soul inside out there would not be a spot on it. I did not care so much for James but Monroe I liked.

"Monroe. Monroe Henry Brown."

Elsie put the baby in my arms, and when I put him to my breast, he latched on fervently. Instantly, I experienced a new kind of love that I had not known existed. I was overwhelmed, scared, and excitedly drunk with this feeling all at the same time. In that moment, I knew I would do anything for my son. Anything at all.

CHAPTER 16

————— ◆ —————

Motherhood

$\mathcal{E}$ lsie said I would be given a week to rest and adjust to caring for Monroe, but when the time passed Abbie told me to rest some more.

"Marse wantin' you to take it slow."

Cherishing Monroe came easy. He had ten little fingers and perfect toes. His skin smelled of powder, and sometimes when I watched him sleep his face would light up in what seemed like a smile. Even though I tried to rest, the moment I closed my eyes his lips started flapping. The boy ate so much that my nipples cracked and bled. But it was easy to forgive him, especially since he favored his father. Essex had stayed on my mind, but Monroe made me miss him in a new way. This child had come from our union, the deepest expression of our love, and I longed for him in my bones.

After Monroe's birth, I stayed confined to the house. Three weeks passed with my attention fully on him. The Jailer had not called me for an evening visit, no work was required, but I itched to get outside and do something more. The promise of spring was in the air and I needed to feel the wind on my face. I took a long piece of material and tied Monroe to my back, the way I had seen the women in the fields do with their babies, and stepped out into the sunlight. As I crossed the courtyard, a group of people chained by the neck trudged along. Once again, the daily dose of misery, the sound of the defeated, the smell of waste and death pushed down my spirit. Elsie had told me I would get used to all of it. After seven months at the jail, I still had not. I suspected I never would.

I had only returned to my work for two days when the Jailer sent word that he wanted to see me. July took Monroe, and Abbie brought me a pail and cloth to wash my face and hands. Between the two of them, they were constantly reminding me to keep up my appearance, but truthfully, Monroe was all I cared about.

I entered the room and stood. When the Jailer saw me, he gestured for me to take a seat.

"Abbie left you a tea cake."

"Thank you." I lifted it from the table. He took pleasure again in watching me eat.

"You seem down," he commented.

"I am fine, sir."

"Maybe you need a change of scenery. Tomorrow Abbie will go to the market to shop. How would you like to leave the baby with July and go with her?"

He phrased this like a question but I knew it was a command. I was supposed to thank him for his kindness but I did not want to leave my new baby behind. I forced my mouth to smile.

"Good, it's settled."

◆

On market day, Abbie had to wait a whole hour for me to get Monroe's tummy full and settle him into his nap. July had been an angel, the way she helped me with everything. She felt like the little sister I never had. Abbie waited at the back door of the house as I slipped on my new bonnet, the Jailer's latest gift; then I followed her through the courtyard. We passed Elsie. She looked me over but, instead of a proper greeting, gave a *tsk* of her teeth. The early spring temperature felt perfect for a day off, and the farther I got away from the house, the more I looked forward to the adventure. When we reached the guard at the jail's entrance, I recoiled at the sound of the whip whistling through the air. Abbie and I exchanged glances and moved even faster. After showing her pass, we were permitted to exit. The heavy gates of the jail closed and locked behind us.

I was finally free.

The notion made me want to throw my arms in the air and spin in circles. A giddiness came over me that I had not felt in months, and I opened my mouth wide, trying to drink down as much fresh air and sunlight as I could hold. When we exited the alley onto Main Street, I surveyed my surroundings. The streets bustled with activity. More people than I had even seen at one time. Businessmen and well-dressed women. Groups of coloreds in simple clothing stood on the corners.

"What are they doing?" I leaned into Abbie.

"Hiring themselves out. Marse write them a note to collect wages."

"Oh."

"Way for marses to make even more money."

I stepped down off the curb, but then Abbie pulled me back as a carriage passed.

"You ain't in the country no more." She chuckled.

I dusted my dress off. "What are we shopping for?"

"Food, material, and supplies."

Wide-eyed, I followed Abbie in and out of several stores, watching her negotiate prices. "Don't think Marse Lapier would agree with that price. Can you do betta than that?" she asked, using her long fingers to smooth out her rough wool skirt.

For such a petite woman she had a good mouth. After we placed the last order at Thalhimer's Dry Goods, she led me down a little backstreet.

"There's a bakery at the corner run by coloreds. We can sit a spell." Then she peeked around and put her mouth to my ear.

"Stop for slaves when they run."

"How do you know all of this?"

"My foot might be lame, but God give me two good ears." She smiled that girlish grin and I squeezed her arm.

When we walked into the bakery, the scent of butter, vanilla, and cinnamon intoxicated me. Abbie asked me what I wanted and I pointed to the biggest piece of apple pie.

"Got a sweet tooth."

"Small pleasure in this bleakness."

"It will get better in time."

Her optimistic view of the future did not catch fire in my heart, but I did not reveal this as we found a bistro table with two seats on the patio.

"How come you never call him Marse?" She passed me my pastry.

I shrugged. "I left my master back on the plantation."

"I ain't never met no woman like you. You don't act like the rest of us."

I stared out into the street unable to explain the world I had come from, and the war that raged inside of me. Mama had told me not to get caught with no slave babies—my only task was freedom. The past few months had devastated that plan, and now with Master Jacob gone, and the birth of Monroe, I saw no way out. Still, I could not crumble.

I took a bite of piecrust and tried to lose myself in its goodness. The flakiness melted on my tongue and made me think of Aunt Hope's sweet treats. I made a note to get an extra slice to surprise July.

Just then, a breeze blew the ribbons of my bonnet, and when I glanced up, a beige woman was sauntering our way. She was dressed finer than Missus Delphina ever had been, even when the plantation hosted company. Heavy jewelry dripped from her earlobes and wrists.

"Beautiful bonnet." She smiled as she passed.

"Thank you." I leaned over Abbie. "Who was that?"

"Corrina Hinton. She the mistress of the jail off Birch Alley."

"But she looks—"

"Yep, she mulatto far as I know. Marses here in Richmond makin' they own rules. She has three or four children with Mr. Omohundro. Come and go as she pleases. I always see her lookin' mighty pretty."

I watched her disappear down the cobblestone street, trying to imagine how she could say yes to this life. But what choice did we have?

"Rumor is she run the business better than her husband. Take care of all they affairs. Marse probably wantin' the same from you."

I looked up. "That is ridiculous."

"Way he courtin' you and all. Have not seen him act like this before, and I been livin' here ten years."

"How come he does not have a white wife?"

"No respectable man would marry his daughter off to the owner of a slave pen. Even though Marse is wealthy, high society southerners consider traders dishonorable. Call them the pariahs of men."

"How do you know so much?"

"Been around long enough to know how things work. That's how I know you the one Marse choose."

I put down my fork.

"Just like Mr. Omohundro choose Ms. Corrina. Better get used to it."

I searched for a way to change the subject. Then Abbie patted me on my arm and told me it was time to go. I did not feel ready to return to my prison, so I asked her to take the long way around. We went through the back way, but even so, I could smell Lapier's Alley before we turned the corner. The stench worsened with every step we took, and then it was insufferable. I covered my nose with my sleeve.

"Avert your eyes," Abbie called out, but I moved mine too late. In the mud laid a half dozen naked bodies tossed at the front of the lot. One was a small child with his eyes still open.

"Wait for the pile to grow high, then bury them all at the same time." Abbie pulled me toward the back entrance. "Don't come this way much."

We crossed behind the buildings where the dogs barked like they had not been fed. Their chains scraped against the earth as they pulled and yanked to be set loose. As we approached the courtyard, a woman screamed in agony. She had blood on her arms; her eyes bulged from her head, and her fingers stretched wide for a young boy being snatched away from her by a white man. The child looked to be about three.

"No, no, no, don't take him," she bawled. Two men pinned her hands behind her back and dragged her in the opposite direction of the boy. Her headscarf slipped off as she twitched to be let loose. She tried to kick but they continued to pull her. I wrapped my arms around my waist as they threw her into the jail. Even with the door closed, I could hear the sounds of her agony. The little boy was tied with a rope and hauled away.

"What is going to happen to him?" I asked, even though I knew the answer.

"Don't like to keep kin together round here. 'Specially mamas and sons."

Abbie's words hit me in the chest. Monroe. I had fallen into a trap. The Jailer had sent me off on leisure so that he could steal my son. I took off running. My shoe slipped off my foot, but that did not deter me. I burst through the side door of the house and shouted.

"July, July!"

No answer.

I moved down the hall toward my room, my heart thumping so loud I could not hear myself breathe. When I pushed through the door, July and Monroe were on the floor. She tickled his belly and he cooed. I swooped him up in my arms.

"I do something wrong?" July stared, confused.

"No, sweet girl." I kissed the top of her head. I rocked Monroe and with the other hand clung to July. These two were my family now, and I had to protect them at all costs.

◆

As I worked in the shed over the next week, the cries of the poor woman being separated from her son rang in my ears. I tried to keep Monroe tied to me at all times. Every evening Monroe slept nestled under my breasts. But even with him so close, my spirit would not rest. In the middle of the night my mind turned over my options. If Monroe and I could get on the other side of the gates, we would run. But the Jailer would never give me permission to take Monroe outside of the jail. I could try to escape in the middle of the night with Monroe, but security on the property was high. It was nearly impossible to move around undetected.

And then Corrina Hinton walked through my mind. She was a woman like me, yet she lived a life better than some white women. Seemed happier than Missus Delphina for sure. Mama's plan had not gotten me my papers, but at least offered me some advantages: Miss Sally's education, never whipped, never worked the fields, always had a full belly and slept in a warm bed. Could I even guarantee that for my son? Our son.

If Essex searched for me, how would he find me here? Seemed near impossible when I thought honestly. Since I'd arrived in the jail I'd hung on to hope that Master Jacob would rescue me, but my dream of escaping this place had died with him. Nothing's more impossible than being rescued by a dead person. It was time for me to become my own savior. As much as the very thought of letting the Jailer touch me repulsed me, as shattered as my heart would be to give up on Essex, the need to protect my child outweighed everything else. My days as a girl were gone. Now I had to think like a woman.

That night I wept through my bath and shed what innocence I had remaining. In my robe, I fed Monroe and rocked him until he drifted off to sleep. When the Jailer sent word for me through Abbie I sighed, pushed myself forward, and opened the closet. Still hanging were the three dresses. I ran my fingers over each one of them, then selected the maroon dress with a lace petticoat.

"Lovely choice." Abbie patted Monroe's back while July threaded me into my corset, same as I had Missus Delphina what seemed like a lifetime ago. Then she held the dress open so that I could step into it. July pulled my hair off my shoulders and Abbie told her to pinch my cheeks.

"You look beautiful."

I kissed Monroe on his temple, closed my bedroom door, and walked slowly toward the parlor. When I turned the corner, the Jailer's mouth broke and the pleasure in his eyes gave me the gall to move forward.

"You are lovely."

"Thank you." I took my seat.

"Will you escort me to my room?"

"No dessert tonight?"

"Is that what you want?"

"Yes, please."

He beckoned Abbie to bring dessert for both of us and a drink for him. He fidgeted in his chair like a surly child who could not wait to unwrap a birthday present. Abbie returned with the two plates. I ate my pie as slowly as I could. Tonight, he did not watch me. He ate his in three big bites.

"Will you escort me to my room?"

I put my plate on the table next to me. "Would you like to hear a song?"

"No."

"Just one? It would please me."

He groaned. "As you wish."

I moved unhurriedly to the piano. I played a love song that I had composed in my head. It was the story of a love triangle.

A girl who loved a boy but had been promised to another. My fingers glided across the keys, pounding out my feelings for my true love but at the same time saying goodbye.

"Come with me. Please?" His voice cracked and pleaded. Then he was standing behind me. "I promise not to hurt you."

I gave him my hand and he enclosed it in his.

"I need something first."

"Anything."

"You must promise to never sell my son away from me."

His eyes went wild and then settled on my face. "Okay."

"And you cannot take a wife. As long as I reside at this jail, your allegiance is to me."

"You have my word." He kissed me on the mouth, and it took everything in me not to gag.

On the march up the stairs, my insides turned and knotted. I had to hold onto the banister to keep from turning back. In his sleeping quarters, a single candle burned next to the poster bed. I entered on shaky knees, then sat trembling on the edge of the bed. He fumbled with his trousers and then closed the door with his foot.

CHAPTER 17

Splintered

S hame rained down on me like angry piss from Missus Delphina's chamber pot. The wetness of dishonor clung to my skin. I had made a vow to belong to Essex until the end of time, but I had given myself to another. I was not sure which crushed me more—the weight of the Jailer's meaty arm across my belly, or my betrayal. The bed creaked as I untangled my body from his girth. I gathered my undergarments from the floor, closed the door behind me, and slipped down the back stairs as quietly as possible.

The jail felt calm that time of night. Even the dogs were silent, but I knew the ones locked inside were suffering just a few feet away. Monroe was snuggled in July's arms on her pallet and I decided not to disturb them. Instead I watched his chest rise and fall, the tight curls on his head bathed in his sweat. Would my sacrifice protect him? Once in bed, I searched for sleep, pleaded with it to put me out of my head, my misery, but it would not come.

When I rose the next morning, it felt like I had spent the night in a boxing match. My insides were sore, and my belly knotted with self-loathing. I stood at my washing basin and scrubbed every inch of my skin, but I could still feel his breath, fluids, and fingerprints all over me.

July was nibbling on a biscuit with jam, and I sat sipping lukewarm tea when Abbie found us at the servants' table in the house shed.

"Morning, Abbie."

"Mornin', Miss Pheby."

"Why you being so formal with her?" July laughed with her mouth opened.

I looked up from my cup, surprised, but Abbie avoided my gaze.

"Miss Pheby, Marse asked me to move your things to the bedroom 'cross the hall from him."

"Abbie!"

She kept her face cast down to the floor, not meeting my eye like usual. The message traveled on the silence between us. The Jailer had told Abbie to address me as such. Sharing his bed had separated me from the others, and I would be treated differently going forward. My face grew hot with embarrassment. July looked from Abbie to me and slowly her jaws closed. "I will gather up Monroe's things."

"Marse wantin' Monroe stay down wit' you." Abbie put her hand on July's shoulder.

"What?" My voice rose, startling Monroe, who slept across my lap. I patted his back but he would not be soothed.

I pushed back from the table, screeching my chair hard across the floor. My son and I belonged together. I would not leave him downstairs. How would I attend to him if he cried in the middle of the night? Monroe continued to fret in my arms, as if he understood our new fate. My bargain with the Jailer seem to already fall short.

"It is what he say. Marse don't like to be question't. Best make haste." Abbie retied her beige apron and then limped ahead of me.

I sat on the bed and nursed Monroe as Abbie gathered my things from the chest of drawers and placed them in a basket. When Monroe settled on my chest, I opened the closet and dug under the chest for my diary. Discreetly, I slipped it into my pocket. Mama's red calico dress hung from the center of the rack. Even though I had washed, repaired, and starched it the best I could, the dress would never return to its regal glory, but I needed it with me. I gathered it in my arms, and Monroe craned his face to feel the fabric. I tried to rest in the notion that he would be just a floor away from me. In the mornings, I could tie him to my back and take him to the sewing shed. We would only be separated in the evening. The split had been ordered to give the Jailer full access to my body at night.

My new bedroom proved more spacious than the one downstairs, by at least a quarter of the size. The four-poster bed draped in lace and the white-and-lavender floral wallpaper made the room feel dainty. A white dressing table stood opposite the bed, with an oval mirror attached, and a cushioned stool. Everything about the room echoed fit for a lady. The wide-plank floors creaked beneath me while I crossed to the window. As I pushed back the heavy curtains, I took in the cobblestone courtyard; a side section of the tavern, not twenty-five yards away; and a full view of the two-story wooden jail. I dropped the drapes back into place. Abbie entered with a water pitcher.

"Who lived here before?"

"Marse's mother use to take this room 'fore she got ill." She poured a glass of water and held it out to me.

"Abbie."

"Make peace with it, Miss Pheby."

"But I—"

"Be best for everyone. 'Cluding Monroe."

I took the glass and drank.

"Needin' anything else?"

I shook my head no, and she limped out, closing the door behind her.

I sat on the edge of the bed, trying my best to take in my new situation. When I stood to leave for my shed something caught the corner of my eye: a dusty leather-bound book on the nightstand near the far wall. I had not been near a book since I arrived at the jail. I listened for footsteps. My heartbeat increased as I turned the book over in my hand. The cover read OLIVER TWIST BY CHARLES DICKENS. When I opened it, I had to press the leaves down a few times at the front and then the back for it to fully spring to life. Mama's voice nagged in my head, cautioning me on the dangers of reading. I returned the book, but as I moved through my day in the shed, I wondered what words I would find on those grubby old pages.

The last girl of the day I was responsible for dressing up had left for the tavern just as the sun bled pink across the sky. I reached for a small tin of lard and massaged the cramps from my palm as Monroe squirmed to be untied from my back. When we got to the house, I ate chicken and dumplings with July and nursed Monroe while agonizing over our first night apart.

"He be fine, Miss Pheby." July pushed her thick braid over her shoulder as she got up off the floor. She had grown the habit of knowing what I thought without me saying it.

"If he wakes in the middle of the night?"

"I will rock him."

"Usually means he needs a change. Dry him good."

We both turned at the sound of the Jailer entering the house. He called to Abbie for his meal. I turned Monroe over to July and made my way up the backstairs.

I paced the floor anxiously, looked out the window, and then stopped at the dressing table. There were a bristle brush and comb set on a silver tray. I did not remember seeing it that morning. I dropped onto the stool and undid my hair. It soothed me to let my locks hang loose and brush my curls free.

Since Abbie had not sent for me, I assumed the Jailer did not need to be entertained, so I changed into my dressing gown. As I pulled back the covers resolved to sleep, I heard the Jailer fumbling on the other side of my door. My stomach burned bitterly at the sight of him. His cheeks were red, his shirt half untucked, and his belly protruded over his belt.

"I want to see you."

He lifted me from the floor as if I weighed nothing, then placed me across the bed. He panted hard as he undressed me, and I shivered under his gaze. Whiskey-scented sweat oozed from his skin and permeated the air around us as he crawled over me.

"You are a sight to behold."

I tried not to show displeasure as the bed made a thud under his hefty weight. He quickly began thrusting into me, pummeling so hard I choked and gasped, like he was forcing my head underwater for too long. When I maneuvered for air, I bit my lip so I would not cry out. Being underneath him was a duty, just like my job in the sewing shed preparing the girls. I closed my eyes and searched for a scenario into which I could escape.

He whispered in my ear, "Oh, Pheby. You are so special. . . ."

His moist hands seemed to be everywhere at once. His cracked lips ran over my neck, breasts, and face, then rested on my cheek. Finally, I heard a gurgle pass through his throat. He raised up on his forearms, stretched his neck back, and squeezed my wrists painfully as he released. When he let me go, I rolled away from him, begging God to make him leave. He snorted and then kissed me on the shoulder before gathering his things and leaving without another word.

I laid listening to the sounds of the house. When I felt sure that he had fallen asleep in his own room, I pulled the book off the nightstand. Under the candlelight, I flipped to the first page and slipped into the world of an orphan boy sold into an apprenticeship with an undertaker.

This became my nightly ritual. Once he entered my room, satisfied himself, and left, I would read, only allowing myself twenty pages so that I could make the book last. *Oliver Twist*, my friend deep into the night, helped me to cope.

◆

"Mornin' Miss Pheby," the boy Tommy greeted me, carrying water to the kitchen for Elsie. It had been a full three weeks, and I still had not gotten used to being called Miss. All of the servants except for Elsie had been nice before, but now they were respectful. Since moving me to the upstairs bedroom, the Jailer had given me full autonomy over getting the things needed for the fancy girls he sold. I had shopped the market twice without Abbie, though Monroe always stayed behind. The dressing of fancy girls became my arm of the Jailer's chattel business and was growing each day. To keep up with the number of girls being sold, I purchased ready-made dresses. Even though I did not sew them by hand, they always needed alterations, which slowed me down. How to sew faster was the thought I was chewing on when July walked in with another young girl, rail thin, with big, hollow eyes that said she had seen too much in a short amount of time.

"Marse said thirty minutes."

I untied the girl's hands. "What is your name?"

"Agnes."

I gave her a pail of water to wash her face with, and then laced her into a corset.

"What you prittin' me up for?" She turned those hollow eyes on me. I did not meet her scrutiny.

"It is my job."

"Where they takin' me?"

This was the worst part: when the girls asked questions. I knew they were frightened for their lives and I could do nothing but feed them, pray over them, and record their stories. I turned her around so that she could not see the worry on my face while I finished getting her ready.

"I am not sure. If there was something I could do for you I would. May God be with you." I squeezed her hand as Basil, the Jailer's manservant, appeared in the doorway of the shed.

"You come for her?"

"Yes, Miss Pheby."

I handed the girl over to Basil. "I have told you that just Pheby is fine."

He stammered, "M-m-miss Pheby, Marse likin' to see you. He in the whippin' room."

I opened my mouth but then pressed it shut. Basil took hold of the girl and left. I had never been to the whipping room, only overheard tales of the horror that happened there. As I walked to the holding pen of the jail, the barks of the dogs grew louder, hungrier. The chains of the imprisoned clinked and clanged. I stepped down the five steps into the whipping room, a dark dungeon, cool and damp. A small sliver of light slipped through a miniature window. When my eyes grew accustomed to the darkness, I saw the Jailer standing tall, wielding a whip that made ole Snitch's whip look like a toy. It stretched out long and hungry, with a split tip. On the floor, a chestnut-colored woman lay facedown in the muck of the ground, stark naked, with her arms fastened over her head in shackles. Her legs were also tied down behind her so that there was no room for her to move. She whimpered softly.

"Come in," he commanded me.

I slithered in with my back nearly scraping the wall.

He twirled the whip in the air, then brought it down on her back. *Thwap. Thwap. Thwap. Thwap.*

The woman cried out after every lash. *Thwap. Thwap. Thwap.*

He stared at me, his eyes daring me to look away. *Thwap.*

Her skin opened and blood seeped from her stripes. *Thwap.*

Thwap. Thwap. Thwap. Thwap.

She screamed until her throat was nothing more than a hiccup. His face became more alive with each swing of the whip. It took everything in me not to shrink to my knees and hide my face in the corner. *Thwap. Thwap. Thwap. Thwap.*

Her voice was no longer audible but her body twitched out her pain, her back completely soaked. The Jailer did not appear to slow down or tire. He tore into the woman like he was engaging in his favorite sport.

Thwap. Thwap. Thwap.

Dear God, had it been an hour? The woman barely moved and I feared she had passed out. My knees wobbled against each other and just when I thought I could not stomach a moment more, the woman gave a shout that sounded like a goat being strangled. Out from between her legs a red mass slithered against the ground. I blinked. It was a baby. It flailed, squirmed, but then fell still.

He looked at me to make sure he had my audience. The vomit in my mouth seemed hard to swallow back, but I forced it down by grinding my teeth. He dropped his arm and called to the two white men who stood outside.

"Get rid of that thing and return her to her master. Let him know I will gladly punish anyone who teaches slaves to read." He looked at me then. "It is against the law."

The men unchained the woman. She appeared dead, but then one of them threw cold water on her to revive her. She jumped and hacked as they carried her away.

He put down his whip and then folded his hands behind his back while taking a step closer to me, his face redder than I had ever seen it. Aglow. Like on fire.

"Something you want to tell me?"

The book. *Oliver Twist*. It had been a trap and I had fallen for it.

"How come you did not disclose that you could read?"

"My mama said to keep it a secret. Now I see why." I looked at the spot where the woman's fluids gathered.

"There are no secrets between you and me." He grabbed hold of my chin and brought his face so close to mine that I was forced to breathe what he exhaled: the scent of her blood.

"If I catch you aiding any slave in learning how to read, I will forget my affection for you and flog you myself."

"I understand."

"We cannot educate these niggers, lest they forget who the master is. Guessing that is what happened to you." He stroked my cheek. I tried not to flinch. Then he had his hand around my neck and was crushing his lips into mine. I could feel his manhood grow against my thigh. I thought he would take me against the wall right there, but then Basil called to him.

"Marse, they ready."

"Mmmm." He pulled back. "Go pretty yourself for supper. I will be up to the house shortly."

As I turned to go, he patted me on my ass so hard, it caused me to fall forward into the daylight. My feet felt spongy, but I willed myself to walk quickly. When I made it to the sewing shed, I closed the door behind me and dropped my head into my hands. Who could whip a woman until she lost her child? Only a monster.

When I crossed my hands over my lap I felt my diary with the log of girls in the hidden pocket of my skirt. What if he had discovered it? I looked over the shelves in the shed and my eyes landed on an old canister covered with dust and cobwebs. I stuffed the diary in the canister and covered it over with old scraps of material.

That evening, his appetite for me was insatiable. The skin on my shoulders and neck were bruised crimson from his teeth. When he finally left my bed, I could not feel my legs. Could not find sleep either. My eyes stayed fixed on a crack in the ceiling. There I watched the dead baby slip from the woman's womb.

Elsie's voice played over in my head. *They call this place the Devil's Half Acre.* Now I knew the devil.

CHAPTER 18

Deliver Me Lord

*I*t only took four months of his regular visits for me to know I carried his child. I felt the pressure across my lower back and my cheeks were fuller, puffy like Mama's, even though I did not eat much. Food stopped agreeing with me again. My breasts throbbed, and the pain his lips caused when he sucked and pulled on them was excruciating. He acted like a baby in that way, always reaching for my breasts, like they gave him life.

He had started falling asleep on my pillow some nights, too exhausted to walk across the hall to his own room. That's when I tried to make sense of him. Besides insisting I watch that awful whipping, he had been consistent in doing things he believed would please me. When he discovered me sniffing flowers out behind the kitchen house, he had Abbie arrange pretty bouquets that she changed out every few days. Gifts of fancy gloves, lace corsets, new shoes, hairpins, and chocolate waited for me weekly on my nightstand. Some days, it felt like I had been living in the jail for two lifetimes, not a few weeks short of a year.

This new pregnancy also made me fret over Monroe's future. The Jailer mostly pretended like Monroe did not exist. I hoped he would honor my request and not separate us. I hated having to rest my hopes on another white man. But it was not up to me. In this world, the men called Master held all the power.

Ever since Abbie had told me the bakery was a stop for runaways, I had thought about asking them to smuggle my boy and me up North and give this new baby a chance to be born into freedom. It was a thought that I indulged in the middle of the night, but the people of Richmond were so afraid of Rubin Lapier that I doubted they would risk their lives to help me. Even before I asked, I would need to find a way to get my son off the premises of the jail—a near impossible feat, because the Jailer's guards watched everyone.

◆

The August heat made it too warm in the supply shed to shut the door, so I kept it propped open and wished for a cool breeze. Lavender plants were stationed at the front of the door to dissuade mosquitoes from bothering me. In those first few months, I had turned the space into a full-fledged dressing room. A sheer piece of material hung from the ceiling to give the old room a sense of warmth when the girls were herded in. Buttons, fringes, feathers, ribbons, lace, gloves, and bonnets—all accumulated from my weekly trips to the market—were organized into drawers. Fabric was rolled neatly and the dresses were hung. I even managed to string together some jewels for the highly prized girls, the ones the Jailer thought would fetch eight or nine hundred dollars. I liked to keep things tidy, since the space was small. I stood sweeping loose ends from the floor when Basil approached with the next group.

There were four fair-skinned girls. They introduced themselves as Missy, Taffy, Beth-Anne, and Brenda. Brenda was the oldest of the bunch. I could tell by the way she poked out her lip that she had lived a life that afforded an air of stubbornness.

"You need to comb your hair," I said, blushing Brenda's cheeks with the rouge I had made from mixing hibiscus flowers, arrowroot powder, and lavender together. One of Mama's recipes.

"Don't want to be made up for them men."

"It will be over soon." I took a small dab to her lips, hoping to achieve a bee-stung affect.

"How you know that?"

"I am a praying woman."

"Way you fixin' us, I say you need the prayer." She pulled back and then spit in my face. I was so shocked that I dropped the jar of rouge and it splattered on the floor, spilling red all over her pretty yellow dress. The other three girls gasped in unison.

"You know I can have you whipped for that." My tone pierced harshly.

"I don't care what happen next. Can't be worse'n what already done happen," Brenda shrieked.

I wiped my cheek. I had a mind to slap the girl across the face myself. What was I going to do about the ruined dress? And my rouge. My thoughts were knotted over how to make her pay for it when July poked her head in.

"Marse ready for them," she said. Monroe cooed at me from July's hip. It had gotten to the point that it was hard for me to work and have him tied to my back.

"Take these three; tell him I need more time with the last one. I will escort her as soon as I can."

July moved into the room, took in the scene. "You need help here?"

I shook my head, motioning for her to go.

"Brenda, where are you from?" I asked, regaining my composure.

"Nowhere."

"Who is your mama?"

"No one."

"Okay, then let me pray with you." I grabbed her hands, but before I could open my mouth she started praying.

"Lawd, I come 'fore you thankin' you for the air I breathe. One of your sheep done deserted you oh Lawd. She is dressed like a sheep but pretendin'. She really a wolf. Change 'er heart Lawd and bring 'er back to your Kingdom. Invite 'er back to you, Lawd, so she can do good and not evil. In Jesus's name."

I dropped her hands. She had a gap between her teeth and she smiled so I could see it.

"I do it for my son."

"You do it for you. Been 'round your kind plenty."

I found another dress. Not as nice as the first one, but I wanted her gone.

"I ain't simple-minded either, if that's what you think. But I can see thangs when I meet people and I sees you." She stared until I dropped my eyes, looked down at my feet like she was a white woman.

Later at dinner, I moved rice and trout around my plate, still thinking about my encounter with Brenda. The Jailer did not notice because he loved the sound of his own voice. I wondered how he cleared his plate with all his talking. When I joined him in the parlor for dessert, he asked me to play. It was a relief to sit at the piano after the day I'd had. I positioned my fingers and let out the anger and the shame. When I finished, I had soaked my dress all the way through.

"Simply lovely."

"Thank you."

"Shall we retire?" he asked, as if I had a choice. The thought of him pumping into me made me ill.

"I am with child."

His eyes opened wide, and it only took a moment before the notion produced a smile, lighting up his whole face.

"Are you serious?" He pulled me to my feet.

"Your child," I said to assure him.

He wrapped me in his arms and brought his face close to mine. I could smell the whiskey on his breath before he kissed me. "You make me happy, Pheby Delores Brown."

His hand rested on my belly. When he looked at me, his eyes said it all. It was endearing to watch, and for a split second, I forgot the evil that lived inside of him. I could see in his eyes an emotion that could only be described as love.

When we got to his room, he undressed me and tucked me under his covers. I closed my eyes, bracing myself for another long night, but he climbed in bed next to me, put one hand on my belly, and used the other to cradle me. Then he kissed my temple and fell asleep.

He still had me in his arms when I awoke the next morning, and my neck was stiff because of it. Brenda was the first thought that came to mind. Was she right about me? Maybe I needed to seek God.

"Good morning." He kissed my cheek.

"I want to go to church on Sunday. Take everyone with me. We used to have service on the plantation. I miss it."

"That can be arranged. That African church is a few blocks away. The others have never been, but I reckon they'll be curious."

"Thank you."

"Thank *you*." He rubbed my belly.

◆

When Sunday came, I had Monroe dressed in a navy jacket buttoned to high-waisted trousers. He wore matching socks, and I combed his hair with a part in the middle. This would be his first trip outside of the jail and I could not wait to see his little face when he saw the horse and buggy, all the people moving through the streets, the stores and city lights.

"Miss Pheby, you lookin' good," July commented on the mustard-colored dress that I wore. I had sewn together a pretty blouse for July out of the extra material from the shed, and she looked lovely in lavender. She was old enough now for a corset and hoopskirt but I did not want men getting ideas about her, especially now that she had received her first blood, so I dressed her down like she was still a child.

I could see the others gathered in front of the house out my window when Abbie came for me. They seemed anxious to get to church, and I did not want to be the one to keep them waiting.

"Miss Pheby? Marse said leave Monroe with Basil. Rest us gon' on to church."

"I am taking him with me."

"Marse told the gatekeeper you ain't 'pose to leave here with Monroe."

I picked up my brush and threw it across the room, angry that he would relay his dirty message through Abbie instead of telling me himself. That bastard. Always separating me from my son. I wanted Monroe to know God. Hear the choir. Catch the spirit.

"Basil ain't so bad. He a good man. Guard Monroe wit' his life till you return." Abbie took my arm and steered me away from throwing anything else. When we got downstairs, she reached for the baby. I kissed Monroe's cheek and then handed him to her. He looked from me to Abbie and started kicking his feet in a fuss. Abbie moved out the back door with him, clicking her tongue against the roof of her mouth to calm him.

Elsie tried looking away when I approached, but I already noticed her checking me out as I came down the steps. We did well staying out of each other's ways most days.

"Miss Pheby," she said, and I did not correct her.

"Morning, Elsie. Ready to hear the word of the Lord?"

"Monroe ain't comin'?" She tipped her chin.

"Might not be ready to sit still for so long." I walked ahead, and July fell into step next to me. We exited through the front entrance. I could hear them singing from the jail as we passed.

The First African Baptist Church sat a few blocks away, at the corner of College and Broad. As we made our way, hundreds of Negroes filed into the street headed toward the church. The women's bonnets framed their beautiful faces and the men dressed neatly. The church stretched in a rectangular shape with its long side facing Broad Street. The foyer was dimly lit, and I could smell the smoke of frankincense and myrrh. Inside the sanctuary there was a wide center aisle with royal-blue carpet. Straightaway I noticed the men moved to sit on the left side and the women to the right. All the children congregated together in side galleries. In the front pews, upper-class whites, dressed in the latest fashions, sat together, with additional white men stationed in the corners of the room and along the back wall, watching. Negroes could not gather, not even in broad daylight to hear the word of God, without being watched.

The church filled fast. The choir walked to the front gallery and began to sing. A lovely pale woman led the massive choir in a few hymns. I recognized one or two. Her voice reminded me of Lovie's from back home, and I longed for our little church service in the clearing on the plantation. Missed Essex holding my hand and smiling at me.

When the choir finished the last note, the white preacher wearing a yellow robe with a gold cross sewn into the fabric walked up to the pulpit. At the sight of him, everyone sat up straighter.

"I want to welcome you to First African Baptist Church. I am Pastor

Robert Ryland. Do we have anyone visiting for the first time? If so, please stand."

My group stood, as did a few others throughout the sanctuary.

"Welcome to the house of the Lord. Please be seated. You are all in for an amazing treat from a Lamb of God. We have Reverend Nathaniel Colver, all the way from the Tremont Temple in Boston. He will deliver the sermon today."

Mr. Colver was a medium-sized white man with tight lips. He stood in front of the congregation wearing his white collar and spoke eloquently. It surprised me to hear him hint at the perils of slavery, and how all people should have the right to live with dignity. When he finished, the same woman led the choir in a final song.

Let Jesus lead me
Let Jesus lead me
Let Jesus lead me
All the way
All the way, way to heaven
Let Jesus lead me, all the way.

They clapped their hands and stomped their feet to provide extra rhythm and I found myself swaying in my seat. The music reached down into my heart and pried it open. I felt appreciation for this encounter with the Holy Spirit. True, I was not free, but living at the jail had taught me that my circumstances could be much worse. Mama always said that a grateful heart served as a magnet for miracles, so I latched onto the worship and gave thanks. I closed my eyes, rocked forward and back, and let their voices engulf me, heal me, restore me, while I prayed, *Jesus lead me. Jesus lead me.*

When the choir finished, I wiped the moistness from the corners of my eyes.

"We better go," I said to Abbie and July, loud enough for Elsie to hear me. July stood and motioned for the boy Tommy.

I could feel the ease and joy between the five of us on our walk back to the jail. Elsie and Abbie chatted about the sermon, and July started singing a Bible song in a voice that sounded almost as good as that of the woman who led the choir.

"I did not know you could sing." I tapped her arm and she chuckled.

The good feeling made me consider stopping at the bakery and purchasing pastries for them, but I decided not to press my luck on our first outing. Perhaps with the Jailer's permission, we would build up to that. We were about two streets from the jail when a little boy ran up to me flashing a wide grin. He looked to be about ten.

"Missus, know where the Lapier jail is?" He bounced on his toes. I saw that he had a note in his hand.

"You all go on around the back way so you can stretch your legs a little. I will take care of him."

They obeyed. When they were out of sight, I read the note, then handed it back to the boy. Shuddering, I took his hand.

"Who wrote this?"

"My marse. Said I get what I deserve. Hoping it a sweet."

The poor boy thought that he would receive a treat. How cruel of his master to send him to the jail, and on a Sunday.

Should be a day of peace.

"I will show you, but let me feed you first."

I took him to the bakery and bought him a pastry. I learned everything about him on our walk to the jail, knowing that he would be added to my diary. When we got to the gate, I told him to hand the note to the guard. They seized him and dragged him toward the whipping room. His big eyes looked up at me, hurt. I turned away and walked toward the house. I could hear his cries as I nursed Monroe and put him to sleep for his afternoon nap. Whenever I started feeling as if I could endure this place, there was always a reminder that I could not.

CHAPTER 19

Keys of Delight

The next day, Tommy found me coming out the house and said the Jailer wanted to see me. I had not spent much time in the tavern, and had to adjust my eyes to see because everything looked dark. The chairs were deep burgundy and the round tables were stained cherry. A long mirror hung behind the bar, and a man in a white shirt was wiping down the countertop. The room smelled like tobacco, musk, and peanuts. The Jailer sat at a corner table in front of his account ledger.

"Pheby." He reached for my hand and squeezed it. Then he rubbed my belly.

He thought the baby to be a boy, but I knew it was a girl by the way my looks had deserted me. My cheeks had broken out in red dots, and my eyes looked too small for my nose. My hands resembled those of a man's, and my ankles were thick like tree stumps.

"You wanted to see me?"

"I need you to play tonight. Important clients coming from Kentucky."

"Here in the tavern?"

We both knew that women were only there to serve drinks and entertain with their bodies. I had no practice with the former and no intention of doing the latter.

"I will be here the whole time. No one will lay a finger on you. You are mine." He smiled.

Essex had said those same words to me, and now look at what I had become.

"Put on a pretty dress and fix your hair. Play something happy. I want these men to spend money."

I nodded and exited the tavern. I had not played in front of an audience since Miss Sally hosted parties at the Bell plantation, but there was little time to practice or pull together a repertoire of music. I had no choice but to make it work.

Monroe and July were out back behind the kitchen playing peek-a-boo. When I walked up, Monroe held onto the side of the table with one hand while bouncing on his little knees. Four teeth had come in, and he drooled all down his chin. He looked so much like Essex that the sensation of it caught me in the center of my chest. As soon as he saw me, he fell to his bottom and crawled along the small patch of grass. I picked him up and nuzzled my head in his neck. Elsie came out the kitchen rubbing her hands on her apron.

"Spoilin' him."

"What is it to you?" I asked.

"Boy ain't gon' know he a slave you keep this up."

"He is not a slave."

She laughed. "You thinkin' 'cause you up at the big house that boy ain't no slave? Chile, you ain't smart as you think."

"What is for dinner?"

"Porridge and carrots. That pleasin' you, Missus?" Elsie mocked me.

"Mind your tongue." I carried Monroe toward the house.

"She gon' learn," Elsie mumbled under her breath, but I kept walking like I did not hear.

I put her out of my head as Monroe and I played awhile. Then I sat him on the floor next to the piano so that I could practice. I made it through my favorite three songs before Monroe demanded to be on my lap. I pulled him up and let him bang on the piano until he giggled and his saliva dripped all over the keys.

◆

That evening, I blended a new rouge, but it did not come out as well as the batch that Brenda had made me waste. I used some anyway to hide the breakout on my cheeks and stain my lips. My hair was styled in a low chignon. When I stepped into the tavern, the Jailer and I locked eyes and he gave his nod of approval. I crossed the room and sat at the piano. The men were already in conversation, and a girl stood serving drinks. Wanting the music to creep up on them, I played softly, almost as if there was no sound at all. Slow and steady, then hitting them with a rhythm that they could rock to. Platters of crab, oysters, and shrimp flowed across the table as I moved from one song to the next. The men grew louder and I played the melody to match their mood. I was having more fun than I had anticipated. Their voices carried over to me and with them brought snatches of conversation like news clippings.

"Abolitionists up north need bullets in their heads. They do not understand our way."

"No room for a Nat Turner repeat."

"Would not be a movement if they did not have help."

"Messing up the biggest business in the state."

"Yankees are damn fools."

"They need to honor the Fugitive Slave Act. It says they must return our property. Against the law."

I played up and down the scales, adjusting the tempo to hear more clearly. When they were all drunk, full, and happy, the Jailer paraded in three girls. They were dressed in low-cut tops, with their bosoms spilling forward. I tried not to consider their faces. A stocky man wasted no time. He took the hands of one girl and headed to his room. Another man pulled a girl onto his lap. I played high up the scale as a girl sat down on the Jailer's thighs. She had almond-colored skin with dark gray eyes. Her hair was smoothed back from her face and her cheeks sat up high, as if they were perched on pillows. Her breasts were large and her waist slender. She draped her arm around his shoulders.

An unexpected discomfort crept into my gut. It was the first time I'd wondered if I were his only lover. I lived up at the house with him and carried his child, but that did not mean there was no one else. But when did he have the strength? Every night he came to me with fury, and he was not a young man. I played and played and the girl stayed by his side. When I glanced up to steal another peek, he mouthed, "Dismissed."

I got to my feet and exited quietly through the side door.

Clearly, I had no cause to be jealous. I did not love him.

I hurried past the jail, ignoring the bark of the dogs and sounds of the defeated. When I entered the downstairs bedroom, Monroe and July slept side by side. I longed to take him up to my room, but I would not chance it. Did not want to cause problems. I slipped into my dressing gown and wished I had a book to read. Since discovering me with *Oliver Twist*, he'd taken the copy. I laid awake until I heard the steps groan under his weight. I listened as he paused at his door and then continued down the hall. My door opened and then closed. The sound of his pants hit the hardwood floor with a thud. Dread passed through me as he lifted my cover, then fumbled for my flesh. Once he was inside of me, we both exhaled.

CHAPTER 20

Second Coming

*W*hen the sun came up on the first Friday of April, I knew that his child would be born before nightfall. The sky had been crying over Richmond for what felt like all of March, and the damp air kept my body aching. For a week now, it had hurt to move, to lie down, to relax, to sew, to even hold Monroe. My manner had been so irritable that the Jailer had taken a respite from coming to me at night. With my protruding belly, there was no room for him anyway.

Abbie came to check on me before she served him breakfast, bringing me a snack while I readied myself for the day.

"Feeling okay, Miss Pheby?" She poured me a glass of water.

I was on my right side, rubbing my belly.

"Time is here."

She gazed at me. "Wantin' me to get Elsie?"

I nodded.

"I's alert Marse too."

The birth pains escalated quickly. Felt like climbing through the woods and up a mountain, then having to slide all the way down on my hands and knees. I rolled into a ball and bit down on my pillow so that I would not cry out every time my stomach cramped. Elsie arrived with a wad of towels. Her hair stood up wildly, like she had been in the middle of fixing it when sent for. She lowered herself down and felt between my legs.

"Head right there. Won't be long."

I grunted.

"Give me a push."

I bore down.

"Breathe now. Push again."

We went back and forth like that, with me breathing and pushing until I felt the baby slip out.

"A girl," Elsie called out.

"I's fetch Marse." Abbie hobbled away.

Tears welled in my eyes as I brought my daughter to my face. "Hello, sugar."

She was white as a sheet. Not a drop of Mama's skin tone in her. She had his emerald-colored eyes and slender nose. Her cry roared from her lungs and her face turned pink. Already angry with me. I squeezed my breast into her tiny mouth. She gummed hungrily until she got the milk to flow.

Emotion overpowered me. We would be a pair, like me and Mama, and I would teach her everything I knew. Not how to be a slave, but how to be a lady. Like Miss Sally taught me. She sucked with her tiny fingers wrapped around mine. That was the picture the Jailer saw when he walked into my bedroom.

He gripped his hat in his hand, while his eyes glistened with tears of joy. I sat up and presented his first child to him. He took her in his arms. I watched from the bed as he cooed at her and kissed her neck. I planned to name her Ruth.

"We will name her Hester. My mother's name." I disguised my disappointment.

"You have done well, Pheby Delores Brown. She is beautiful." He snuggled her to his chest. "I will give her the world."

◆

The Jailer constantly visited us, wanting to hold Hester and talk to her. I wondered how he conducted any business at all. He spoiled us completely, having Abbie fluff my pillows and bring meals to my room. There were toys and blankets for Hester but nothing new for Monroe. I tried not to worry about the Jailer's lack of attachment to my son. If we were going to have a family, however unconventional, I wanted Monroe to be a part of it, but he showed no interest in my boy. Still, I wanted Monroe to get used to his sister, so July and I developed a system. Each morning after the Jailer left for his business, I brought Hester to the downstairs bedroom so that he could interact with her. While I sat in the room with the two, July kept watch for the Jailer from the window. I did not know if he would approve of the visits or not, and I decided not to take any chances of upsetting him when things were going so well.

Monroe treated Hester with wonder during our visits, touching her hands and kissing her face. Since he was recently weaned, I did not nurse her in front of him, so when she started up a fuss we would have to go. Those visits were the best part of my day. When Monroe settled down from the excitement of seeing her, I held them both in my arms and sang every children's song that Mama had taught me. In the time that I had lived at the jail, those moments were the closest semblance of peace.

When Hester turned three months old, the Jailer decided to throw a party to celebrate her birth. In her honor, he invited three couples: Silas Omohundro, Hector Davis, and David Pulliam, all jail owners and deal-ers of the chattel business in Richmond, and their companions. I had not heard of or met most of these couples, yet he wanted us to move heaven and earth in preparation to receive them.

"I want everything perfect. Nothing is too good for Hester," he re-minded me daily. He had only given us one week's notice about the party, so we all buzzed around like blue-arsed flies trying to prepare.

To get ready for the festivities, Elsie slaughtered a pig, July picked veg-etables from the garden, Tommy polished the silver, Basil whitewashed the outside of the house, and Abbie went to the bakery for sweets. Elsie got mad when she realized she was not making dessert, but when she baked anything but her apple pies, she usually added too much filling and the result was a hot, bubbling disaster.

The Jailer insisted that a dress be tailored for me. The German seam-stress he sent me to on Grace Street did not seem pleased to work for me at first. She carelessly took the wrong measurements, and when she wrote them down she seemed surprised when I corrected her. She tried to dis-suade me from the material I selected, saying it was too expensive. When I used the name Rubin Lapier, she fell over herself to help me. I was an-noyed but also impressed by the power being associated with him wielded.

The day before the party, I rearranged the furniture in the parlor to make it more open for guests, assembled centerpieces for the dining room table, and helped Abbie dust. Abbie had no experience tending a party, so I taught her how to set a table properly and explained the way white folks like to be served dinner.

"Back straight and stiff. Seen but never heard."

City life was different from plantation life. There was no punkah, a fan used to keep the flies away and the room cool. I hated opening the windows because of the odor and sounds coming from the jail, but the house sweltered in summer so I had no choice. The candles that I scented with perfume worked at masking the smell, kept the mosquitoes out, and added a loveliness to the table.

In the afternoon, I propped Hester on the bed. She chewed on her hand while July laced my corset.

"Is that good?"

"Tighter."

"Ma'am, you red in the face."

"I can take it a little tighter." I held my breath.

When July finished with the corset, I slipped into my hoopskirt. The gown had a white-and-blue delaine skirt and bodice with a satin trim. It was the most elegant and elaborate garment that I had ever owned. When I caught myself in the mirror, my first thought was that Mama would have been pleased at how I had made the best out of my situation. When I was growing up, she constantly reminded me to never be a slave in my mind. Tonight's gathering served as my opportunity to honor her wishes. As I slipped into my satin shoes, I tried shooing away my second thought, but it pressed hard against my temples. What would Essex think of me? Had he too found it necessary to move on? I shoved those feelings aside.

July slipped Hester into a white satin gown with a light blue ribbon around her head so that we matched. The Jailer knocked before entering my room. His navy waistcoat with a floral cravat also complemented my attire.

"You look lovely." He pressed my cheek to his.

"Thank you."

"I have a surprise. Bring Hester."

July picked up the baby and we followed him downstairs. In the living room stood a man next to a wooden box camera resting on a thick stick.

"Our first family photograph." He held his hand out to me and guided me to the Queen Anne chair.

I pursed my lips. A family photograph without Monroe. I knew by now not to question him. I forced glee into my eyes and clung to Hester.

◆

The guests arrived one couple at a time, with just minutes between them. The Jailer had me stand next to him to receive each pair as they crossed the porch and entered the house.

"Hector, my friend, may I present to you Pheby Delores Brown, mistress of the Lapier jail and mother of my firstborn daughter, Hester Francine Lapier."

It was the first time that he'd introduced me that way, and I felt the color rise in my cheeks.

"How do you do?" The man kissed my hand.

"Congratulations. Motherhood suits you," said the woman with him. "I am Anne." She was nearly white.

The second couple arrived, David and Helen. Basil served the wine and Tommy held a tray with small snacks of olives, peppers, soft cheese, and crusty bread. July had the difficult job of collecting gifts for Hester and dashing to the back room to check on Monroe. Now sixteen months old, Monroe had become quite confident on his feet, and I worried that he would get hurt.

Next, a man of small stature with a long mustache arrived. On his arm was draped a beautiful woman decked out in a cream-and-burgundy dress. It was finer than anything I had ever seen, better even than the pictures in a catalogue. When she brought her black-rimmed eyes to mine, I recognized her as the woman I'd seen on my first trip to the market. The one who had complimented my bonnet.

"Silas Omohundro, may I present to you Pheby Delores Brown, mistress of the Lapier jail and mother of my firstborn daughter, Hester Francine Lapier."

"How do you do?" The man kissed my hand.

"I am Corrina Hinton," the lovely woman breathed in my ear as she pecked my cheek. Her perfume smelled heady; it took my breath away.

Silas and Corrina made a most handsome pair. She too was very fair, and carried herself in such a stately manner that I shrank in her presence.

"May I hold her?" Corrina reached for the baby. Green and red gemstones dripped from her fingers, and gold bracelets adorned both wrists.

"Beautiful. Just like her mother." She smiled at me and then handed Hester back.

The Jailer had hired a violinist for the evening, and we all made our way to the parlor to be entertained. As the gray-haired violinist played, I felt the tune move through me, and could not help but wonder what we would sound like together. The Jailer must have read my mind, because just then he called my name.

"Pheby, dear, would you honor our guests with a selection on the piano?"

"Of course." I smiled sweetly.

All eyes were on me as I sauntered toward the piano. The instant my fingers grazed the keys, I felt at ease. The moment rivaled old times on the plantation, with me entertaining important guests and being admired for my talent. The violinist accompanied me perfectly, and we each paused to give the other a chance at a solo. Then we ended with one last piece and moved through the notes in concert. Everyone applauded. The Jailer looked at me approvingly just as Elsie rang the dinner bell.

"Let us eat." He led the way to the dining room.

It was not nearly as impressive as the one on the Bell plantation, but for a city home, I imagined it suitable. The mahogany table seated ten people comfortably. July reached for Hester and then the Jailer pulled out my seat opposite his at the head of the table. Another first. Though we had been taking meals together for months, I had always sat to his right, never opposite him, never with company. The couples sat in the middle of the table with the men closest to him, and the women closest to me. The first course was pea soup and sweetbread. The men chatted, falling into a comfortable conversation of their own, while we women glanced around and sipped daintily from our spoons. I racked my brain for an interesting subject. Since I had never entertained as hostess before, I had no idea what to talk about. I opened my mouth to make a comment on the weather, but Anne spoke first.

"You are gifted on the piano. How long have you played?"

"Feels like most of my life. I started very early."

"And your dress is gorgeous. Where did you get it?" Helen put down her spoon.

"A German seamstress on Grace Street."

"Hilda?" Corrina raised an eyebrow. "We live on the same street. She is tightly threaded until you get to know her."

"I have had my moments with her too," chimed Helen.

"She did not seem to want to work with me until I threw Rubin Lapier's name into the conversation."

"She can be peculiar like that, but once she warms up to you she will go above and beyond your request."

"Did she make your dress?" I asked Corrina.

"Oh, this?" She looked down like she'd forgotten what she was wearing. "Silas sent for it from New York. A gift for giving him his first daughter. We have four sons."

"I do not know how you keep it together, Corrina, and still manage to look like that." Helen flicked her hand and we shared a low laugh.

My nervousness started to wane as Abbie and Elsie served the next course. Pork legs, dumplings, and potatoes with stewed vegetables and gravy.

"Delicious," Corrina commented.

She appeared to be just a few years older than me, and so beautiful I found it hard to look at her without staring.

"Finding a woman to cook to my tongue has been trial and error. How long has she been with you?"

"She was here before me."

"Lucky." Corrina ate some more.

Besides the scrape of forks and knives the entire party fell silent as everyone enjoyed their meal. Elsie had outdone herself with the flavors and seasoning. After having seconds, the Jailer pushed back from the table.

"We will take our dessert and cordials in the parlor," he told Elsie, and then showed the men out.

"Missus, would you like your dessert served here?" Elsie's tone pretended at passiveness, but by the way the three women eyed each other, I knew that she had not succeeded.

I placed my glass down on the table and looked at her pointedly until she dropped her eyes. "Yes, please."

When she exited the room, I sighed more loudly than I'd intended.

"You all right?" Anne touched my arm.

"Yes, of course," I said, searching for a new topic. "How long have you lived in Richmond?"

Anne replied. "I was born not far from here. Hector took possession of me when I turned thirteen. You?"

"A little over a year." I dabbed my chin with my napkin. "Born in Charles City."

"Well, I have been here eight years. Still cannot adjust to the filth of the city." Helen pouted.

"I love the city," Corrina replied. "There is much more opportunity here for women like us. If we were on a plantation, the best we could hope for was a position working in the big house. Here, we are running our own homes."

The other women nodded in agreement as Elsie brought in a silver tray with slices of pie, and blueberries and cream, and placed them on the table. We ate and talked about our children, the endless shopping and management of the servants and food supply. From these women, I discovered that Richmond was second to New Orleans in the slave trade and that there were several jails, holding pens, and auction houses similar to ours scattered within a few-block radius.

As the evening progressed, Anne shared that her older brother, who had lived as a free man in Anne Arundel County, Maryland, had turned up missing a month ago. She feared that he had been stolen and sold South. Corrina squeezed Anne's hand as Helen confessed to the guilt she nursed over families being separated at auction.

"Sometimes I feel their blood on my hands."

"None of it is your fault. I have learned that all we can do is pray for change," Corrina offered, and I felt less alone with my own shame in preparing the girls for sale.

Abbie hobbled in with a carafe and poured each of us a glass of red wine, which lifted the mood. I had never had more than a few sips prior, and after finishing my first glass I felt loose and free.

"Who have you hired to tutor the children?" Helen asked Corrina.

"William Cawfield. He has been amazing."

"You will have to put us in contact with him."

"Silas has started looking at boarding schools in Lancaster and Philadelphia for the older two."

"So much to think of." I fanned myself, thinking about my own education in Miss Sally's parlor, which I had been fortunate enough to get, and the one in Massachusetts that had never come to pass.

Corrina touched my wrist. "I was like you once: young. This life forces you to grow up fast."

Helen finished her wine. "Your daughter will be educated just the same. Never too early to think about a tutor."

"She's only three months."

"Time seems to slip away in dog years," Anne agreed. "My oldest is already eight and it feels like I just carried her."

Corrina sipped. "Our children are our legacy. We must educate them, and then get them out of the South."

"That is my daily prayer. For my children to be completely free," Anne breathed.

Corrina took my hand in hers. Her touch was soft and soothing. "You must also demand respect. That cook does not respect you. I would have her sold. Do not care how good she salts pork."

"You just want her for yourself," Helen teased, and we all giggled.

When I had lived on the Bell plantation, I'd lived in isolation between the loom house and the big house. This budding relationship between these women was all new to me, and it was, apart from my children, a ray of light in an otherwise grim time. By the time the dessert tray was cleared away from the table, the many glasses of wine had gone to all our heads.

Helen kept us laughing with stories of her thickheaded house servant, and as I chuckled at yet another tale, I heard the Jailer make a loud grunt from the parlor. Then something crashed to the floor.

"Excuse me." I rose from the table and walked to the entryway. I was immediately caught off guard to see two of the girls used for entertainment at the tavern in our home. He had one of the girls draped across his knee, and was spanking her with the back of his hand. His forehead was wet and his slack eyes revealed that he was drunk.

"This is how you do it."

The other three men were caught in the middle of cheering him on when I stepped into the room. They looked away and straightened up in their seats.

"Pheby," he called to me. "Come, this one loves a good whipping. Give her a slap on the old arse."

I tried to hide the disgust from crossing my face as the other three women appeared at my side. David rose from his seat and beckoned to Helen.

"Ladies, you ever see a good arse whipping? This one likes it rough," he slurred.

Silas stood and smoothed out his jacket. "We had better go. It is getting late." He reached for Corrina.

Hector followed his lead. "Thank you for a very nice evening."

"Where are you going, boys? We are just getting started." The Jailer turned the girl loose and she scurried from the room. "The night is young. We have not had our cigars."

"Next time." Hector shook his hand.

Abbie gathered everyone's things and stood at the door with Tommy to hand them out. The women bid me goodbye, and then followed their men across the courtyard. When they were all gone, I burst.

"Why would you do that?"

"Do what?" he roared.

"Bring them in here. Tonight of all nights. I thought we were celebrating our daughter. This is not the tavern. It is our home." I had spoken without thinking of the consequences. And now I braced myself to be slapped. But he just grinned.

"All in the name of fun. Get the stick out of your arse, would ya?"

I was spitting mad. This was my first attempt at friendship. Being with women who understood my experience of the last year and a half, and he'd ruined it with his crude ways. I turned to go.

"Where are you going?"

"I need to nurse the baby." He pushed up from his seat, grabbing my arm and pulling me back toward him.

"Do not turn your back on me."

"That hurts."

"You do not do that." His face shifted.

The two girls in the hall flinched at his tone. I then recognized the one with the gray eyes as the girl who'd sat on his lap in the tavern. The baby started to whine.

"Would you rather she starve?"

He let me go with a jerk. I marched down the hall to the nursery and slammed the door. July rocked Hester.

"Unhook me from these things!" I cried out. July fumbled with my hooks and ties and released me from the dress. I was in my chemise and bloomers when Hester found my breast. Monroe placed his head on my lap. Though I was trying to make peace with my fate, I was reminded again that the Jailer was an uncouth animal. It took everything in me to calm down. I stayed in the nursery with the children until they were in a deep sleep before taking the back stairs.

When I reached the landing, his bedroom door was slightly ajar. As I passed, I heard the springs of his mattress, so I glanced through the gap. That is when I saw him with the cat-eyed entertainment bent over the side of the bed. His hands cupped her dark breasts as he pounded into her flesh. I moved quietly to my room. Moments ago, I'd been the mother of his firstborn, mistress of the jail; now I was reduced to the woman across the hall while he bedded another. I placed a chair against my door to bar him from entering, then searched for sleep.

CHAPTER 21

Sissy

The entertainment had a name: Sissy. Where she came from or when she had arrived I did not know. Hard not to picture him plucking her off the auction block in the same fashion he had me. Three days after the dinner party, he moved Sissy into the room above the tavern. A small space but private, one that she did not have to share. Her new jobs included working alongside Elsie, boiling the laundry, canning vegetables, and passing out the meals to those in the holding pen. Given her promotion, I spent several days worrying over my status as mistress of the jail. Even though I did not love the Jailer, I suffered through our arrangement for the safety of my children, and I could not let another woman threaten my position, not until I figured out a way to get them to safety.

On my shopping day, I ran into Corrina at Thalhimer's buying dry goods. She convinced me to stop with her at the bakery. Over tea and crumpets, I confided my fears surrounding Sissy.

Corrina brought her eyes to mine. "You have given him a daughter white as snow. His allegiance is to you. Sissy is nothing more than his black concubine; all men have one or two. Even though white men do not consider us women fully human, they cannot stop lusting for our flesh." She took a deep breath. "Rest assured, you are his prized yellow wife. Just make sure she respects you and knows her place." I carried Corrina's words with me from the bakery like armor and shield.

The servants and I had been attending the First African Baptist Church regularly. I still could not take either of my children from the jail. This week Abbie stayed back and Basil was permitted to go. The next week someone else would be on rotation. When we gathered in the courtyard, I noticed that Sissy had joined us for the first time.

"Morning," she said without looking at me, then went and stood out of view behind Elsie, as far away from me as possible.

We passed through the front gate and made our procession to the church. Basil was the closest person to me, probably ordered to protect me. I had not exchanged pleasantries with Basil often, but he wore his devotion to the Jailer in his posture, always anticipating his next need and moving when told. He had been walking slightly behind me, and I slowed until we were side by side.

"Basil."

"Miss Pheby." He kept his eyes on the ground.

"Nice day."

"Any day 'bove ground good for me."

"How long have you been living at the jail?"

"Round 'bout seven years, ma'am."

"Where are you from?" Basil's story had not yet graced the pages of my diary.

"Stafford County. Born on Ashby plantation."

"How did you get to Richmond?"

He looked the other way. I knew I asked more questions than he was accustomed to answering. Even around the jail, I did not see him talking much. Not even to Abbie, for whom I suspected he had affections.

"Ran 'way. Sent here for a whippin'. Then Marse decided to buy me."

"He whipped you first?"

"Worse 'n ten marses."

I wondered how he lived with being loyal to someone who had treated him so cruelly.

"You like it here?" I do not know what made me ask that.

"Like city life betta 'n plantation life. Little more freedom. Out in the country had me thinkin' every day bout dying. Was worse 'n hell. Now, things ain't so bad. Marse treat me real good."

We arrived at the church. Basil held the door open for all of us to pass through. The choir was already singing, and Elsie moved to the front of the church and started clapping and praising right along with them. We filed into the pews in our usual formation. Men to the left, women to the right. We had been attending so often that it was almost like we had assigned seats. I sat on the end and swayed to the music. The choir always put me in a good mood, and I pondered what it would be like to play that organ up front and accompany them. The organ could not be too unlike the piano. Different sound, but I knew that given the chance I could do it.

"Today there is cake and lemonade in the church hall. You are all welcome to join and fellowship," announced Pastor Ryland.

Elsie did not wait for my nod, just started down to the basement with Sissy behind her. I signaled to the others that it was fine to go. Pastor Ryland had a sack filled with letters, and as members passed by, he handed the unopened mail to the addressees. I had heard from Corrina that they were notes sent from people who had escaped to the North and contained news of their arrival. The men in the tavern often spoke against Pastor Ryland's mail deed with repulsion, calling him a traitor, but it did not deter him from handing out the letters each week at the end of service.

I closed my eyes and used the peaceful time alone to pray. After the week I'd had, I needed to get my head straight. When I opened my eyes, Pastor Ryland stood in front of my pew.

"I did not catch your name, ma'am."

"Pheby Delores Brown." I extended my hand.

"Thanks for bringing your people to hear the word of God. It makes a difference in their lives." He removed his spectacles. "You are over at the Lapier jail, right?"

"Yes."

He looked around to see if anyone was listening to us. "Hard place. How are you faring?"

"Fine. Just fine."

"I pray for Rubin Lapier all the time."

I gave him a questioning look.

"His exercise of overt cruelty is beyond the sanctions of the Bible." His face contorted.

"Is that why you give out the letters?"

"My role is to preach the gospel and bring as many to Christianity as I can. Not to be a policeman."

"Well, it was nice to meet you." I pushed myself to stand. I suspected that he could be trusted. Still, I could not take any chances, not even with a man of God.

"Hoping to see you next week." He placed a hymnal in my hand. We exchanged looks. His eyes were kind. "As long as there is breath, there is hope."

"Thank you." I slipped the hymnal into my purse and fastened it.

◆

That evening the Jailer sent word through Abbie.

"Marse say he want you at dinner tonight."

More than a week had passed since the last time we had eaten together. "Very well."

I allowed her to dress me in a simple plaid dress with my hair pinned at the nape of my neck. The children were settled with July in the nursery, and after peeking in on them, I entered the dining room. He was sitting at the table when I arrived. When I moved to the seat at the other end, he beckoned me.

"Sit here, dear."

I gathered my skirts and sat to his right. The pins in my hair were pinching my scalp and I touched them lightly to rearrange them.

Abbie served pork and dumplings with rice. I guessed we would be eating pork for the remainder of the month, on account of Elsie slaughtering that pig for Hester's introduction party. "You are cross with me."

I said nothing.

"I cannot take it when you are cranky. I have missed you."

I wanted to comment on his new source of pleasure but I bit my lip. No sense in showing a hand of jealousy. That was not going to get me far. I knew what he needed to hear, so I forced the words to exit my mouth.

"I . . . have missed you too. We must not quarrel, it is not good for the children."

He smiled sloppily. "Shall we retire?"

"It would please me to have a run with the piano."

"Very well. I would be honored to hear."

We moved into the parlor. Abbie brought him a nightcap and I took my seat. I closed my eyes and then played the tune that I had shared with the violinist. The tempo and timing sounded beautiful, like a coveted piece of silk floating in the sky.

When I was finished, I had released as best as I could my resentment toward him.

"It is time to get you back over to the tavern. It has been so quiet without your music."

I stood, walked to where he was, and made myself kiss him on the cheek. He seemed startled by my aggression, but eagerly took my hand and led me to his room. Once the door was closed, I kissed him again, then reached for his trousers and unbuttoned them. He moaned in my mouth as I undid his shirt and slipped it over his shoulders. I had learned that when I pretended to want him, our encounter ended much quicker.

The Jailer was not good at all with the straps and pulls that held me in my dress, so I removed his clumsy hands and pushed him down on the bed. His eyes quickened with anticipation as I laid down and pulled back my dress, eager to get my duty over with. While my body suffered through his rough touch and grunts of delight, I closed my eyes and let my mind escape inside the tune I had just played on the piano. When he had his fill I tried rolling away, but he clung to me possessively and breathed into my neck. "I love you, Pheby Delores Brown."

I swallowed back the bitter taste in my mouth and forced a smile, hoping this meant we were back on decent terms.

CHAPTER 22

The Hickory

The smell of smoke woke me from my stupor. And then there was the yelling and running that rose from outside the window. I turned toward the Jailer's spot but he was gone. It was the first time that I'd stayed all night in his bed. I hurried to my room, dressed in something that I could serve in, and beat it downstairs. Abbie met me at the foot of the steps.

"What happened?"

"Tommy set the haystack on fire. Know it an accident, but Marse mad as a March hare."

When I rushed out the back door, Basil and Tommy were running back and forth from the well with buckets of water, passing them to Elsie and Sissy, who were dampening the fire. The Jailer stood there with his arms by his sides, tapping his left foot but not lifting a finger to help. I grabbed a pail. Abbie and I worked one side of the fire while Elsie and Sissy worked at the other. When we finally got the flames to submit, we were all hot, flushed, and exhausted.

"Follow me," he said to no one in particular, so we all dropped the supplies and went.

When we turned into the courtyard, a coffle was being led into the jail. Four other groups were washing up and preparing for auction. He walked down into the cellar and headed for the whipping room. I did not wish to follow, but because it was little Tommy I went, hoping that my presence would force lenience. Especially after last night. I stood with my back against the damp wall and sweated.

"Basil, strap him down."

Basil did not hesitate. He grabbed Tommy by the arm and pushed him to the ground.

"But it was an accident, Marse," Tommy cried out. My, how he had grown since I'd arrived. He stood at least three inches taller and his voice had deepened.

Basil handcuffed his hands to the ground and then put his feet in the ankle beads. The ledge under the window held his collection of weapons and restraints: a whip about nine feet long made of tough cowhide, a cobbing board full of angular holes, various hickory sticks, more cowhide, lead, ropes, two clubs, various shackles, and a chain. He studied the weapons, pondering over them like he was trying to decide between wearing a white shirt or a blue one. He reached for the hickory stick and in a blink he tore into Tommy's flesh. *Thwap. Thwap. Thwap.*

We stood in line, watching Tommy's skin break loose and the blood begin to seep. *Thwap. Thwap. Thwap. Thwap.* With each swing the Jailer looked brighter; the sheen glistened high in his face, and any connection that we'd shared the night before seemed forgotten. He behaved like an animal who had finally cornered his prey. Tommy was just a boy, I wanted to scream out. *Thwap. Thwap. Thwap. Thwap. Thwap. Thwap.* My stomach curdled, but I knew if I averted my eyes he would be upset. This was his show and we were supposed to learn from his performance. *Thwap. Thwap. Thwap. Thwap.* The blood poured and mingled with the last victim's in the mushy ground. Tommy's voice had grown weak and his breathing dropped shallow. *Thwap. Thwap.*

The hickory stick swung through the air and then onto Tommy's back, breaking in two. The snap of the stick brought the Jailer's awareness back to the room. Tommy's back looked so red that I could not see where the skin started and the wounds ended. It was all a messy blob of puffy flesh and blood. No one moved out of fear that anyone could be next. The Jailer tucked his shirt back into his pants and ran his right hand through his hair.

"Basil, get him cleaned up. Fix the situation with the hay. Rest of you back to work."

I walked the few steps to the supply shed. I had some salve that I made of mutton suet and dandelion roots. I carried my medicine bag over to the kitchen house. When I entered, Elsie had Tommy laid out in her quarters, on the same pallet where I had nursed my fever when I arrived. She dabbed at his back with a wet towel. I watched as she washed his wounds, and then I knelt beside Tommy and went behind her rubbing in the salve. He winced. I held his head and gave him a sip from the brown jar, Mama's strongest pain medicine. He fell right asleep. But then as I turned to leave, he lifted his head.

"Marse said for me to—"

"Hush now, boy," I said, gently pushing his head back down on the pallet. "Get a little rest. Be back to check on you after a while. Stay on your stomach so your back can heal."

◆

I found it impossible to concentrate on my work after doctoring Tommy. The Jailer could easily afford more hay. I knew that the beating was more an example of his power than anything. He liked to keep his foot on our necks, squeezing until it felt like we could not breathe without his permission.

There were no girls today, so I set about the task of mending things needed—blankets, socks, old shirts—and I stitched together clothes for the field hands out of burlap. I preferred to have some pieces on hand for those who came to the jail with nothing. Especially in the colder months. When I finished, I crossed the courtyard to prepare for dinner. Basil jogged up to me.

"Miss Pheby, Tommy got a fever."

I went back for my bag and headed over to the kitchen house. When I reached the top of the stairs, I saw Tommy shivering on the pallet. I lifted the brown jar to his mouth.

"Bring some onion to put by his bed," I called down to Elsie.

I smeared another layer of salve on his back, knowing that I had better hurry or the Jailer would be irritated with me for holding up his dinner.

"I will be back soon as I can. Do not forget about the onion," I said to Elsie. She bent her shoulders over a pot of stew and grunted.

When I reached the house, he was already there.

"I just need a minute to check on Hester. Do you mind?" I asked nicely. More kindly than I felt, but I knew the way forward to keep the peace.

"Yes, bring her to dinner so I can see her."

I headed to the nursery. Monroe had his arms up right away, demanding that I hold him. I gave him a quick peck on the forehead and reached for Hester. Monroe started to cry. July grabbed him up and started kissing his neck and belly, but he refused to be pacified. He wanted me.

"Baby, I will be right back. Stay with July."

"No, Mama. Mama!" His arms flared in the air.

I knew the Jailer did not like to wait, and after today, his patience would wane. I hugged Monroe to my chest, kissed his face, and then handed him to July. When Hester and I walked down the hall, I could hear my son screaming for me. "No, Mama, come, Mama."

I walked into the dining room, handed Hester to her father, and then took my place at the right of his arm.

"My lovely ladies." He smiled. "Let us eat."

And we did then, as I listened for Monroe.

———— • ————

CHAPTER 23

Barefoot

*W*hen Isabel was born on April 20, 1855, her skin looked as fair as Hester's, but her mannerisms and the way she held her head reminded me of Mama. Joan arrived eleven months later. She had a hint of my mama's color and proved to be a fussy baby. I could barely work without her tied to my back. She refused to let any of the fancy girls in the shed hold her, and she never quite took to July or Abbie. Soon as Joan could hold her head up, my belly swelled again.

If I had to guess, I would say that Hester was the Jailer's favorite. He spent most of his free time in conversation with her. By the time she was four, her mind absorbed everything, it seemed. The Jailer allowed me to read to the children, and Hester had already begun to pick up on three-letter words. She was clumsy on the piano, but I made her try her scales for at least fifteen minutes each day. She hated it, and we quarreled during every lesson. She shared her father's likeness in that way. Stubborn as a nail. The only person she did not hassle too much was Monroe.

Those two were like two sides of the same coin, inseparable. They ran and played behind the house in the small garden, made up games, and shared toys. When I taught Hester, I sent Monroe off so that the Jailer would not suspect that I educated him too. Monroe's learning took place in private, during the hours that I knew we would be alone. I reminded him constantly that no one could know of his lessons. Each time we studied together, I told him about the slaves who had their eyes burned out with lye when their master found out that they could read.

"Am I a slave, Mama?" he asked after our last session in the back of the stables.

I scratched my head at the difficulty of the question. "In some way, all the people who live at the jail are servants of Rubin Lapier, because he owns it."

"Even you?"

I swallowed. "Even me."

"But he is kind to you." He broke a piece of straw in two. "He hates me."

"That is not true."

"It is. He always tickles and plays with Hester, but not me."

I pulled Monroe to my chest. "Tickle her like this?" I started under his arms and moved down to his ribs until he fell out in a fit of giggles. I hoped his laughter would help him to forget.

The windows at the back of the house were open, and the breeze kept the children cool while they relaxed. We used the drawing room for a play area because the nursery had gotten quite crowded. Isabel slept across my lap. Joan had just begun holding her head up without support, and put everything within reach into her mouth. July had gone to the kitchen to fetch the children a midmorning snack of apples and peanuts.

Hester and Monroe were playing their favorite game of hide the puppet. Monroe had hidden the puppet and called out "warmer" or "colder" as Hester dashed about the room to find it. She was usually good at finding the puppet, but that morning she seemed frustrated and could not uncover it. Then she started to cry.

"Monty, I want the puppet."

"You got to find it," he teased.

"Mama, make him give it to me."

"Find it. You are getting warmer."

Hester stomped her foot and started wailing. Usually when she acted like that Monroe would stop the game and give her what she wanted. Today, he did not give in. It had reached the point where the noise rattled my nerves, her crying and him teasing. I had just resolved to put an end to the game when the Jailer walked through the door. His boots clunked heavily against the hardwood floor as he grabbed Monroe by the arm and dragged him across the room to the nearest chair.

"Dear," I tried coaxing, "the children were just playing."

He ignored me, flopped down in the wing chair, threw Monroe over his lap, and started pounding him on the backside with his large palm. *Woop. Woop. Woop.*

"Papa, stop!" Hester cried out.

But he kept hammering. *Woop. Woop. Woop. Woop.* As Monroe's face turned from scared to horrified, I silently thanked God that I had not allowed the Jailer to keep whipping tools in the house. His hand came down on my son like a clap of thunder. *Woop. Woop. Woop.*

"Enough!" I called out, pushing myself from my seat.

Hester ran over to her father and forced her body under his arm. "Papa, stop hurting Monty. Stop it, please." Tears spilled down her rosy cheeks, and her hair came undone. When he saw her distress he stopped, discarded Monroe to the floor, and swept her up in his arms.

Monroe crawled across the hardwood and found a hiding space on the other side of the table. He did not utter a sound of pain. I had taught him to be quiet when the Jailer came around. Mama always said, *Less trouble finds a quiet soul,* and I had instilled that in my boy.

The Jailer stood and headed for the door. As soon as it closed behind him, I reached for Monroe. Only then did he start crying.

"Told you he hated me."

I held him tighter. "He does not hate you."

"He does," Monroe hiccupped.

Hester came and put her arms around him and we stayed like that until Monroe calmed down. When Hester asked him to play the game again, he declined.

◆

The Jailer returned to the house for his supper, calling for Abbie.

"Yes, Marse." She limped into the dining room. "Needin' more bread?"

"Have the boy's things moved over to the kitchen house."

"Why?" My voice cracked.

"I will not have a nigger tormenting my child."

"He is my son."

"He will still be yours living in the cook's house. 'Sides, it's time for him to start working."

"He is five years old."

"If he were on a plantation he would be in the fields by now."

"He is not on a plantation. I want him here."

"It is final." He slammed his fist on the table.

Abbie scooted from the room. I pushed my plate away, refusing to eat. July passed through the hall with Joan on her hip and clutching Isabel's hand.

She paused at the door. "Afternoon, Marse. 'Scuse me, Miss Pheby, should I put the girls down for a nap?"

I nodded, then noticed his eyes take in her slim waist and rounded hips. July's hair was so thick and long that I implored her to keep it wrapped, but she was young and busy, and often forgot. I feared for her, and tucked her away with the children as much as possible. Beauty was a curse for a slave girl.

"Go on," I said, waving them away, "Mama will be there shortly to give you a kiss."

He put down his fork. "I need you at the tavern. Important guests will be here within the hour. Go get ready to play."

◆

The Jailer was sitting at a round table with five men when I entered. The lights were low, so I concentrated on every step to the piano, careful not to misjudge my feet and fall. My mind was not on the chords or the melody that I played, but on my son. How could he move him out of the house like that? Monroe would never hurt his precious Hester. They had played that game countless times. What was Hester going to do without Monroe? What was I going to do without him?

The Jailer drank until inebriated. The entertainment girls pranced around the room in low-cut dresses and too-potent perfume. Sissy stood next to the Jailer, and though I had grown accustomed to seeing her at the tavern, my discomfort at the thought of them together had not lessened any. She had gained a little weight in the face, probably from spending her extra time around Elsie, eating the leftovers in the kitchen and sampling Elsie's pies. Sissy did not come near the piano, and instead worked the opposite side of the room, as if there was an invisible line between us. Once I saw the men choose their girls, I slipped out.

I suspected he would not be home soon, so I walked over to the kitchen house to peep at Monroe. Elsie was bent slicing beets on the long table, and Monroe was mopping up the debris. The one thing I could rest on was that even though Elsie did not like me, she adored Monroe and acted something like a grandmother to him.

"Mama!" he called and rushed into me.

"Hey, baby." I kissed his forehead as he tried to wrap his arms clear around my belly. I could sense Elsie watching me. Judging me.

"Get you anything, Missus?" She spit between her teeth.

"Just take care of my boy." To him, I said, "Be good and listen to Aunt Elsie. I will just be up at the house. I will come for you when I can."

"Why can't I come now? Marse say I have to stay here?"

To hear Monroe call that man Marse made me cringe. "Yes, for the time being."

"What I do?"

"It is 'what did I do,'" I corrected him. I knew the more that he stayed away from me, the more common he would sound.

"Everything will be all right." I took his hand and led him out of Elsie's earshot. We stopped behind the Wintergreen Boxwood bush and I crouched down until we were eye to eye.

"Me and Hester always played that game." He kicked a pebble.

"'Hester and I.'"

"Hester and I."

"You did not do anything wrong, son." Then I pulled his ear to my mouth and whispered, "You his slave in name only, never in your mind, boy. You are meant to see freedom. It is my solemn promise to you."

"Me and you both, Mama, right?"

I picked a lint ball from his cotton shirt, avoiding his eyes. Did I even dare contemplate freedom or had that dream died when Master Jacob passed away? And get buried even further with the birth of each of my daughters? Truth of the matter was, most days I only thought of liberty for my children. Particularly Monroe, because as long as I pledged my loyalty to the Jailer, our girls seemed destined to live a decent life.

Grabbing both his hands, I said, "I will always protect you. Now listen to Aunt Elsie and remember the things I have told you."

As the days passed into weeks, I did not get to visit him daily like I wanted. He for one was busy fetching buckets full of water three times his weight, running errands, and stacking firewood. Between prepping the girls for sale and playing at the tavern, I scarcely had time to visit our daughters in the nursery. This new baby felt bigger than any I had carried. Every step I took felt like moving in slow motion. Once the child arrived, I planned to make it my last. The recipe to make this possible resided in my diary, and I planned to use it.

◆

My head was resting on the side of the table in the shed when Basil and a new girl walked through the door.

"You all right?" she asked me.

"Yes, fine." I forced myself up. She was pretty enough and did not seem to need much fixing. I selected a blush-colored dress for her, and as I fastened her into it, she told me that her name was Florence. I was in the middle of collecting her history so that I could scribble it into my diary when the birth pain hit me. It came hard and so fast that I doubled over. Then water gushed down my legs.

"The baby." I could not help but bear down.

"Want me to get someone?"

My teeth started chattering. Florence stood in the door and screamed, "Needin' some help. Somebody, help."

I felt the baby slip down. I held onto the table and squatted.

"No time," I gritted between my teeth. "Have you . . . done this before?"

Florence nodded. She took off my dress and removed my bloomers. By the time she crouched down on the floor, the head had started crowning.

"This baby ready to see mama," she said, and then reached down and caught it. "It's a boy." She held him up for me to see.

He did not cry out like the other children.

Florence cut the cord with my shears, then wrapped the baby in a soft piece of material. I eased down onto the floor, feeling cold and wet. As Florence covered me up I thought, *A boy. His first son.*

May God show him favor.

─────── • ───────

CHAPTER 24

Sons, Then Heirs

God did not show him favor.

Abbie had settled us in my room and the baby burned hotly in my arms. It had been two hours since his birth, and he still had not latched on for a feeding. I worried, and when he dozed off, I thought hard on what Mama would do. The Jailer pushed my door open and entered.

"Is it really a boy?" he asked.

"Yes."

He moved to my bedside and carefully picked up the baby from my arms. Tears were in his eyes. He has cried over the birth of every one of our children. This time was no different.

"We will name him Rubin."

I knew that I would not call my son Rubin, and settled on Bin for myself.

"Something is wrong. Didn't you feel how hot he is? I think we need to send for the doctor," I told him.

Concern crossed his face as he returned the baby and then left the room. It was not long before I heard an insistent rapping on my door. The gray-haired, hunchbacked doctor entered my bedroom carrying a big black leather bag, with a stethoscope around his neck.

"May I?" He took the baby from me and started unwrapping him from the blankets. After conducting a full examination of Bin, he lowered his eyes and declared that he had puerperal fever.

"He will only last a few more days. I am so sorry."

The Jailer rubbed my cheek with his hand and then walked the doctor out. I wanted Mama. Most times to sense her was enough, but this was the first time in a while that I'd wanted her physically. There had to be a cure. I needed my diary with the recipes, so I gave Abbie the baby and made my way down the stairs. I could feel the blood gathering between my legs but I had to save my son. I crossed the courtyard and then reached for the tin container that hid my secrets. By the time I returned to my room, the blood had soaked all the way through my skirt.

The diary bulged in my hand, nearly full from all the girls' stories I had collected over the years. In the front were Mama's recipes, and I turned the pages until I found it. The tea was meant for adults but it was all I had. I tucked the diary under my pillow, called to Abbie, then rattled off a list of what I needed from the market.

While I waited for her to return, I tried to get the baby to suck. He would for a few seconds and then give up. I kneaded my nipple and tried to make the milk come down to make it easier for him. He took a swallow and then fell from my breast.

"Come on, Bin, just take a little bit for Mama," I coaxed.

I knew I had no business getting out of bed again, it had so exhausted me the first time, but when Abbie returned with the ingredients, I made my way over to the kitchen house.

Elsie opened the door. "What you doin' here, Miss Pheby? Should be restin'."

"Doctor said the baby is not going to live long. I have got to try to save him." I held up the bag with the ingredients.

"What you needin' me to do?"

"Help me make this tea." I sat down on the chair in the corner and gave Elsie the instructions on how to brew it. When she finished, she brought me a taste.

"Little more apple cider vinegar and I will be on my way."

Elsie poured the tea into a pot and then helped me up from my seat. I thought she would just hand over the pot but she carried it to the house for me.

Abbie rocked Bin near the window. "Ain't moved much since you gone."

I eased back on the bed. His body still burned hot, and his skin looked grayish.

"Hey, sweet Bin," I said. He opened his tiny slits of eyes and looked at me for the smallest second. I took it as we had an understanding. I, as his mama, was going to do everything to keep him alive. He was going to drink the tea and let me work a miracle.

I used a dropper to feed him the tea around the clock, every hour on the hour, but saw little improvement. Abbie prayed, Elsie sang, and July mostly kept the girls occupied.

By the third night of our around-the-clock vigil, Bin's breathing had grown shallow. Abbie was sitting at the foot of my bed, Elsie in the chair in the corner when Bin started crying, loud and steady. I looked down at him in my arms. It was the first time I'd heard his voice. I tried to soothe him with my words. "It is okay, Bin. Mama's right here."

He gave a shudder and then a small sigh. Everything in him went still. An icy feeling traveled up my arms.

"Noooo," I cried out, but Bin was gone. Even though the doctor had warned me, I sat in disbelief.

Elsie came for the baby. "Abbie, get her to sip from the brown jar. She in shock."

Everything inside of me was shattered and thrashing all at the same time. I felt worse than I did when I was sold, when I had lost Essex, worse even than how I felt when mama died. This one pierced me down in a place deep, and the pain kept hemorrhaging.

"Come on, Miss Pheby." Abbie tipped the jar to my mouth, and then everything went blank.

When I woke up, the sun had gone down and the curtains were drawn. The Jailer laid next to me. His arms wrapped around me like a cradle. When I turned toward his face, his cheeks were moist, and his eyes were red too.

CHAPTER 25

——— • ———

Undone

I could feel myself dying, week by week. I could not eat, could not sew, did not want to be bothered with any of the children. I just stayed in my room, staring at the wall. When I did push myself up from my pillow, my hair stayed on the sheets. It dropped out by the clumps. The Jailer worried sick over me. He even had the doctor bring me opium drops, but I refused to swallow them. Mama had cautioned me against white people's medicine all my life, so I knew better.

My breasts had filled to the point of pain, puffing out like tightly packed water balloons. Abbie covered them with cabbage leaves to dry them out. Two weeks passed, and nothing revived me from my grief. Then Abbie appeared at the door with Monroe.

"Marse went in to town. Be quick," she said to Monroe and pushed him toward me. He seemed to have grown a full inch.

"Mama, what is wrong?"

My face opened into a smile as I made room for him next to me on the bed. I smothered him against my breasts and kissed both of his cheeks.

"You okay, Mama?"

"Yes, baby. Now that you are here."

He looked around, eyes bulging over my delicate things. That is when I remembered that he had never been to my room.

"You sick?" He touched my forehead.

"A little."

"Want Aunt Elsie to make you some tea?"

I nodded.

"I made you something." He reached into his pocket and then held up a bracelet woven from straw.

"Did you do it all by yourself?"

"Tommy helped me."

"I love it, thank you."

Abbie entered. "Better get goin'. Hear the carriage."

Monroe kissed my temple, and I grabbed his face and whispered, "Remember the things I have told you."

He nodded his head and then followed Abbie out. I slipped the bracelet on my arm and then crossed it over my heart.

◆

The following day, the Jailer appeared with a box.

"For you, love."

I sat up. Inside there were several books. I pulled the heavy one off the top. It read EMMA. I opened it and started flipping through the pages. The Jailer kissed me on the forehead and then left me alone. I read *Emma* deep into the night, not stopping unless I had to relieve myself or when Abbie begged me to eat something. The story delivered me from my feelings and provided the escape I needed. By the time I finished the book, my appetite had returned. Then I read *Jane Eyre*. When the Jailer noticed my improvement, he called me to the parlor. I had taken my meals in my room until then, and my legs were a bit wobbly on the stairs. I appeared in my dressing gown.

"My love." He seemed startled. "You will catch a draft."

"I am fine." I sat on the edge of the piano stool.

"Would you play something for me?"

I turned toward the piano, but my fingers would not gobble up the keys. I could not locate a single song inside of me.

"Maybe another time."

"How about 'Pretty Dreamer'? I would love to hear that," he coaxed. "Just give it a try."

I turned my legs toward the piano again. Placed my fingers on the keys and pressed down. The first sounds rang out harshly. Then I pressed again.

And again. Slow and steady, low and melodic, and then up the scale. More color, more light. The song picked up and I found myself playing notes in staccato. I moved my fingers back and forth across the keys until they were tender and I breathed freer than I had in weeks.

"Brava." He clapped.

When I turned, wiping the sweat from my brow, I saw that the girls had joined us in the room.

"Mother, lovely." Hester clapped.

"I want to play like that," said Isabel. "But where is your pretty dress?"

I chuckled lightly. Joan made her way to me and crawled into my lap. She stuck her pointer finger in her mouth and sighed. I fingered her damp curls from her forehead.

"I have hired a tutor to start working with the girls," the Jailer informed me. "She will be here day after tomorrow. Would you remember to dress for the visit?"

"She will," answered Hester. "Of course Mother will."

◆

On the morning that the tutor was meant to arrive, Abbie came in with a sweeping new dress.

"Marse said for me to run you a bath and wash your hair."

I followed Abbie to the bathing chamber. A claw-foot porcelain tub sat in the middle of the room, with steam rising from the water. When I sank my body down in it, my first bath in three weeks' time, I exhaled. I knew that I had to let my grief go. My son would be in my heart every day, but I had to move on. Abbie soaped my thinning hair. I had taught her to use egg yolk and warm water to give it a healthy glow.

"It will grow back," she whispered. "I rub your scalp good, then pin it. Nobody know what's missin'."

After oiling my skin and dressing, I had to admit that the weight on my chest had lessened. Abbie encouraged me to brush my cheeks with rouge and stain my lips.

"Now you look like the lady of the house." She smiled, and I felt grateful for her friendship.

July brought in the girls; they were all dressed, and their hair had been combed and tied with bows.

"Mama, you look beautiful." Hester put her arm around my waist. Isabel tugged on my hand.

"Miss Pheby, Miss Grace here to teach the girls." July bounced Joan on her hip.

"Let us head into the drawing room so that we can meet your new tutor. When we are finished listening to Miss Grace, we will have cookies and tea."

Isabel's face lit up. She had a sweet tooth like her mama. When we entered the room, Miss Grace appeared younger than I had imagined. I estimated her to be around twenty-five years old. Her skin was pale even for this late in the season, and her body looked rail thin. She had dressed her hair elaborately and pulled it tight away from her face.

"Good day, children." She removed her gloves. "Shall we get started?"

"Yes," said Hester.

"I will be in the sewing shed." I had taken Joan from July, and now balanced her on my hip. "Girls, remember to pay attention. July will stay here in case you need anything."

This became our weekly routine. The kids would be tutored by Miss Grace and July would stay in the room to supervise while I took Joan with me to the shed. I instructed July to listen to the lessons but to keep her face blank and feign disinterest. Any questions after the lesson, I would answer for her. She was a quick study and learned how to spell all the girls' names and read a few simple sentences in only a few weeks.

◆

Sissy had kept the fancy girls dressed and going in my absence. When I returned to the shed, she was kneeling near a girl, hemming the bottom of her skirt.

"Morning, Missus," she called out.

"Morning." I breezed by her, deciding to take inventory so that I could get ready for my next trip to the market. "How many are we expecting today?"

"Three mo' after this one."

"Any supplies running low?"

"Bloomers." Sissy heaved herself up by holding onto the sewing table. When she stood, her belly rounded in front of her. Surprise lodged in my throat. I had to swallow a few times for the news to settle right in my stomach. I did not have to inquire after the father. Obviously, the Jailer had done this.

"I will finish up here, Sissy." I dismissed her, then turned my attention to the girl to be sold, asking my usual string of questions to distract myself from the emotions that overcame me. I did not love him but we had a family. Sissy's child would, I assumed, work his property, while mine were educated and presented to society as his daughters, but even that reasoning did not diminish my bitter feelings.

I learned from July that Monroe had been spending more and more time in the stables, working with Tommy to help with the horses of the men who traveled to the tavern. When I visited him, he showed me a few coins that had been given to him. Fitting he would be a stable hand just like his father.

Once I returned to work full-time, Sissy went back to her other jobs, leaving me alone in the shed. The Jailer took me moving about as a sign that I was well enough to visit at night. He returned with his usual lust for me, and it did not take long before that familiar fatigue hit. I knew soon enough that Sissy was not the only one with his child. Never had the chance to fix myself after my son's death, so here I carried again.

◆

Two weeks later, Sissy gave birth to a boy. Walnut-colored skin with her gray eyes. Abbie reported that the birth proved difficult but that Sissy was recovering fine. Although the Jailer had never asked me for a son, it was hard knowing that the one I had borne had died and hers thrived.

"Mama?" Monroe called to me from the door of the stables. Hearing his voice snapped me out of my head. My boy stared up at me with a piece of straw hanging from his mouth. Essex used to chew on straw. I made sure the Jailer was not around, then followed him inside to our secret hiding place behind the haystack.

"Hey, baby." We embraced. The baby fat had gone from his face. I leaned down and whispered into his ear. "When is your birthday?"

"February 6, 1851."

"Count to twenty."

He cupped his hands around my ear and counted. I wished I had a treat for him.

"Guess what?"

"What?"

"Tommy said he gon' teach me how to ride a horse."

"That will be nice."

"You know how to ride a horse, Mama?"

"A little, but I know you will be better at it than me."

"How you know that?"

"'Cause it is in your blood." I nipped his nose with my finger and kissed his cheek.

CHAPTER 26

Fly Birdie

*B*asil was gone.

No one knew what had happened to him. The Jailer had sent him to Rockett's Landing to pick up a coffle, something that he has done twice weekly since I had lived at the jail. This time he did not return. The Jailer had his britches in a bunch over his escape. Had every patroller in the state looking for Basil. I was surprised by the whole thing because Basil appeared so loyal. Never hesitated when the Jailer asked him to do anything. He had us all fooled, and I secretly prayed for his safe passage.

As I moved through my tasks, I could not help wondering how Basil must have planned and plotted his escape for months, years even. I pictured him making friends at the dock and consulting with the free blacks on the best way to travel north. If I had known his plan, I might have begged him to take Monroe to freedom. This jail was no place for a Negro boy, and Basil's running reenergized the notion that I needed to get my boy free. In some ways, I had been lulled into passivity, but now I felt awake.

Every evening over dinner, I had to endure the Jailer's bouts of anger over losing what he called his best nigger. Three weeks passed with no leads. Basil had vanished without a trace. After getting the report from the patroller, the Jailer decided to take matters into his own hands. He stormed down to the docks and picked up three men. I could hear them from the shed pleading their innocence, but the Jailer had them strapped down. The whip seemed to whistle through the air for hours. When he finished, none of the men could stand. But that did not stop him from having them thrown into the jail. His message rang clear: if anyone hid Basil they would pay with their lives. By the end of the month, the Jailer was at his wits' end. He drank more and slept less. I coaxed him to take it easy but he disregarded me.

The thing that pushed me over the edge was his determination to show no mercy. I had not known how truly brutal he could be until the morning he sent for Abbie. This time he did not force me to watch, but I could nonetheless hear her call out in pain. The cries had an almost feral quality to them. When she was carried back to the house by Tommy, the metallic smell of blood clung to her skin long after he'd beaten her. Since she and Basil had been lovers, the Jailer now blamed her for his escape. I nursed her back to health best I could, but being under the whip had struck Abbie dumb. She became clumsy and her memory grew short once she returned to work. On top of everything that July already did for the children, she now had to pick up Abbie's slack.

◆

On May 30, 1857, Katherine, our fourth daughter, was born. Elsie had been ill with fever, Abbie still a useless wreck, and July busy keeping the children entertained. When the birth pains came, I pulled her from my womb myself. As soon as I saw her tiny face, I pet-named her Birdie. She would be my last little bird. There would be no more. When my blood stopped, I fixed myself to make the children stop. I had given him enough.

Sissy worked in the kitchen cooking until Elsie could get back on her feet. Her bigheaded son sure loved Monroe. He cooed and giggled whenever Monroe stopped to play peek-a-boo with him. I was standing in the garden watching Monroe carry slop buckets, amazed at how strong his little arms were, when the Jailer startled me with his presence.

"Pheby. Need you at the tavern, now."

"Would you like me to change?" I asked, knowing he would not want his clients to see me in my simple housedress.

"There are but ten minutes to spare."

I untied Birdie and handed her over to July. Abbie was slow, but after fidgeting with my straps and pulls, she got me into my lavender calico dress. I twisted up my hair and made haste. I slipped in unnoticed and started playing a classical song that made me think of home. When I peeked over the top of the piano, I saw the Jailer sitting with four men at a table. One of the entertainment girls brought over a platter. I recognized two of the men as Silas and David, his jailer friends with the wives whom I adored. From eavesdropping on the conversation, I found out that the other two men were politicians. I had seen neither before. The Jailer's cheeks were red, and I could ascertain from his tone that he was riled up.

"How does my boy just walk away with no trace?" He was yapping on about Basil again.

"I have never lost a nigger," the Jailer fumed.

"Some of them plan their escape for years. Sneaky."

"Yankee abolitionists are not making it easy for us. Do they not recognize the law? That we have got papers on them?"

"They think differently."

"Foolishly."

"Did you get wind of the nigger in Massachusetts, causing a ruckus?" asked the politician on the right.

Silas nodded. "What is his name? Essex Henry."

I missed a note on the piano but quickly recovered. Had I heard him right?

"Yes, that boy Essex Henry is causing so much trouble, the federals had to get involved. He is in custody now, but they are planning to bring him back to Virginia, where he belongs," answered the politician on the left.

"He needs to be punished, and punished good."

David put down his glass. "We need to send a message that we will not stand for this."

"Bring him here," the Jailer growled, and the hairs on the back of my neck stood to attention.

The politician on the left clapped the Jailer on the back.

"That is what we came here for, Rubin. To get you on board."

"These niggers need a good showing of what happens when they fix it in their head to escape."

The politician smiled. "Thought you were the man to do it."

The Jailer smiled back. "I will get justice on this nigger for every slave who has run off, or even thinks about running off. Plan it big. Open up the courtyard for folks to come from miles away to see. I will scare them straight. You have my word."

One of the politicians stood up. His belly was as big as the Jailer's. "I will inform the authorities and get back to you with a date. Now, can I indulge?" he said, pointing to one of the girls. The Jailer waved his hand for the man to go.

I played and played and played. *Essex has been captured. My Essex is coming here.* Everything in me started aching for him at once, but on the same notion, I was desperate over his fate. With Basil having run, the Jailer would be ruthless. He had been merciless in his punishment before. But now, there was no telling what he would do. God help us.

PART THREE

Bully Trader

CHAPTER 27

---•---

Auction

*A*fter overhearing the men speak of Essex being sent to the jail for punishment, I found it impossible to rest that evening. After minimal sleep, I awakened to the sound of hammers pounding, objects falling, and loud shouts. July pushed open my bedroom door.

"What is the meaning of so much noise?"

"Marse having the pen cleaned out. Ain't never smelled nothing so bad." She pinched her nose and slid my window closed.

My stomach knotted. The jail had not been cleaned in the six years that I had lived here. All of this for Essex's arrival? I waved off breakfast and headed outside. The odor was so putrid that I ran back to the big house and told July to keep the girls locked up in the drawing room. I felt sure they would fall ill if they inhaled the fumes. On my way to the shed, I gave Monroe and Tommy lavender-scented cloths to tie over their mouths and noses.

"Use this as a barrier to breathe until the odor subsides," I instructed.

Monroe stood still while I looped the cloth behind his neck. His head rose past my waist now and he was due for a haircut. Working with Tommy had broadened his shoulders and he had lost all traces of baby fat. It was hard to believe he was only six years old.

While Tommy mucked the stall, he told me that in preparation for the fugitive's flogging, all punishment and trading had been ceased on the property for forty-eight hours.

"Marse said that was enough time to clean the pen and paint the tavern and big house. People coming from miles away to see."

I leaned into the boys. "This is no time for mistakes. Do not give him any reason to find fault with you."

Tommy nodded his head, but Monroe's eyes widened with fright.

I pulled him to my waist and held him tight.

"Mind your tongue and stay close to Tommy. I will be near, watching over you always." I squeezed his hand.

The courtyard was noisy with the drumming of sledgehammers. Four strapping men were erecting a platform stage. Men and women, threaded together by chains and ropes, sat along the cobblestone pavement while a horde of others shoveled out pounds of sticky bodily waste, rotten debris, and even a small lifeless body. I hacked at the sight and overpowering smell, and then removed a cloth from my pocket and tied it over my nose. Little children sat at the women's feet, and a baby with big hair cried, refusing to be soothed by her mother's arms. A bony girl leaned as far as she could with her ropes and vomited. It was the toxicity in the air making them sick. Noxious enough to poison. Something had to be done.

"Pheby." The Jailer stood in the door of the tavern, dressed for a day of business.

"Good morning."

"What do you think?" He gestured to all the work going on, seemingly unaware of the dangerous odors.

"I am concerned about their health. The stench is no good for them to breathe. Especially the children." I pointed to the crying babies. "We must find temporary housing until the cleanup is finished."

"They are nothing more than something to sell. Like furniture." He reached for his pocket watch, opened it, and then returned it. "An advertisement ran today in the classified section, inviting nearby men to come with their family members and property to watch the flogging."

"Has anyone passed around water?"

"Enough with that." His eyes held mine, then he patted my bottom and steered me toward the shed.

◆

The baby's cries carried on persistently through the night. I could not lie in bed while the infant suffered, so I slipped out of the house and went to the shed for my medicine bag. When I rounded the courtyard, the people were still bonded, woven in packs along the ground. Some slept, but most were wide-awake. I walked through the rows following the sound of the child. When I located the mother, I reached for her baby. She turned her back and shook her head no, frightened that I meant them harm.

My eyes were soft. "Let me help."

She looked me over and then held up the baby.

The little girl's skin flamed with fever. I rubbed a lemon balm on her palms and chest, behind her ears, and on the soles of her feet. To her mother, I extended my canteen of water. She drank deeply. Once I finished with them, I moved through the row, feeling foreheads and doling out medicine. Then I closed my eyes and prayed.

The next morning, I was exiting the tavern with a package of books that had been delivered for the girls, when the Jailer and Monroe strolled past me. Since he had never taken an interest in my child, the alarm of them together rang in both of my ears.

"Can Monroe carry these books for me up to the house?" I called out.

But he ignored me and shuffled on with Monroe at his heel. I could feel my son's trepidation but he did not chance a glance at me for reassurance. What could he have done to be beaten at six? But then they walked past the whipping room, away from the jail, and out the front gates. I sighed a small relief, but then realized that I did not know which fate would prove worse—Monroe being stretched out, or Monroe leaving the property with the Jailer alone.

As many times as I had pictured Monroe's first time off the grounds, he was always with me. I would show him the shops, point out the carriages, walk with him along the river, show him the city lights, buy him a pastry, and let him sit in the café to enjoy the smell of butter, vanilla, and sugar.

I wanted to chase after them but knew that doing so would make matters worse. Seeing my daughters would ease me some, so I went over to the house to get my thoughts together. July greeted me at the back door with Birdie on her hip. The baby cooed when she saw me and reached for my chin. I crossed into the drawing room, where the other three girls were playing on the floor.

"Mama." Joan rushed into my arms, her fingers around my neck.

"Can you play with us?" Hester begged with two hands in front of her.

"What are you playing?"

"Auction," chimed Isabel.

I looked at them, confused.

"Let us show you how it is done." Hester led me to the chair. "Joan, you be the buyer. Isabel, get on the block."

Hester held up her hand to Joan. "This here is a fine girl. Who has one hundred dollars for her? Do I hear one hundred dollars?"

"One hundred," cheered Joan.

"Two hundred, anyone two hundred?"

"Two hundred."

"Three hundred. Three hundred. Someone three hundred."

"Three hundred. That is it," Joan called out.

"Sold for three hundred."

Isabel started fake crying. "But I do not want to leave. Mama." She held her arms out to me. "Mama, help me."

Joan started dragging Isabel away.

I sat stunned. "Stop it! Where did you learn this game?" My nostrils flared from one child to the other.

"We saw the niggers playing it in the courtyard while they were waiting to be sold," Hester offered. "Now it is my turn to be sold."

"You were sold last time! It is my turn." Joan pushed past Hester and stood on the footstool. "Mama, do you want to get sold?"

I bared my teeth. "That is enough. No more of this. I never want to see this game again! And we do not call them niggers, they are people. Am I clear?"

The girls looked confused at my outrage, and I pushed up to my feet. "When folks are sold, they never see their families again. What if it were Monroe?" I let slip.

"Something happen to Monty?" Hester's eyes widened.

"Nothing is promised. You hear me? This is people's lives you are play-ing. Now go wash up for lunch," I raised my voice.

July entered the room and ushered the girls off. I returned to my post.

◆

The Jailer had rented a woman named Janice to help me with the sewing for the fancy girls. When we had finished up for the day, I returned to the house to help July settle the children for the night. I had just rocked Birdie to sleep when Abbie called to me. When I found her, she was staring out the back door at the garden.

"Abbie, did you need me for something?"

Abbie looked up at the ceiling and scratched her dry right foot with her left toe. Her apron was filthy around her waist.

"Forgot what I wanted again."

"Did he send for me?"

"Yes. Marse said join him for dinner."

I moved her short hair back from her forehead. "You feeling all right?"

"Yes, Miss Pheby. Just fine." She smiled.

But Abbie was not fine. She had slipped away little by little since Basil ran off and the Jailer's whipping. With Monroe gone and Essex's impending arrival, I had little time to help her through her pain. I tipped a bit of perfume to my wrists while July fastened me into a plum-colored dress. When I walked into the dining room, he stood while I took a seat at his arm.

"How was your day?" *And where is my son?* I forced a sweet smile.

"If I say they are furniture, you say okay."

"Okay."

"You do not go behind my back embarrassing me with your mercy."

How did he know that I'd administered medicine and water to the ones left outside?

"I do not like it when you disobey me." He wiped his mouth.

My head tilted toward my lap in a way that I hoped looked submissive.

"There is no room for pity in this business. Do you understand me?"

"Yes, I understand. It will not happen again."

"I have been too lenient with you. That is my greatest mistake. You forgot I am your master."

"I did not."

"Say it." He slammed his fist on the table. "Say it, goddamn it!"

"You are my master."

"I have spoiled you." He threw back his drink, and I sat stiff as a board.

"Upstairs," he growled.

I stammered, "W-w-would you care for dessert? I could play you a song."

"Now!"

I pushed back my chair, dropped my napkin on the table, and moved toward the stairs. His heavy footsteps echoed behind me but could not compete with the pace of my racing heart. In his bedroom, he slammed the door behind him. Then forced me onto my knees and pushed up my dress. I could barely breathe as he wrapped his meaty hand around my throat and entered me.

"You are mine, Pheby Delores Brown. I am your master. Say it."

I choked for air and forced the words out.

He loosened his grasp but continued to drive into me. He had been crude before but never like this. I tried to disappear in my mind, but the searing pain of him ripping apart my insides kept me present. It did not matter that I lived in the big house, had his children, helped run his business: I was the same as those chained up in the courtyard awaiting sale. My status did not protect me from the grip he had on my hair, the bites he put on my neck, and the beating and hemorrhaging of my female parts. I bit my bottom lip and endured it all. When he finally passed out across his bed, I crawled to my room, closed the door behind me, and refused to cry.

◆

I had just finished soaking in the tub and massaging ointment into my bruises when I spotted Monroe walking through the courtyard from my bedroom window. His back was bent and his head hung low. It took everything in me not to shout out my window for him to come to me. My son, a pawn in a game he had no business playing. If only I could bury him in my floorboard along with the money I pinched off from my trips to the market, the diary, Mama's red dress, and Essex's necklace—all the things dear to my heart. But I could not. I needed a plan.

CHAPTER 28

The Boston Lion

*M*ost everything to do with the transportation of slaves happened in the dead of the night, while the more fortunate were
tucked away in their beds. Essex was due to arrive on July 16, and the Jailer
had spent every waking moment in preparation. Though I had seen hor-
rors, I had not seen his desire for punishment reach such a fever pitch as it
did now, and his heightened attention kept me in a constant frenzy. I could
only imagine how much worse it would be if he were to discover that Essex
was Monroe's father. Only now was I grateful that the Jailer disregarded
Monroe, because if he really looked him dead in the eyes he would see the
resemblance to Essex. If that were to happen, I was certain my beloved
would not make it out of here alive.

On the eve of Essex's entrance into Richmond, the Jailer refused to retire even though it had grown late. Instead, he waited in the parlor, drinking whiskey and eating peanuts. I hoped his heavy consumption would
not cause him to behave foolishly. To ease his tension, I offered to play for
him, but he was not in the mood for music and sent me up to bed. It was
just as well; I had a better view of the courtyard from my bedroom window
anyway. There I perched on my chair and waited. I tried to read by candlelight, but my mind was so distracted with thoughts of Essex that the words
blurred together. I wondered what he would be like. Would he remember
me? Had he searched for me? Had he taken up with another?

Even though I had anticipated his arrival, I was ill prepared when the
gates were thrown open and Essex shuffled in with his head down. My
arms broke out in goose pimples. Flanking him on either side were four
white men. Straightaway, I could see that the journey had taken a toll

on him. His white shirt had been completely soiled, the hair on his head wildly overgrown, and his beard matted with dirt.

The Jailer stumbled across the courtyard, belting out directions to the drivers, blocking my view of Essex with his large girth. I wanted to bang on the window and shout Essex's name, but then the driver holding his chain yanked him forward. Essex lifted his head, taking in his new surroundings.

"Look up, sweetheart. I am right here," I whispered in vain.

When the men moved him from the courtyard to the jail, I did not realize that I had been holding my breath until I sat down feeling faint. My need to see Essex consumed me, but sneaking out at that moment would prove dangerous. Besides, the guards were with him and I had not heard the Jailer return to the house.

I imagined what my first conversation with Essex would be like. The sound of his voice as we caught up on the last six years, and his reaction to having a son. I had not been privy to any updates from the Bell plantation and I wondered if he had news of Lovie or Aunt Hope. I was so wrapped up in my fantasy that I did not know that the Jailer had entered my room until he reached for my waist and lifted my dress.

◆

It had been decided that the flogging would take place on Saturday. Just two days away. In preparation for the big event, the Jailer had people on the half acre busier than a moth in a mitten, stacking chairs, setting up tables, lugging liquor, prepping food, blowing up balloons, organizing games for the kids and instruments for the bandstand. The night before the flogging, he had decided to entertain his colleagues, local politicians, and important plantation owners. The tavern had been rearranged to allow women to attend more comfortably, and lounge chairs had been set in the right corner for them. I did not realize how many meals I had skipped until July fastened me into my evening gown and it hung as if I were wearing one of Elsie's dresses. The Jailer did not seem to notice as we received his guests.

Silas and Corrina, David and Helen, and Hector and Anne arrived together. Sissy and the other girls worked the room with drinks and passed hors d'oeuvres. My assignment was split between being by the Jailer's side and playing the piano. It was a blessing when he nodded for me to play. The women's conversation eluded me as my head was focused only on seeing Essex.

When I took a break, Corrina came to me.

"You are extraordinary. You should be playing in concert halls."

I dabbed at my brow. "Maybe in another lifetime."

"How are the girls?"

"They are all fine. And your children?"

"Two are away at boarding school. The house seems empty without them, but I know it is for the best."

I shifted from one foot to the other.

"Must be difficult managing with all the attention and traffic."

I gave her a strained smile. As much as I adored Corrina, I knew that if I wanted to steal away to see Essex, time was of the essence. The Jailer sat in conversation with three men, and Sissy had just passed him a fresh drink. I had about twenty minutes before I would be missed.

"Speaking of which, I better run over to the house and check on them. My little Birdie has been nursing a cold."

Corrina leaned into me. "If you ever need help with anything, please consider me a friend."

We exchanged looks and I squeezed her hands before exiting through the side door. Two gentlemen smoked in front of the tavern but they had their backs to me. My thoughts of getting to Essex were so loud that I could not hear the dogs barking in the distance. As I turned the corner, I collided with someone in the dark. He put his hands around my arms to keep me from falling.

"Miss Pheby, you all right?"

It was Tommy.

"Yes."

"Marse sent me to fetch you. He wants to introduce you to a friend."

I dusted my sweaty palms against my dress and then followed Tommy back into the tavern, where I stayed for the remainder of the night.

◆

The summer heat had made sleeping with the windows closed unbearable. On the morning of the flogging, I woke in a pool of sweat. I could not conceive how Essex was faring at the top of the jail in such a small holding space. When I turned to rise, the Jailer entered my room fully groomed.

"Wear your finest dress and jewelry that reflects your status as mistress of the jail. The children should also look their best."

I bolted up. "Honey? Might we leave the children in the drawing room? I fear the blood might give them nightmares, especially Hester." I evoked the name of his pet in hopes of gaining favor. He looked at me and then sucked on his tooth.

"Very well. Have July stay with them."

I waited for him to shut the door behind him before I threw back my covers. It was one thing for him to see me in the night, but quite indecent for him to see me undressed during daylight hours. When I arrived at breakfast, he had a morning ale with his potatoes, bacon, and biscuit. My hands shook as I clung to my teacup.

"Today feels like my birthday."

I forced a smile but my insides turned over on my lap.

By nine o'clock, I did not see a cloud that would provide an ounce of shade. The spectators had been gathering since seven, and the courtyard was nearly filled. Ladies carried umbrellas to shield themselves from the sun, and their house girls held onto picnic baskets with snacks, beverages, and lunch. Most of the workers squatted on the cobblestones. Some had small sheets to sit on; others were forced to sit on the hot gravel. This performance of showing off his power by the Jailer was as much for them as it was to entertain their masters. It surprised me that so many owners had brought their children along with them, and I felt grateful that I was allowed to keep the girls away from the scene. It was bad enough that they lived on the half acre of the Lapier jail. God bless them if they had to also witness human flogging.

Once satisfied that my daughters were settled in with July, I found Abbie. Thankfully, she had her full mind today and could help me dress. She buttoned me into a light-blue-and-white printed gauze dress. My hair she pinned into elaborate rows at the nape of my neck, and then covered it with a matching bonnet. I felt sickened, prettying myself for such a barbaric display of power, but recognized my tasks. When I descended the stairs, the Jailer waited for me by the front door. The sight of his face lit like it was Christmas made bile rise in my throat.

"You look lovely, my lady." He took my arm.

We walked side by side to the courtyard. The crowd clapped and parted to make room for us. When we reached the stage, the Jailer reached for my hand and escorted me to the top of the platform. I folded my wrists in front of me, hoping that when Essex laid eyes on me he did not feel betrayal.

The Jailer looked out onto the audience and grinned. "Mighty men and women of the South, we will not stand idly by and let our niggers run away to the North. The Bible says that all slaves shall obey their masters."

Cheers roared from the crowd.

"I am here today to demonstrate what will happen to those who disobey the law and God's plan."

More cries of joy.

"Punishment to the highest extent for those who go against our institution. Let the flogging begin." He raised his hands and the crowd shouted.

"Justice! Punish him! Show no mercy!"

The door to the holding cell clicked open, and two white men dragged Essex in. His hands were in irons in front of him, feet chained together, and he only had on one shoe. My throat filled, and I lowered my head to hide my dismay. The Jailer stood stiffly on the stage as they dragged a limp Essex up the steps and onto the platform. When he reached the top, he glanced over at me. His eyes narrowed a bit; then they widened in recognition.

Sissy and Tommy approached the stage. Sissy carried a big, steaming pot. As I moved out of their way, I saw boiling pods of hot peppers. What was this man planning? I silently prayed for Essex's safety as I stepped past the crowd of slaves and over to the side where the white women stood with babies. Close enough that if the Jailer called to me I could come, but not front and center to Essex's misery. The mob continued to shout and taunt. When the two white men stood Essex on his feet, he raised himself to full height and looked the Jailer square in his eyes.

"You better look away, boy."

Essex did not budge.

"Very well, you want to be a show-off nigger. Let the punishment begin!" he called out.

The crowd clapped and whistled. Men stood shaking their fists in the air and the women shouted out until their faces were inked red with hatred. I felt alone in my repulsion at their glee at human suffering and searched the crowd for a kind eye, but there were none.

The Jailer pointed to the pole that stood in the center of the stage, and the two white men holding Essex pulled his arms above his head and fastened him by his thumbs to the pole. Essex grunted as he was raised so high the big toe of his shod foot barely scraped the ground. His shirt was then cut away from his body and his back on view to the crowd. He had a smooth and strong back that showed no signs of previous whippings. Even though I stood in the shade, the heat felt excruciating.

Tommy presented the Jailer with a tray of three weapons. He reached for his cowhide whip and snapped it between his fingers. Then he twirled it in the air and crashed it against Essex's back. *Thwap. Thwap. Thwap. Thwap. Thwap. Thwap. Thwap. Thwap. Thwap. Thwap. Thwap. Thwap.*

The Jailer paused, and then Tommy dipped a rag into the steaming pot of hot peppers. He then washed the rag across Essex's gashes. The scalding liquid bubbled in the wound. Essex cried out in such violent pain that I instinctively moved forward, but then just as quickly I was jerked back.

"Best not 'rupt Marse's work. Don't want no more trouble on your boy," whispered Elsie.

"Where is he?"

"I told him stay in the barn. Ain't want him seeing this."

I thanked her for protecting him. The whip sang through the air, and he was at it again. *Thwap. Thwap. Thwap.*

I counted twelve lashes. Tommy again washed the gashes with boiling water. The scene played out again. Twelve lashes. Scalding hot pepper water poured into his skin. Again. Again.

Again.

Essex sounded like an animal being slowly slaughtered; each time the guttural noises became fainter and fainter, as if he were drifting toward unconsciousness. His one toe had stopped reaching for the ground and his arms went limp.

Again. Twelve lashes. Hot pepper bath. Twelve lashes. Hot pepper bath. Twelve lashes. Again. Again. Again.

I turned my head, but that did not exempt me from counting each lash. It seemed that even the crowd had had enough. Children started crying. Women walked away with their babies, covering their ears. The men only grunted. Then the Jailer finally stopped. If my count proved accurate, Essex received ninety-six lashes, but the hot pepper bath probably made it feel like five hundred.

"Take him." The Jailer dropped his whip.

The two white men took Essex down, his body like a rag doll.

Blood ran in every direction.

"He needs to be nursed," I said to Elsie.

"Marse will send for us when he ready."

As soon as the men and Essex left the stage, Tommy washed the floor down, and then a local band stepped onto the platform. In a matter of minutes, they were playing festive music. The scene transformed from beastly to boisterous in the blink of an eye. House girls approached their families with picnic baskets. The entertainment girls walked around giving out licorice to the children and ale to the men. I stood back and watched as the Jailer received pats on the back from his colleagues for his fine performance, his hands and shirt still splattered in Essex's blood. While he remained occupied, I returned to the house, where I found the girls in the drawing room.

Hester was reading a book while Isabel and Joan worked on a puzzle. Birdie was nestled on a floor pillow fast asleep. I collapsed into the chair and removed my bonnet.

"Miss Pheby, you all right?" July rose and poured me a glass of water.

"I will be fine." I drank it down and willed myself to breathe.

"Why are so many people here?" Isabel jumped up and tugged on the hem of my dress.

"'Cause Papa had to flog a nigger who ran away." Hester looked up from her book.

"Hester!" My hand flew to my mouth in shock. "I told you about using that word."

She looked bashful. "Just repeating what Papa said."

"I do not want to hear that talk again or you will be punished."

"But, Mama—"

"That is enough." I held my hand up to silence her.

"Can I get you something to eat?" July touched my shoulder.

"No, thank you. I am going to freshen up a bit."

In my bedroom, I looked out on the courtyard at the people laughing and being merry. I resented them all. Before I could chew completely on my bitterness, I noticed that the red flag had been raised, which signaled that the auction for today was set to begin. I dabbed my cheeks with rouge and then hurried off to do my duty.

When I arrived in the shed, my helper, Janice, already had the girls dressed and lined up to make the procession over to the tavern for the sale. I felt so troubled over Essex being without medical care that I could not remember any of the girls' names. I only cared about getting over there to clean and dress his wounds before they became infected. Janice and I worked hard preparing and moving the girls, hour after hour, with little downtime. By the time I walked the last group across the courtyard, the party had died down, the band was packing up, and only a trace of blue remained in the sky. My back throbbed from the long day, but I felt determined to get to Essex.

At the tavern, the Jailer was surrounded by men. They were drinking and talking loud. Half-full dishes of food were laid out on the table. As I turned to leave, he called my name, then motioned for me to play. At the piano, I went through my repertoire of songs, starting from light and airy and moving to hard and robust. I tried to lose myself in the music as I often did when playing in the tavern, but I could not stop picturing Essex or his injuries. Finally, the Jailer stood and stumbled with his group of men to the door. I watched as they clapped him on the back and congratulated him again before leaving.

"Anything for the cause," he hiccupped. There was a red stain streaking his shirt, and his cravat had come undone.

"Pheby?"

I hated the way he made my name sound like a question, when it was most certainly a command. I moved away from the piano and followed him out the door. He put his arm around my shoulder to steady himself as we headed toward the house.

"Fine performance today, was it not?"

"You outdid yourself."

"Gave that nigger a whipping that he will never forget."

He pulled me tighter and kissed me on the neck. When we reached the parlor, he called to Abbie for a drink.

"Honey, you go up and I will bring your nightcap to you."

He leaned in and kissed me on the lips. "Such a smart girl. It is why I chose you to be mine."

I went to the bar and poured him a healthy shot of whiskey. My hands were shaking as I listened for his footsteps on the stairs. When I did not hear any sounds, I carried the drink to my room, removed a dab of sleeping powder from my medicine bag, and mixed it into his drink.

"Here you are."

He sat on the edge of his bed trying to remove his shoes.

"I will help you undress," I offered.

The Jailer drank the whiskey in one gulp. I took my time removing his shoes and then his socks. Once I had his pants around his ankles, he collapsed backward onto the bed and started to snore. I returned to my room and removed my jewelry, then dug in my closet for the necklace that Essex had given me before he escaped the plantation. I changed into a simple work dress and took what I needed from my medicine bag, sliding them into the hidden pockets of my skirt.

The stairs in the big house usually groaned under the weight of the person descending the steps, but years of going up and down to check on the children had taught me which spots to avoid if I wanted to move undetected. I poured a canteen of water and wrapped up some leftover ham and bread. Outside, I slid along the shadows of the courtyard. The square remained cluttered with rubbish. I looked over my shoulder every step of the way until I stood in a dark corner of the jail. Essex was being held in the garret room, a small space at the very top. When I climbed the stairs, the key hung on the hook outside of the room. I had to bend and crawl through a trapdoor to get inside. It was pitch-black until I lit the candle and closed the door behind me.

"Essex?"

CHAPTER 29

Reunited

*H*e did not answer. When my eyesight adjusted to the light I saw how tiny the room was: only about eight feet wide, and there was no bed or chair for comfort, just a rude bench fastened against the wall and a coarse blanket. Essex laid flat on the floor and did not move at the sound I made as I entered. His arms were shackled, his feet fettered, and the smell of infection setting in was nauseating.

"Essex." I knelt beside him, touching the top of his hair with my fingertips.

"That really you?" He looked into my eyes in a way that rearranged my soul. My skin sweltered under my clothing as I pulled him to my breasts. I had forgotten how good it felt to be seen by him.

"It is me."

He tried to roll from the plank floor, but his chains and wounds made it near impossible. I cupped his shoulders to help steady him. His skin sweated hot. The fever would claim him if I did not act fast. He grasped my hands in his and brought them to his lips. A tingling sensation passed through the center of my chest.

"Not much time."

I helped him to his feet and over to the bench. After the flogging, one of the drivers had covered him with a burlap shirt, which was now embedded in his wounds. I tipped a canteen of water laced with medicine from the brown jar to his lips. He drank with thirst, and I had to pull the jar back so that he did not drink it all. Once I could see that the medicine had made him numb, I started cutting away the material with my shears, trying hard not to tear at his skin. With every pull, Essex cringed, and I whispered how sorry I was for everything.

When I started contemplating my list of sorries, the trail led me all the way back to the Bell plantation. Sorry that I ever came up with the plan for him to run. Maybe we should have waited it out. If he had never run, then perhaps she would never have sold me, and I would be living in Massachusetts with my free papers. Essex could have stuck to his original plan of buying himself from Master Jacob, and I could have persuaded Missus to give the black baby to a woman in the fields without Master knowing anything. Now look at us. Essex had become the most wanted fugitive in Virginia, and I was bound to the Devil for the sake of my four daughters. I had made this mess. All my mistake.

"Ain't your fault," he babbled, as if he heard my thoughts.

I put my concentration on the work ahead. Never had I seen wounds as deeply lacerating, and I had to labor cut by cut to clean them. I rinsed his bruises with water and then let them air dry before smoothing on salve. Essex remained stoic throughout. Once I finished dressing the wounds, I pulled the food from another pocket and watched him eat.

"He treating you okay?"

My eyes looked away. The air between us became stifling but silent as he finished the last bit and then licked his fingers.

"If you are happy—"

"I have not depended on being happy since I left the plantation." My voice boomed. "This here is surviving." I thumped my fist into my chest.

"Did not mean—"

"And you have no idea what surviving has cost me. My bruises might not look like yours but they are there."

Determined not to let my emotions fall, I focused on the small window.

"There wasn't a girls' school in Massachusetts I didn't search, some of them more than once. Looked for you on every corner in Boston."

"Missus sold me. Then a few months later Master passed away."

"What about Ruth?"

I told him about Mama dying, and how Missus had traders snatch me on the day of the funeral.

"Would give anything to go back to that place and protect you Pheby."

His comment hung in the air. We both knew that there was no protection for us when white folks made up their minds on how to handle us.

"I have thought about you every single day since we have been apart, Pheby."

My fingers moved like I was knitting. It calmed all that roared inside of me.

"You have a son," I blurted.

When he turned to look at me, his chains rattled. "Am I hearin' you right?"

"His name is Monroe Henry Brown. Six years old and reminds me so much of you."

"Our son?"

I looked him in the eye and ran my fingers over his face.

"Only takes one time."

Essex reached for my hand through his shackles. "I need you to get a letter off to my friend. He will get the three of us up North. I promise you that."

"Rest and get back your strength. You will need it here." I pulled out the hymnal that the preacher had given me and tucked it between his fingers. "Keep this hidden. I will come again as soon as it is safe."

◆

The next evening, I mixed sleeping powder into the Jailer's drink again. When he fell asleep, I took the same route to see Essex. This time I smuggled in green beans, chicken, biscuits, water, salve, and more of Mama's pain medicine. As I crept through the courtyard, I reasoned that I would only dress his wounds and feed him. But when he begged me to stay, I could not resist. Every second with him felt like it could be our last.

With a handkerchief I produced from my pocket, I wiped his mouth.

"Thank you kindly. That was ten times better than the chicken feed they gave me in Naw'fok." He grimaced.

We sat side by side on the narrow bench. Every time he moved his chains clattered, and I could see fresh pain flash across his face as he searched for comfort. It angered me. No purpose in having him tied up like an animal in this small space. The Jailer was just being a dictatorial arse. But after all I had sacrificed, I did not even have the authority to unloose his shackles. To take our minds off his circumstances, I asked him to tell me about his journey.

"What you want to know?"

"Your story?"

He rubbed his swollen ankles together. They were tied so closely that his walk was more of a waddle.

"Well, running ain't for the weakhearted. Them woods get mighty terrifying at night when you out in the middle of nowhere by yourself. Worst was when I came upon a wolf."

"How do you know it was not a coyote?" I teased.

"I know a wolf when I sees one, and I was sure she had a notion to tear me to shreds. I climbed up in a tree and stayed there for three days waiting for her to pass. It wasn't until I saw four runaways below that I came down."

"They saved you?"

"Ain't need much saving but I sure needed food." He chuckled. Still had that hearty, deep-throated laugh and it reminded me of home.

"I still had the pass you wrote me. My plan was to get to a boat and beg passage up to Baltimore, so I stayed close to the water."

"What was the worst part?"

"Being hungry. Never enough food or fresh water. I went days without eating."

He had stuck to Aunt Hope's plan the best he could. By the time he made it to Baltimore, the fellow she had told him about had moved on. But just using his name had gotten him a job working the docks.

"That is how I saved money to get on to Philadelphia."

"I always wanted to go to Philadelphia."

"Ain't never seen that many freed men and women in one place in all my days. They sure could dress. But I only stayed a few months; always had in my mind that I needed to reach Massachusetts to find you. The farther north I got, easier to breathe. Air different up there."

As I listened to him, I could not help but wonder if he had taken up with another woman. He did not disclose, and I could not bear to ask.

"What caused your capture?"

"I reckon my love for horses."

Essex, slowly and, from the looks of it, painfully stretched his legs out in front of him and told me about his jobs in Boston. During the day he worked at a clothing store; in the evenings he tended to people's horses.

"Word spread that I was the horseman, so I became easy to find." He shook his head, and I could see that the memory sat fresh.

"The day I was taken to the ship became a day of mourning for the city."

Essex described the scene for me. Thousands of protesters, organized by black and white abolitionist groups, had lined the streets of Boston to watch him walk in shackles toward the waterfront, where the vessel waited to carry him back to Virginia. Every business along the route to the ship was draped in black sheets and the American flag hung upside down. A coffin sat in the middle of Main Street with the words HERE LIES LIBERTY.

"We sailed for eight days and I was treated fairly on the ship. Naw'fok was a different story. People shouted and spit at me, threw things at me all the way to the jail."

He looked over at me. "I would do it all again because I finally found you. You still so lovely."

I blushed and squeezed his hand. "Our son is in danger. We need to get him to freedom."

"Us to freedom." He leaned in and kissed me. I'd forgotten how good he tasted. Desire for him pulsated below my navel and rested like a weight against my thigh. I pulled away.

"Who do I need to write?"

Essex dictated what he wanted me to say, then had me repeat the address until he felt convinced I had it committed to memory.

"I have never stopped loving you, Pheby."

"Hush now." I put my finger to his mouth. Then my lips were on his and we kissed again. "You get some rest." I blew out the candle. As I locked the door behind me my whole face smiled. Essex could always lighten my mood, even in the worst situations. That is when I saw Sissy on the balcony watching me. Her room sat atop the tavern, directly across from the garret room. I made eye contact with her, lifted my skirts, and hurried along.

My breath quickened as I slipped back into the big house. When I reached the hallway upstairs, the Jailer's bedroom door sat ajar. I knew that I'd left it closed. I crept to my room as quietly as possible, but a creaking floorboard betrayed me.

"Pheby?"

"Yes?"

The mattress squeaked as he got up; then he was standing in the doorway in his sleeping gown. "Where did you go?"

"To check on the children?"

He looked me over, then demanded that I come to his bed. I had no time to write down the message or the address that Essex gave me. I needed to smother the Jailer's suspicions. When I laid down next to him, he tucked me in the crook of his arm and began to breathe heavily. In my head, I recited the address and the message until they sounded as familiar to me as my own name.

CHAPTER 30

The Letter

*M*ost days I pressed through my work unprompted: tended to the fancy girls, raised our daughters, tried to keep Monroe safe, and aided the half acre in running properly. There was little in my daily activity that spoke to me. After spending two nights with Essex, I felt something turn inside of me. It happened as fast as the sun slipping behind the clouds. My spirit had been asleep, and now I was awake and thirsting with purpose.

I imagined myself as the heroine from one of my novels. I would get that letter off to Essex's friend in the North so he could reclaim his freedom and take our son to safety. But I needed a plan. There was no way I could risk entering the post office and customhouse on Main Street unaccompanied. It would get back to the Jailer before I made it home. I would have to find someone to do it for me. Who could I trust? I moved through my morning routine considering my options.

"Miss Pheby." July stood in the doorway with her long hair in a single braid. She had grown so much in the six years that we had been together. With her pouty lips and bright eyes, she was more beautiful than most of the fancy girls I dressed.

"July, you have to tie up your hair."

"Forgive me, ma'am. It just takes so much time."

"Better that you are overheated than draw unwanted attention from the men at the tavern."

She shifted from one foot to the other.

"Beauty is a curse for a slave girl." I fidgeted with my hair. "It is what my mama always told me."

"But you are mistress of the jail."

"Not by choice," I let slip, then changed the subject. "It is almost time to celebrate your birthday."

"Oh, Miss Pheby." She beamed.

When I had first arrived at the jail, July had told me that she did not know her birthday. We decided on the first day of September because it was easy enough to remember. In a little over a month, the girls and I would celebrate her sixteenth year of life with her favorite lemon cake and present her with small tokens of our affection.

"I's here to remind you the dressmaker comin' to measure the girls for they fall wardrobe."

I tapped my forehead. With everything going on with Essex, I had plumb forgotten.

"Have they had their breakfast?"

"Yes, ma'am. They are in the drawing room playin'. She be here directly."

"Very well, I will be right down."

When July closed the door, I put my chair in front of it. Then I pulled up the floorboard for my ink bottle and ledger. I removed a page and jotted down all that I could remember that Essex had said, along with a few sentences more. I would have to steal into the Jailer's library and remove an envelope. I tucked the letter into my secret pocket and covered the floor with the rug.

Hilda, the dressmaker, arrived tugging her wooden trunk on wheels, with all of her supplies.

"Good day." She removed her gloves and bonnet and handed them to July. Her hair was mostly white, but her cheeks were cheery and she gave us all a big smile.

"Thank you so much for coming. I know this is a busy time for you."

"It's always my pleasure to visit with you and the little darlings." She smiled.

The girls took turns greeting Hilda with how do you dos, and little curtsies. Then they sat at the foot of her trunk waiting for her to open it. Hilda handed them each a book with the latest pictures in girls' fashion. Their eyes shone as they paged through catalogues. July sat between Hester and Isabel, and her demeanor brightened too. That was when I decided to have Hilda make her a dress as a birthday present. She could wear it to church and when we attended the state fair in October.

Abbie hobbled into the drawing room with tea and biscuits, which she set up on the buffet. Birdie squirmed around in my lap until she was satisfied, then stuck her finger in her mouth.

"I am first," said Isabel.

"No, me. I want everything in yellow," piped up Joan.

"Mama," Hester cried.

"I think we should go in age order, from youngest to oldest."

"No fair." Hester balled up her fist.

I took her arm and whispered in her ear, "Always save the most elaborate dress for last." I winked, and she returned my grin.

"Let's go, little Miss Joan, hop up on my footstool." Joan did as she was told, while Isabel watched and Hester opened her book.

With everyone occupied, it was a good opportunity for me to step aside. I beckoned to July, my most trusted confidante. "Hold Birdie. If he comes home, just whistle."

She nodded. After peeking out the window to make sure no one was approaching the house, I made my way down the hall to his library. I sat down and quickly recopied the letter on a piece of manila stationery. As soon as I felt certain the ink had dried and it would not smudge, I folded it and placed it inside the envelope. When I returned to the drawing room, Joan was holding out a beautiful peach fabric.

"Mother, what do you think?"

I touched her cheek. "It is beautiful, darling."

Birdie reached her arms out and I picked her up, hoping that she would calm my thundering heart.

Hilda hung her measuring tape around her neck. "All done."

"Wait, there is one more." I pointed to July. She looked at me, confused.

"For your sixteenth birthday, dear. Hilda will make you a lovely dress of your own."

"Really?" Her cheeks blushed with disbelief. "Thank you, Miss Pheby."

I watched as Hilda measured July. It was not with the same gentle care as she did the girls, but July did not seem to notice.

"Which fabric should I pick?"

"You should select what makes your heart spin in circles."

She ran her fingers over a mint-green pattern that I could already envision her wearing. When Hilda had finished with July, I sent July and the girls into the dining room to have their supper.

"Your girls were a delight as always." Hilda talked through the pins that she had in her mouth. "I do not usually have the opportunity to fit such young girls. You give me a wonderful challenge."

"I am certain the dresses will be gorgeous."

She closed her trunk. I looked over my shoulder to make sure that we were alone, then took a few steps closer to her.

"Hilda, I need a small favor."

A look of concern crossed her face.

"It is small. Just a letter that needs to be posted. Would you do it for me on your way back to the shop?"

"Does Mr. Lapier know about this?"

"Well, no. It is a surprise for him. An inquiry for his birthday."

She removed the pins.

"Of course, there is something in it for you." I produced a small purse from my pocket and handed it to her. When she did not deny me, I put the letter in her other hand. She dropped the envelope and purse into her larger bag. A sense of relief drifted down my spine.

"Please see that this stays between us."

She nodded.

"When will the dresses be ready?"

"In a few weeks. I will be in touch." She moved from the room with her large trunk trailing behind her. I hugged myself to celebrate my good fortune.

◆

Once I got the girls settled in their afternoon play, I left in search of Monroe. I found him in the stables sitting atop a pile of hay.

"Mama! Tommy teaching me how to change the horse's shoe."

"Is he catching on?" I kidded.

"He a natural, Miss Pheby." Tommy's body had caught up with the size of his head.

"I need to borrow Monroe for just a few minutes."

My son dusted off his knickers and fell in step next to me. Just a few weeks ago, he'd run and jumped when he saw me. Since the Jailer had taken him off the half acre, he had become cautious in my presence. More subdued.

"Where we going?"

"Where are we going?" I corrected gently.

He repeated my sentence.

"To help Sissy move a few things." I turned my face so he could not see my lie. We climbed the outside steps that led to the top floor of the tavern.

"It stink bad over here." He touched his nose.

"It is coming from the jail." I held my breath too.

"Is that where the prisoner is?" He pointed to the garret room.

"Yes."

"Marse whip him real bad? Hope I never get whipped like that. Tommy show me his scars."

"I will protect you always. Do not worry, son." I kissed the top of his head and immediately felt shame. Deep down, I knew that when it came to the Jailer's will, my promises were just dust.

We stopped in front of Sissy's door, and I hoped that she was not there. I knocked, then coughed. A shadow moved toward the window of the garret room. Essex had to be standing on tiptoe to peek out the high window, because all I could see was his forehead and eyes, and the bridge of his nose.

"Mama, you okay?"

"Yes."

Essex's chains clashed together as he moved closer and his eyes fastened on Monroe.

"Do you know him?"

"Why do you ask?"

"He is looking at you. Better not let Marse catch him." He grabbed my hand. "Sissy not home. We better go."

I glanced back at Essex and nodded my head. I walked Monroe back to the stables. Sissy came from the kitchen house and stopped me.

"Miss Pheby, may I has a word?" Her smooth brown skin shone with oil, and her dress looked of good fabric.

"I have work to do."

"Won't take but a few seconds."

I followed her to the spot behind the kitchen, between the two blackberry bushes.

"What is this about?" I cocked my head with impatience.

"I knows you sneakin' to see the prisoner at night."

I tore off a handful of berries and placed them in my mouth.

"I keep your secret from Marse, but you has to do somethin' for me." Sissy stepped closer. She smelled of licorice root. "When Daniel is old enough, wantin' you to teach my boy how to read."

"That is against the law."

"Well, I knows you teachin' Monroe."

In that moment, I could see what the Jailer saw in her. The boldness. Accommodating her would be foolish, but denying her request could be too. It had been impossible for me to forget the day he'd forced me to watch the horrible whipping of the woman who had taught others to read. Him beating her until she lost her baby. It was one thing to teach July in secret; she was under the roof with me. Monroe was my son and worth the risk. I had no choice but to take my chances.

"Thank you for your concern, but there is nothing to be told."

"Sure about that?" Her cat eyes caught the sun.

"Good day, Sissy." I lifted my skirts and left with my head held high. Such a simple country girl. I could not let her believe for one second that she could intimidate me.

When I reached the drawing room, the girls' tutor, Grace Marshall, was finishing up a lesson on addition. July was sitting guard with her knitting needles in her lap, absorbing the lesson as I had instructed her.

"The girls are doing very well. Hester has advanced to multiplication."

Grace showed me the problems that Hester had worked on her board. "Joan needs to practice words that sound the same but are spelled differently." She gave me a list. I thanked her.

While July packed up their school things, I moved the girls into the breakfast room so that Abbie could serve dinner. Once we were washed and seated, Abbie announced, "Marse said eat wit' out him."

"Is he coming home?"

She shrugged.

I had planned to sneak out to see Essex, but I could not leave the house until the Jailer passed out. After getting the girls to bed, I waited in the parlor for him, hoping that he would return and quickly have his way with me so I could give him the sleep aid. After an hour of reading, I paced the floor of the parlor. What could be keeping him? I had grown anxious to get over to Essex and tell him all that I had accomplished. When the clock struck ten, I knew that the Jailer would be cross if I was still awake, so I gave up my vigil.

"Abbie, I am going to retire," I called out.

Abbie must not have heard me, because she did not light the candles in the hallway or in my bedroom. I struck the fire and lit the candle next to my bed. When my eyes adjusted to the light, I felt an onset of dry heaves. I tried reaching for the pitcher of water, but then my dinner traveled up my throat and spouted from my mouth all over the floor. What a mess I had made. I wiped my lips with the back of my hand, and picked up the envelope that sat on my pillow. It was the letter I had written to Essex's friend. Hilda, the seamstress, had betrayed me. I choked and then retched again.

CHAPTER 31

My Charges

I must have fallen asleep because the sun was up when July's hands were gripping my shoulders.

"Missus, wake up," she cried.

I jerked forward so fast I experienced a rush of dizziness. My fingers wrapped around the arms of my chair to steady myself. July's eyes were red rimmed, and she had missed a button on her blouse.

"What is wrong?"

"Marse took the children from me. They in the carriage headin' way from the jail."

I jumped up. "All the girls?"

"Monty too."

I ran from the room barefoot. The quick movement caused my hair to come loose, but I did not stop to pin it. At the side door, Abbie was sweeping the dust away.

"Marse said for you to go to the supply shed. Left work for you there."

"Where did he take the children?"

"Sorry, Missus. Him gone."

I hurried across the courtyard, feeling every crack and crevice of the cobblestones strike my naked feet. The entrance gate was closing.

"Hester!" I shouted.

"Mama?" she called back, but I could not get past the two guards to follow the carriage out. One man grabbed me and restrained my arms behind my back, while the other blocked the gate with his breadth.

"Let me go."

"Mr. Lapier ordered you to stay put," said the one holding me, smelling faintly of tobacco.

I yanked away from him. "Do not put your filthy hands on me again."

The guard at the door looked at me through his blond bangs and snickered. I rolled my shoulders back and spit on the ground in front of him. As I turned to march away he grumbled, "Nigger bitch."

My face went hot as I stooped down, picked up a rock, and threw it at him, narrowly missing his head.

"You will be sorry. Both of you."

July was standing at the door when I returned and walked me to the breakfast room. "Miss Pheby, let me clean you up."

Abbie hobbled in. "Want some eggs and biscuits?"

"I want my children!" Before I could think it through, I had grabbed Abbie by the shoulders and was shaking her. My fingertips pressed into her flesh. She looked terrified but I could not stop myself, even when her eyes rolled back. I was angry at her for becoming this shell of herself. I wanted the old Abbie back.

"Miss Pheby." July wrapped her arms around my waist and pried me off Abbie. "Stop this. You know Abbie suffer from a broken heart and God knows what else."

I let go. Abbie gasped for air and dropped to the floor, her lame leg stretched out in front of her like a piece of wood.

"Come sit. Let me get you both some tea," July offered.

I backed down into the stuffed chair, aware of the ache in my feet. Small pebbles had cut into my skin, and I drew them out one by one. The Jailer had never taken the children anywhere without me. Who would care for them and tend to their needs? Then it dawned on me.

"Did Sissy go with him?"

"Yes, Miss Pheby." July sat a hot cup in front of me. "She won't let nothin' happen. Try not to worry much."

I pushed the cup away and stood up. Abbie was still crouching on the floor in the corner rocking and murmuring *Jesus*.

"Where are my shoes?"

"Miss Pheby, you are soiled. Let me dress you, please."

"Just a pair of shoes will do."

July sighed and then placed a pair at my feet.

Perhaps I should have changed and dressed for the day, but I was in no mood to play mistress of the jail. What did that title get me anyway? Had not protected me or my children from his evil reach. My babies were all I had, and I would rather die than to let something happen to them. Hilda, the seamstress, was a snake for betraying me.

And what of Monroe? I could not stop picturing my boy on an auction block with his sisters watching. Only then would they understand the full picture of this life we lived. I willed those thoughts away, knowing that if my brain kept traveling down that path, I would lose my mind as Abbie had.

When I entered the shed, my helper, Janice, sat on the metal stool rolling out burlap and humming to herself.

"Morning, Missus. Marse said for we to make shirts, pants, and plain dresses."

"Any girls today?"

"No, ma'am."

"Did he say anything else?"

Janice looked me up and down. "You okay?"

"Did he say where he was going?"

She shook her head and picked up the shears. I decided that Janice could handle the simple task of mending basic clothing without me. I needed to find someone with answers. As I walked out the door, I saw Clarence, the Jailer's right-hand man, unlocking the tavern. He wore a waistcoat and a shirt whose sleeves seemed too short for his long arms. When the Jailer left the premises, Clarence had the responsibility of running the property.

"Pheby."

"Clarence." I stared at him.

"Anything I can do for you?" He brushed crumbs from his red beard. He stood tall like a tree, and I was forced to look up.

"Did Mr. Lapier say when he would return?"

"No, he did not."

"Usually gives some indication of when to expect him back."

"Not this time." His eyes took in my hair curled over my shoulder. That was when I remembered that I had not pinned it back up.

Beauty is a curse for a slave girl.

"I will be inside if you need anything. Anything at all." His cheeks blushed crimson and his eyes lingered a beat too long.

I wrung my hands until they throbbed. I felt like I was being strangled by my own saliva. As I passed through the courtyard, the people to be sold for the day were standing at the water trough, bathing and grooming for auction. There were women with small, sparsely clothed children at their knees, an old woman who could barely stand without leaning heavily on her walking stick, a group of men with thick irons around their necks, wearing nothing but the look of malnourishment. Many of their lives would be changed for the worst today, and the sorrow of separation stretched beyond the Lapier jail in Richmond. Rumors had swirled for years that some free blacks from Philadelphia had even been kidnapped to be sold farther down South.

From the tobacco South to the cotton South, families would be torn apart and roots shredded. Mothers would hold their young for the last time and cry out for God's mercy as they were stripped away. For the first time in a long while, I felt united in experiencing their pain. Living in the big house and bearing the Jailer's daughters had given me a false sense of protection. Now that he had taken my family, I saw that we were all the same. Elsie had been right from the beginning. My children and I belonged to Rubin Lapier. We were his property. He could do with us as he pleased. Including our daughters, and especially my son.

I had wandered behind the stables—a habit I had of always checking for Monroe. Tommy did not hear me approach because he was chopping wood.

"Give me the axe."

He turned, startled. "Miss Pheby."

"I said give it to me."

He handed it over to me by the wooden handle. I walked over to the wood he had been chopping and thrashed the axe in the air. It flew down hard onto the wood. There was something satisfying about seeing the wood split down to the fleshy middle. Like I was killing it at the heart. I swung the axe again and again. Chopped until my shoulder blades burned, and my palms were raw with blisters. My hair held onto the wood chips and was matted in sweat on my neck and cheeks. When I could chop no more, I sat on a stump with my knees pulled up to my chest. The midday sun was hot on my skin, but that did not give me the power to move. I had no place to go.

"Missus?"

Elsie tramped with a heavy foot. I could hear her long before she stood in front of me. Her green scarf was knotted at the front, where a patch of gray sprouted from her widow's peak. She cupped a bowl covered with a cloth napkin and stopped in front of me, blocking the sun.

"Marse love him chil'ren."

"You warned that he was the devil. I should have listened better."

"No sense rakin' ol' bones. I could have been kinder."

I regarded Elsie. It was the first time that I noticed the stoop in her back and the wrinkles set on her face.

She extended the bowl to me. "Brought you some mutton stew."

I bit my lip. Aunt Hope used to make mutton stew.

"Try a little. Good for your nerves."

I took the bowl and spooned up a small bite. Then another. The stew started coating my belly. It tasted delicious, and took restraint for me not to lick the inside of the dish.

"July done made you a bath. Go on 'fore the water get cold."

"Did Sissy say anything to you about where they were going?"

"'Fraid not. But Marse sweet on those girls, and Monty know how to be a good boy. Go on now," she urged me.

I stood and did as I was told.

CHAPTER 32

———— • ————

Back Talk

*W*hen I entered my bedroom, the window was open to the breeze and the floor had been scrubbed of my waste, the awful odor replaced by the scent of the lavender flowers in the vase beside my bed. July must have heard my footsteps, because she knocked on the door the second I closed it behind me.

"Miss Pheby, ready for a bath?"

"No."

I could see through her eyes my disheveled appearance. "It is hot and ready."

"Tell Abbie I said for her to get in."

She tilted her head. "Your bath, ma'am?"

I nodded.

"What if Marse returns?"

"Keep watch. Hurry on before the water becomes tepid."

July closed the door behind her. The stew had given me a sounder head. From the window, I stared out at the courtyard. I could not see the garret room from my view, but I thought about Essex. His back needed a fresh layer of salve. Clarence would be watching the jail, but at this point what else did I have to lose? I decided to wait until the cover of night before making my move to see him.

To pass the time, I pulled up the floorboard and removed my diary. The pages swelled with my note keeping. So many names collected, so many lives affected. Many stories I remembered without reading. There was Susan, who had come with a broken toe. Her master had smashed it with a hammer when she had refused his affection. I boiled comfrey leaves, mixed them with vegetable oil to make a poultice for her, then wrapped it in a clean cloth. I found a big pair of shoes for her to walk in to give her foot room to heal.

Little Hally arrived too young to receive a man, but her beauty astounded. She fetched the price of a full woman. I remembered hugging sweet Hally to my breast before letting her go, and did not sleep for many nights fretting over her fate. Chubby-cheeked Ginny giggled after every word she said. She was childlike in a curvy body. My little Joan took to Ginny right away, and Ginny turned out to be one of the few people who could hold Joan without her making a fuss. Nancy had a twin brother named Cudjoe who was locked up with the men in the jail. Nancy could not bear being separated from him and was the only girl who ever tried to run. She did not make it as far as the middle of the courtyard before she was clubbed over the head and dragged back to me. I iced her bruises down and let her sip from the brown jar. She recovered in the kitchen house for four days before being sold to the highest bidder. Cudjoe went to someone else.

When I flipped to the front of the diary I could hear Mama's voice whispering in my ear. Her recipes read like a love letter to me. I uttered her prescriptions for lockjaw, dropsy, and cow sickness until I felt her presence in the room. My eyes closed to the wisdom she conveyed. I could not decipher the words exactly, but I sensed them taking root, meant for later. I inhaled the faint scent of hemp from her hair and peace descended over me.

When my eyes fluttered back open, the half acre was asleep. I shook the cobwebs from my bones and then stood at my bedroom door listening. There was no movement. I slipped out the house, hiding in the silhouettes of darkness until I made it to the jail. When I unlocked the garret room my hand flew to my nose. The smell of waste assaulted my stomach, and I swallowed down the need to throw up.

I hacked. "Hello?"

I did not want to close the door behind me, but I knew it was best to secure our secret meeting.

"Essex?" I lit the candle.

"Pheby." Essex moved along the back wall.

Once my eyes adjusted, I noticed a pail of dingy water in the right corner. It was meant for him to drink and bathe in, but there was no pot. He
used the left corner for his waste, and the funk reminded me of when I'd
been in the jail with sticky defecation up to my ankles. My throat clenched
and I willed myself not to be sick.

Essex's clothing hung from his frame and his hair was matted on one
side. I wished I had the key to free him from the shackles at his hands and
feet. He stopped halfway to me.

"I's sorry you have to endure this. I am a proud man."

"It is not your fault. I will bring things to get you cleaned." I sat on the
bench.

"You look like you had a hard day."

"The Jailer intercepted the letter that I tried to post for you. He has
taken my children away, including Monroe. I do not know where they are."
My voice cracked.

"Monster." Essex waddled to where I sat, bringing his stench, but I kept
my face pleasant.

"Thank you for letting me see my son."

"He is so much like you."

"My life changed in that moment. Pheby, you must get off another
letter. It is our only opportunity at freedom."

My temple pulsed. "Did you hear me? The man took my children. There
is no telling what he is capable of doing."

"While he is not around, you have a good chance."

"He has eyes everywhere. You do not know him."

"You sleep in the big house with him. I am sure you can get around it."

I whipped my head and slapped him across the face.

"What was that for?"

"You come back here with your big city ideas. Because of you, my children have been compromised."

"I did not mean to upset you. I am sorry."

But his words fell on deaf ears. My forehead blazed hot and my hands
made fists at my side. "Being with you is what got me in this mess. I should
have minded my business where you were concerned."

"Do not say that. Everything I have endured was to bring me to you."

"You are dangerous, Essex Henry."

I removed the bread and water flask from my pocket and thrust them onto the bench.

"If anything happens to my children I will never forgive you."

"Pheby, wait." He shuffled toward me, but I moved faster. When I locked the door, I heard a quick movement below me.

I paused, and then out of the shadows jumped a black cat.

CHAPTER 33

---•---

The Vigil

For the next few mornings, July appealed to me to change out of my soiled dress but I refused. The dress marked my vigil, and I would wear it until my children returned unharmed. Three excruciating days had passed, with me worrying until my mind played hoaxes on me. From the shed, I thought I heard Joan's sweet voice calling, *Mama!* I leaped up twice, only to realize that it was the wind. Elsie forced more stew on me, and Janice kept setting water within arm's reach. But I did not require their watching. I wanted Monroe, Hester, Isabel, Joan, and Birdie to come home.

To escape the depression, I sewed and mended every pair of socks; knitted hats and scarves; repaired sheets, curtains, towels, and tablecloths, and did not stop until my hands stiffened. When Janice noticed my discomfort, she took my palms and massaged them with lard until my muscles relaxed. Janice had soothing eyes. Not bothered by my poor hygiene, she stayed by my side until I went up to the house each night. Her silent companionship reminded me of when I used to work side by side with Mama in the loom house. Words were never necessary, and for that I was grateful.

Around suppertime, Elsie came to the shed holding a bowl. The bite between us had lost its teeth. She had cared for my son in ways that I could not with him living in the kitchen house. Nursed his fevers in the middle of the night, gave him extra helpings of food, support, and love. I accepted that Monroe was her boy too.

"Missus, I don't think the prisoner bein' fed 'nough. Permission to take him somethin'?"

I had let my grudge against Essex get the best of me.

Suddenly, I felt ashamed that it had gone on for this long. The poor man was suffering, and now at my hands.

"Yes, please."

She hurried off with the food. When she returned, she had her hand over her mouth.

"What is it?"

"Poor man smell worse than hog slop. Terrible how he bein' treated. Shame 'fore God I tell you." She clucked her tongue and walked heavily toward the kitchen house.

Had I forgotten about Essex? I made up my mind that I would shake my grief and anger and go to him. Before leaving the shed for the night, I wrapped up a burlap shirt and some pieces of fabric I had cut out to make trousers. July had been working in the kitchen helping Elsie since the children had been taken away, and Abbie served me dinner alone. When I'd had my fill, I told her to leave the leftovers for me to clean up and take an early rest.

"You sure, Missus? Don't mind hangin' 'round."

"No, get some sleep. You have been working hard."

Her fingers clawed at her scalp.

"Abbie, I apologize for grabbing you the other day. My mind has not been right. Please forgive me."

"'T's okay, Missus. You got your own troubles."

"Go now." I pushed her.

Once she hobbled down the hall to her room, I wrapped up the remaining carrots and sweetbreads in a cloth and stuffed it along with the water canteen in my hidden pocket. In a clean rag, I placed lye soap, shears, a needle, thread, and a candle. I tied the bundle like a satchel around my waist and then covered the bulk under my skirt. By the back door, I had left a pail of clean water with a small jar of the Jailer's whiskey inside of it. I grabbed it and then made my way through the shadows of the buildings.

The bucket was heavy and I dampened my brow before unlocking the door to the garret room. The stench hit me all at once.

When I lit the candle, Essex was lying on the floor, clinging to the hymnal that I'd given him on my first visit. Essex had not been taught to read on the plantation, but I imagined the hymnal offered him comfort nonetheless.

"Sorry for your trouble," he called.

I rested the bucket at my feet, turned my back, then reached under my skirt to remove the bundle.

"Let me help you up." I reached for his elbow until he was steady on his feet; then I took the scissors and started cutting him out of his clothing. The shackles prevented me from removing them any other way.

"Don't have to do this."

"Be still." I breathed through my mouth.

Flies hummed in my ears, and I had to stop cutting to swat the mosquitoes nipping at my wrists. I could only hope that his smell had not attracted any larger vermin. When I peeled back the soiled shirt, I was relieved to discover that the material had not set into his wounds. Scabs had formed. There was no sign of new infection. I traced his scars, then turned to examine his chest. His shoulders were a solid mass of muscle, his stomach drum tight, a firm slab of elastic. The shears trembled in my hands as I cut off his trousers. My resolve weakened, and I peeped down.

Waste was clumped in the seam, and I gagged as I removed the breeches from around his thick legs. Essex hunched his shoulders until we were nearly at eye level. Besides his shackled hands covering his manhood, he stood there naked. The soiled items I balled together and carried outside the door.

"Why are you doing this?" he whispered.

"Sorry it has taken me so long."

"I made you upset."

"No excuse." I dipped the rag in the water and then lathered it with lye soap. When I took the cloth across his shoulders, he winced.

"I know it is cold. I could not risk heating it."

I washed his neck and chest, then moved with care across his tender back. Essex relaxed into my touch. Every place I wiped sent an unexpected yearning through me. Never had I seen a man completely naked. The Jailer never even removed his shirt. I gave Essex the rag and motioned for him to wash his male parts.

I could feel the rhythm of his breath pulse inside my chest when he shook his head no and handed it back to me. I lowered the rag over his thickness, and as I massaged him clean, he released a deep-throated sigh that tugged at my inhibitions. He had grown under my touch, and I tried to deny the swell of my breasts straining against my blouse. I soaped down his thighs, then poured clean water from the canteen to rinse his feet. The fetters around his ankles had cut off his circulation, causing them to be heavy and swollen.

"They must hurt."

"I have missed you, Pheby." He stepped closer to me, and then his lips were on mine. My body sank against his bare skin, and we kissed and licked with impatience. I could feel the contours of his muscles pressing through my skirt. The time we lost had not reshaped my longing for him. The same passion I had felt for him in the stables took over my good sense. I bunched my skirt around my waist and pressed my fingertips into the wall. Essex lowered his shackled hands over my neck, down to my waist, and thrust me forward. We fit like two missing pieces of a jigsaw puzzle. His chains rattled, mimicking the sound of our rhythm.

"I love you, Pheby. You still mine." He hummed a slow ballad in my ear. Our hips thrust in unison until we could no longer hold the tempo. I rested my head against his mouth and bit my lip to keep our secret between us.

CHAPTER 34

Little Time

*W*hen I could think clearly, I helped his arms over my head and untangled us. The washcloth hung on the edge of the pail, and when I reached for it Essex stopped me.

"I want your smell. It will keep me alive in here."

I blushed, smoothing my hands over my skirts. Essex had always said the most endearing things. New life surged through me as I draped him in burlap. I stitched roughly, sewing loose so he could pull his trousers down and up with ease to relieve himself. Once he dressed, we moved to the rude bench. I extended the cold food.

"I have managed a spoon." He pointed to the one on the floor and I rinsed it with the canteen water.

"How?"

"Friends in the prison below. I tell them my story. They slip me things through that little hole in the floor. Tobacco, small treats, news." His eyes got big. "Heard Missus Delphina lost Master Jacob's fortune."

"What?" I turned.

"Married a man who gambled away the farm, then left her for another."

"Any children?"

"Not that I know of. Living out her life on her parents' farm. Say she a little touched in the head too."

"She reaped what she sowed." I smirked, remembering my curse, and a peace that I had not felt in a long time washed over me.

"Cheers." I handed Essex the jar of whiskey. He sipped with thirst, then handed it to me.

"No, thank you."

"Never drank before?"

"Only wine."

"Dulls the senses." He motioned to me.

I gulped until my tongue puckered and my throat burned.

"That was terrible."

"Just wait for the warmth." He took it back from me.

I rubbed my chest.

"Any word on the children?"

"Nothing."

"You must get the letter out."

"It is too perilous."

"I have promised to get us to freedom and I will. It is the only way."

He passed the jar back, and I braved another gulp from it. "I do not know who I can trust, who else to ask."

"Pheby, remember when we were on the plantation? It was you who hatched the plan for me to run. Brought in Aunt Hope. You can do this. Otherwise, I will die here. I am sure of it."

"Do not say such things."

"You said it yourself, I am trouble."

I kissed his lips and then stood to go. Time had gotten away from me.

"Can you stay? Just a while longer?" he pleaded. "It is so lonely in here."

My head told me to resist, but my mouth said, "Few minutes more."

I settled in next to him. We talked and giggled as the whiskey slipped between us and we traveled back through time. We visited the happier moments we had shared on the plantation. At some point the bottle and Essex's voice must have lulled me to sleep, because the next thing I heard was the sound of the gates being thrown open and the thud of horses trampling in. I bolted up.

The carriage had returned.

"I have to go."

Essex squeezed my hand, but I had no time to return his affection. The carriage was back. My children. I threw open the door and locked it behind me. Clarence came out of the tavern as my foot hit the last step. Disgust for me crumpled his lips. I realized that I had not considered my appearance.

My hands went to my hair and I pinned back what I could while hurrying toward the courtyard.

"Mother," Hester shouted, and leapt from the carriage. She wore a new dress and bonnet made of a rich cranberry color. She had grown in the time we'd been apart.

I took off at a run.

"Darling." My arms were around her.

"Mother, why are you not dressed? You look like the help." Before I could respond, Isabel and Joan were upon me, throwing their arms and limbs around, jumping into my arms. I nearly toppled over from the weight of them, but Clarence lent a hand to steady my shoulder.

"We have missed you." The girls tugged on me.

"And I have missed you."

Sissy exited the carriage with her son, Daniel, in her arms asleep.

"Missus." She too wore a new dress, I took note, before she hurried off.

"I am glad you have returned," I addressed the Jailer.

Birdie squirmed in his arms. I approached the carriage. There was no sign of Monroe. I made my lips pleasant, despite the color I knew had darkened my cheeks.

Where was my son?

"Pheby."

Birdie's cry escalated, but instead of passing her over, he held her tighter. His cheeks looked even fuller than before.

They must have eaten well on their journey.

"Would you like me to take the baby?"

Birdie's voice shrilled in my ears.

"Please." I reached for her.

Clarence leaned over and whispered something I could not hear. Then the Jailer stood, gave her to me, and followed him into the tavern.

I clung to Birdie, patting her back until she settled.

Tommy took the reins and led the horses to the stables.

Where was my son?

Birdie and I found the girls in the drawing room. Isabel and Joan were fighting for space in July's lap, and Hester rested her head on July's shoulders.

"We missed you so," said Hester. "We must never be apart from you again, July."

"I will always be here for you, sweet girls." July squeezed all three.

I sat down and Birdie wiggled off my lap and over to July.

"Tell me about your trip."

"Papa took us to the hot air balloon show. It was magnificent," said Hester, who ran down their entire three days' events.

"Did Monty go?"

Joan smacked her lips. "No, we dropped him off at a house on a big land."

"A plantation," Isabel explained. "Papa called it a plantation."

"He is staying to work."

"I begged Papa to let Monty come but he said no." Hester cast her eyes down, like she thought I would be disappointed in her effort.

"Well, I am glad you girls are back. How about we have some pie to celebrate?"

"Before supper?"

"Yes, before supper and then after supper." I made my voice light.

They cheered, and I willed their enthusiasm to quiet the thump in my head.

CHAPTER 35

Beautiful

At first light, Abbie knocked on my door. "Morning, Missus. Marse requestin' you take breakfast wit' him."

"Will you help me dress?"

"'Course."

It was rare that we had breakfast together, and I did not take it as a good sign. Abbie pulled tight on my corset, and I had to remind myself to inhale. I slipped into a pair of wooden shoes and followed her down the hall and into the dining room. He sat in a white shirt with blue suspenders. His hair had been brushed away from his face and he looked recently shaved.

"You look nice," I offered, taking my seat at his elbow.

"You have been busy since I have been gone?"

I placed my napkin on my lap and did not respond. Abbie poured hot water into my teacup.

"Abbie?"

She hobbled toward him with the teapot. "Tea, Marse? More potatoes?"

"Fetch July for me."

Abbie hobbled out. I sipped the tea, my stomach raw with fear. July glided in with her hair in a long braid. Her blouse clung tight. I made a note to swap in new clothing for her.

"July, prepare a bath for yourself. When you are clean, meet Pheby in the supply shed, where she will dress you."

"For what?" I blurted.

"I have a buyer who insists on taking her today." His lips curled.

I fought for air. "What about the children?"

"They will adjust."

July looked from him to me, her face frantic. "Marse, why you sendin' me away? I been good to your family."

"I am not. It is your mistress."

July's eyes welled up. I had been her protector since I arrived and now I had failed her.

"Can we talk in private?"

"There is nothing to discuss. That will be all, July." She ran from the room.

"Please, stop this. I will do anything."

"What is it about these niggers that make you disobey me? I told you to stop with your mercy. Now you are aiding my prisoner!" His fist slammed against the table, causing the dishes to rattle in place. "You are an embarrassment."

"July is our family," I pleaded.

"There is no such thing as family, only business." He dropped his napkin in his bowl and walked for the door. "Have her ready in an hour."

I threw my teacup on the floor and stomped it with my foot until it shattered into tiny pieces. I picked up my chair and slammed it back down in place.

Abbie met me at the back door. "You gotta do somethin'."

I staggered down the steps and dragged myself to the supply shed. My love for Essex had cost me my sweet July, who was family in all but blood. He did not need to use her to make his point; he'd already taken my son away. Now I had lost them both. I clawed at my forearms until they stung with pain.

Time ticked—I had to pull myself together. I wanted July to have the dress that Hilda had made for her birthday even though it was still a few weeks away, but before she put it on I needed to sew in protection. Through my tears, I attached two secret pockets. One I filled with coins and the other a pouch of herbs, like Mama had made for me when I moved up to the big house.

July entered the shed with red-rimmed eyes, her hair damp.

"I am so sorry." I wrapped her in my embrace.

"I's scared."

"I know. You are the closest thing I have to a younger sister. If I could change your fate I would."

"You can change Marse mind. He listens to you."

I wished I could hide her. This was my cross to bear and she needed to see my strength. "Not this time."

I dried her tears with the back of my hand, showed her the inside of the dress, and told her about my gifts. Now it was my turn to lace her into a corset. I pushed it below her ribs, laced it through, and fastened the strings when tight. July had a real hoopskirt, not the grapevine I'd come to the jail in. I added rouge to her cheeks and made her lips appear bloodstained. Her thick hair I piled onto her head and then dabbed her neck and wrists with perfume. Maybe being pretty would make her luckier than most.

"Don't make me go," she cried again.

If I had to throw her to the wolves, then she needed to come out of the battle standing. I grabbed her hands tightly in mine.

"You are only a slave in name. Never in your mind. Remember all that I have taught you. Try to be useful in the big house and keep your education hidden."

She nodded.

"Lord protect her." I spit over her shoulders like I had seen Mama do, then pulled her along.

Elsie, Sissy, and Janice stood behind the shed to see her off. I hoped that the girl's teacher, Grace Marshall, was keeping them occupied and that none would run from the house. That would only make this moment more difficult. Tommy darted from the stables and threw his arms around July.

"Shame 'fore God." Elsie slapped her hands together. "Raised her up from a girl. Shame 'fore God."

My knees wobbled as I led July away from the crowd and opened the door to the tavern. The Jailer waited at his usual table, where he was sitting with a tall, skinny man. Between them sat July's papers.

When I stepped back outside I bent over and howled.

CHAPTER 36

Falling

Grief rose like a wall around me. Everything that had happened was my fault. July being sold. Monroe not returning home. Essex withering away in the prison cell. The guilt of failing them all suffocated me until my bones felt heavy and exhausted. I took to my bed early without dinner, but the next morning I still overslept. Abbie had to rouse and remind me that July was gone. "I tried gettin' them dressed, but they wantin' July."

When I opened the door to the nursery, they ran to me.

"Mother, Abbie said July was gone. When shall she return?" Hester wrangled with her hair.

"She promised to play dolls with me today," Isabel pouted.

I stumbled, then collapsed into the rocking chair. "Girls, July went away."

"For how long?"

"When will she return, Mama?" Joan clutched my hands.

"She is not coming back. She has been called to do another job."

Isabel wailed. "She is my best friend."

I moved to comfort her, but she screamed, "I do not want you. I want July!"

I pulled my robe tighter against my chest.

"Me too, I want July!" hollered Joan. "Who will rub my back?"

"Me."

"No! You will not do it right."

With me working in the shed and playing in the tavern, the girls relied on July for their every need. They were more accustomed to her than they were me. Isabel threw herself on the floor and started kicking her feet. I pulled her up in my arms and rocked her.

"Girls, it will be okay."

"Feels like I have swallowed a rock," said Joan. "My belly hurts."

I brought her into my lap too. Hester rested her head on my knee.

"We will get through this, I promise."

When the older three finally settled down, I held Birdie and read them each the book of their choice. Then we colored pictures.

"For July, when she comes home," said Joan, her eyes big and hopeful. I patted her head as Abbie shuffled in.

"Marse wantin' to see you in the parlor."

It was early for him to be home for supper. Even earlier for him to fancy a drink. I handed Birdie to Abbie and then made my way to the parlor. I wore my simple work dress, with even less attention given to my hair.

The Jailer's mouth creased. "We are going for a carriage ride. You look as if you could use some fresh air."

"But the girls? With July gone, who will care for them?"

"Sissy will arrive shortly. Dress in something presentable. We leave directly."

I pressed my tongue against the roof of my mouth, even though I wanted to scream. I returned in a summer calico dress with a lace-front bonnet and gloves to match. The August high-noon sun made my head sweat, but the wide brim concealed my displeasure at leaving the girls behind. The Jailer's new driver, Hamp, extended his hand to me so that I could rise into the carriage. Hamp was a big man, copper-colored, with thick lips and an arrow-shaped scar in the middle of his forehead.

"Ready, Marse?"

The Jailer nodded his head. Hamp stepped into the coach box and commanded the horses by clicking his tongue.

◆

Once we rode past the city limits the landscape changed. The cluster of houses and buildings were replaced by vast green fields and rolling hills. The air smelled fresh and crisp. I had grown so accustomed to the odorous jail. The dewy air started to reset my brain. For a few moments, even my sadness took a reprieve. I had brought a ball of yarn with me and knitted mindlessly. I willed myself to just be.

We traveled for half the day before Hamp turned the carriage onto a long dirt road. My hand flew to the carriage handle as we hit a bump. The horses began kicking up dust, and as I lowered back the curtains a large house came into focus.

"Do you love him?" It was the first words that the Jailer spoke to me on the drive.

"I realize you came from the same plantation. Make sense that you would want to help him. Do you love him?" He eyed me.

I parted my lips, with the intention of looking sincere. "No."

He turned back to his papers, stuffing them into his briefcase. Hamp stopped the carriage. The house was a brick Georgian-style mansion with Palladian-inspired side wings, and white shutters. It loomed larger than our house at the Lapier jail, but appeared about half the size of the one in which I had grown up. I did not know where we were or why, but I hoped with every fiber in my body that Monroe was near. A short, wide man with silver hair and a hearty smile greeted us at the door of the home. Two black-and-white dogs wagged their tails at his feet. A young brown girl stood waving a fan to keep him cool.

"Welcome, Rubin. Wonderful to see you, old pal."

"This is Pheby Delores Brown, mistress of the Lapier jail."

"I am Henry O'Keefe." He kissed my hand and led the way through the front door into the foyer. The ceilings were high and the space cool.

Henry called out, "Polly."

A thickset woman descended the sweeping stairs, sliding her hand along the wrought-iron banister. She wore her blonde hair in a bun, and her cheeks were sprinkled with girlish freckles. Her attire was plain, a simple skirt with a small hoop, a blouse, and no jewelry. My dress had wrinkled from being in the carriage for so long, yet hers still paled in comparison to mine.

Rubin kissed Polly's hand. "Lovely to see you again."

"Likewise," she said to him, but she had not taken her eyes off me.

"This is Pheby," her husband introduced.

"Nice to make your acquaintance."

"Dear, take Pheby into the sitting room for tea. Rubin and I will be back in time for dinner."

Polly's hand went to her throat, and she swallowed for several seconds before leading the way. The sitting room was a square space off the entrance to the house. The curtains were drawn over the large windows, and I could see the Jailer and Henry stroll toward a small outhouse that I assumed to be Henry's office. A molasses-colored woman stood clutching a platter with a teapot, cups, and saucers. Once we were seated on opposite settees, she placed the tray in front of us and poured.

"Where are you from?" Polly's saucer shook in her hand.

"Charles City."

"How did you come to be with Rubin?" Her gaze met mine over the rim of her teacup. The nervousness in her eyes betrayed her intention. She wanted to know whether I was a nigra or white. Whether he owned me or if I was his wife. I sipped my tea, then took my knitting from my bag and resumed my stitching.

When my shoulders relaxed back in place I responded, "You have a beautiful home."

She pursed her lips and nodded her thanks. It would have pleased me to chat like friends, but Polly abandoned her attempt at conversation when I refused her question. We sat in silence. I knitted while she stared out the window. Finally, the dinner bell rang.

"Betty," she called to the woman who had served tea. "Show Pheby where she can wash up."

"This way."

Betty led me to a small room adjacent to the kitchen prep area, and my stomach growled at the smell of savory meat. We had missed lunch, and I'd only picked at my breakfast. As I rinsed my hands up to my elbows, I heard Polly's voice through the thin wall.

"I do not want any nigras sleeping under my roof 'less they work for me."

"Quiet your complaints."

"And for them to sleep together. A white man and his nigra? I will not have that sin in my house, Henry."

"Stand down, Polly. Rubin is our guest and you will do as I say. Now, pull yourself together and be a good hostess."

◆

Dinner tasted delicious, and after we'd had orange pudding for dessert I feigned exhaustion and retired to the guest quarters. It was an adequate room with a bed and dressing table. As I changed into my sleeping gown provided by our hosts, I could hear the Jailer's boisterous laugh drift from the back porch. No doubt the whiskey flowed, and he pulled heavily from his pipe. Where was my son? I strained to pick up the men's conversation, but I could not make out the words over the constant calls of the cicadas. The moment I found rest, the Jailer opened the bedroom door. He undressed gauchely and slipped in next to me. When he reached for my gown, I hoped it would be over quickly.

◆

The next morning, Henry O'Keefe offered to give us a tour of his plantation.

"Nice to stretch your legs before the long ride back."

I followed the men. On our walk, I noticed Polly disappear into the kitchen house. If she was like Missus Delphina, she would be going over the menu for the day. Henry pointed out his various outhouses, and I faked interest. Then he showed us to his stables.

"This here is Gold Charm." Henry pointed to a horse with a dark, velvety coat. Henry's chest poked out with pride over his prized steed. When I moved in closer, down on the ground kneeling before the horse was Monroe. I bit my tongue to keep from calling out at the sight of my son.

"Your boy has been the biggest help. Sure you don't want to sell him to me? For such a young fella, he is mighty gifted with my horses."

Monroe looked up, but he did not dare run to me or even acknowledge our connection. He wore the breeches I'd sewed for him, but had on a rough burlap shirt that I did not recognize.

The Jailer looped his arm through mine. "I am not going to sell him today, but that could change. I will keep your offer in mind. Come along, boy," he summoned.

Monroe dusted off his knees, then followed us out of the stables trailing a few feet behind, the way a boy would walk behind his master. When we arrived at the carriage, Hamp helped us in, and then Monroe climbed into the carriage box alongside him. Betty appeared carrying two baskets. She handed one to Hamp and the other to me.

"Miss Polly wish you a safe journey."

"Please pass on my appreciation."

Hamp clicked his tongue, and the horses pulled away.

Relieved to have Monroe back, I still worried over what he'd endured on that plantation. I wished I could hold him in the carriage with me and rock away his confusion but babying him would not help his situation. By the time we reached the jail, the sun had slumped down behind the buildings and the journey had provided me with a clearer look at our future.

When we came to a rest in the courtyard, the Jailer lifted my hand to his mouth and eyed me. "Consider this a fresh start. No more middle-of-the-night missions. If you disobey me again, I will sell that boy to the highest bidder."

"Thank you for showing him favor," I responded, not for one second doubting the validity of his words. But I also knew that I would not honor his request.

CHAPTER 37

Come by Here, My Lord

*W*ith all the commotion of Essex's arrival, we had stopped attending church service. I missed the cool breeze of our walks, the soulful singing of the choir, the pastor's heartfelt sermon, and the belief that Jesus could make everything all right. When Sunday rolled around, I insisted that we attend. The Jailer permitted me to take all the girls except for Birdie. One of his children always had to stay behind, along with Monroe, as insurance we would return. Sissy stayed in the big house with Birdie and her son, Daniel. Abbie, Elsie, and Hamp, the new driver, accompanied us.

My daughters loved the production of preparing for church, picking out pretty dresses and having their hair curled at the ends. As soon as we walked through the double doors of the sanctuary, they found their place in the front of the children's section with the other girls and boys of distinguished families and honored guests.

Three rows from the back, on the women's side of the church, I spotted Corrina Hinton sitting alone. I removed my gloves and took a seat next to her. The organ started up and the choir sang "Come by Here."

"Good day."

"Pheby, so nice to see you." She swayed.

"Feels good to be back. Needed something to help restore my faith."

"Trying times," she sang, keeping in step with the choir.

I sang back, "He sold July."

We both kept our heads facing forward, but she reached for my hand and patted it.

"Life here ebbs and flows. There will be rough patches but you must stay strong."

"Corrina, I need your help."

"Whatever I can do."

The choir finished and the crowd shouted in unison, "Praise the Lord! Amen! Glory be!"

Once the cries began to die, Pastor Ryland walked into the pulpit and gave his welcome address.

Corrina dabbed her handkerchief at the corners of her mouth while whispering, "Ears watch and eyes listen here. Meet me inside the bakery on market day."

I nodded.

"Tell the woman with the cleft chin that you are meeting me."

My hand covered hers, and then I turned my attention to the gospel.

◆

On Wednesday I went to the market. I put in my weekly order at Thalhimer's Dry Goods and went to Hilda's competitor on Franklin Street to order ready-made dresses. When I had completed all the tasks on my list, I meandered to the bakery. I loved that I could taste cinnamon and nutmeg in the air. A woman with a cleft chin served behind the counter. There were two white customers in line ahead of me, and after she aided them, I whispered that I was meeting Corrina. She did not raise her eyes, but handed me a swirl pastry and pointed to the seat away from the window. I ate slowly and waited. After about ten minutes, a little girl around Hester's age came to wipe my table. When she finished, she motioned with her shoulder for me to follow her.

We walked behind the counter, through the kitchen, and down steep, narrow stairs. The place smelled of dust and cement. We turned into the tunnel on the right. Since we carried no light, I touched the chalky wall with my left hand so as not to lose my balance. At the end of the tunnel sat a small table with a candle burning. Corrina sat there with a notebook and a teacup.

"Sorry I do not have a second cup to offer you."

I dropped into the seat opposite her. The girl disappeared the same way she came. When I felt sure we were alone, I muttered, "Thank you for this."

"I have not done anything yet."

I took a deep breath and told Corrina everything, from my life on the plantation, the promise of my freedom, my love for Essex, being sold on the day of my mama's funeral, and giving birth to Essex's child to the anguish of the Jailer selling July because of me.

"It is only a matter of time before he sells Monroe. I need to get him out of here."

"By himself?"

"And Essex."

Her eyes opened wide. "How would you get them off the property? I am sure they are under lock and key."

"I am working on that now."

"They will need money."

"I have it."

She sipped. "Rubin Lapier is feared. You know they have nicknamed him Bully behind his back?"

"Yes, I have heard."

"Let me see what the friends can do."

"Thank you, Corrina."

"Do not thank me yet. Your request will not prove easy."

◆

I had no opportunity to see Essex, because the Jailer had me playing in the tavern with him until he closed for the night, then insisted that I sleep in his bed. His way of keeping an eye on me. The only time I could visit Monroe was at first light, before the Jailer roused for his day. When I left the big house to find him, the girls were still nestled in their beds but the guards were all at their posts. A coolness followed me as I trekked over to the stables, carrying apples and pears to sustain the boys through the labor of their day. When I reached the stall, Monroe had already headed to the well to draw water, and Tommy was sweeping the stables and stacking hay.

"I need to talk to you," I whispered, looking over my shoulder. Tommy led me to a corner in the back of the stables. I pulled his ear to my mouth and whispered directions.

"You sure, Missus?" I could not mistake the terror in his eyes.

"I do not want any of you to end up like July."

At the mention of her name he started to weep. "My sister."

I never knew. I pulled him to my breasts and rocked him. He stood stiff in my arms, unaccustomed to affection.

"Listen to me and do what I say. I will reward you. It is my promise."

As I left the stables, I spotted Monroe carrying water up to the kitchen house. I watched as my son balanced a strip of wood with metal buckets hanging from each side. Backbreaking work for such a young child. When I was his age, I was learning to play piano, how to add, and to read simple books like *Little Boy Blue*. On my way to the shed, I glanced up toward the garret room where Essex resided and prayed under my breath for God's guidance. A full week had passed since I'd seen Essex last, and I did not want him to lose faith.

◆

The next Sunday I prepared the girls for church. This week Tommy put on a clean white shirt and attended with us. Abbie stayed back with Birdie, and Hamp remained at the jail to clean and repair the wagon. Sissy held the younger girls' hands and Hester walked beside Elsie. Tommy and I were side by side; he slowed down a bit and uttered between his lips, "I figured it out, Missus. Take a few more days."

"Good. No one is to know."

"I real careful."

When we arrived at First African Baptist, I quickened my pace and walked up the stone steps. The greeters bid us all good morning and then we entered and found our places. Elsie and Sissy liked to sit as close to the pulpit as possible, as if the word of God could only be found in the front few pews. Corrina sat in her same pew, and I took a seat beside her. While singing the hymns, we talked to each other.

"The friends are afraid. Moving the fugitive is too dangerous. We can help with your son."

"It has to be both or he will die."

Corrina folded her hands gently in her lap.

"Please. I can pay more."

She sang on, "I am so sorry."

CHAPTER 38

Grounded

I did not know what had spooked Corrina, but I had too much at stake to give up now. There had to be another route. I laid in bed next to the Jailer, waiting for him to fall into his deep sleep. Once his breathing changed, I crept from his bed and walked down the hall to my room. I pulled up my floorboard, retrieved a slip of stationery, and crafted a letter. After the ink dried, I folded it in half, took coins from my stash, and slipped down the back stairs. Abbie's room was a few inches bigger than the closet that Missus Delphina had made me sleep in back at the Bell plantation, and her door stayed slightly ajar.

"Abbie," I hummed.

Her eyes fluttered. I put my fingers to my mouth and crawled inside next to her, though there was hardly enough room for the both of us. I pushed her headscarf up over her ear. "I need a favor."

She nodded.

I whispered my instructions. Her eyes went big, but then she bit her bottom lip and quivered.

"It is the only way." I pressed the letter and the coins into her hand. "The woman with the cleft chin."

She nodded her head.

I slipped out and then returned to the Jailer's room. When I pushed the door open, he sat bare chested and wide-awake. His eyes sliced into me.

"Where have you been?"

"I went to relieve myself."

"I do not trust you."

"I am wearing my dressing gown," I said softly.

My feet carried me toward the bed and he reached over and grabbed my arm roughly, pinning me against the mattress.

"Is it that nigger again?"

"It is indecent for me to use your chamber pot."

He climbed on top of me and held my thighs in place with his knees. "What is it about him that makes you disobey me?"

"You are hurting me."

He bared his teeth. "You stay on the premises from here on out. No market and no more church."

Then, to my relief, he let me go.

The next morning, I rubbed balm on my bruises and then hid them under a sweater. The girls barged into my room as I slipped into my shoes. Abbie entered behind them.

"Missus, you wearing that?" she said, referring to my simple work dress.

"How come we cannot go to the market?" pouted Joan.

"Papa prefers that you mostly leave the half acre with him. For your protection."

I raised my eyebrow at Abbie. "I have sewing to do, so you will go to the market alone."

Hester pulled my arm. "Protection from what?"

"There is ugliness in the world that beautiful, smart girls like you have no business being around."

"I am brave," said Joan.

"That you are." I leaned down into their little faces. "You be good for Sissy today and Abbie will bring you back a delicious treat from the bakery. How's that?"

All three ivory faces smiled up at me.

When we got downstairs, Sissy came through the side door.

"Mornin' Missus."

"Sissy."

"Come along, girls." She took them to the drawing room.

Abbie dragged herself into the dining room and cleared the Jailer's dishes from the table. Her hip knocked against a saucer; it fell to the floor and shattered. I bent to help her. We were both on our knees when I caught her pinched expression.

"It will be okay."

"Missus, I's scared. You ain't been whipped before."

"We must be strong."

"Marse sold July." Her eyes shifted, wild with fear. "God only know what happened to that girl."

I grabbed her hands to steady them. "You can do this. We must or he will die."

"I's want freedom too. Promise me." She lifted her eyes.

Abbie had never asked for anything. Always did what she was told. "I promise."

Abbie pulled herself together and I followed her out into the courtyard. The sun beamed down so brightly I pulled my bonnet lower over my face to protect my eyes from the glare. The same two men were always stationed at the gate. They asked Abbie for her pass every week, even though going to the market on Wednesday was the routine. She produced the paper and disappeared beyond the wall.

I passed by the stables on my way to the shed. Monroe stood holding a shovel in his hand but stared out into the bushes. Being away from us on that plantation had changed him. I'd thought giving him time alone would help him snap out of it, but he continued to be withdrawn.

"Son."

"Morning." He glanced at me, then picked up the shovel.

"You all right?"

"Yes, ma'am."

"Baby, what was it like working on that plantation?"

His face went dark and his shoulders shrank. "It be well as 'spected."

"Expected. People will judge you on the way that you speak."

He backed away from me. "Silver-head man did not like me speaking like white folk. Showed me a man with his cheek gone and told me to watch my uppity ways."

My teeth gnawed at the inside of my jaw. "You are not a slave."

"I am, Mama."

"In name only, son. Not in your mind. Never in your mind."

"I am a slave. No more pretendin'."

"Monroe."

He covered his ears. I grabbed his arms and spun him.

"Look at me."

He drew his eyes up.

"You are the great-grandson of Vinnie Brown, who was the grand-daughter of a Mandara queen before she was stolen off her land. Your grandmother was Ruth Brown, healer and medicine woman of the Bell plantation. Your blood runs deep." I reached for his chin, but he pulled away. "What of my father?" My mouth gaped open. He had never asked before.

"Who is he? Know it ain't Marse, 'cause he hates me."

I did not know if I should tell him the truth or not. Just saying the words out loud could put them both in danger.

"He was a good man. Who loved me and would have loved you. Now, focus on being a good helper."

"Now that July been sold, I gotta feeling I's next, Mama. Ain't nuttin' you can do to stop it either."

"Nothing."

"Nuttin'. Ain't gettin' my face cut up," he spat. Tommy returned.

"Monty, Hamp needin' us to help unload the wagon. Wood just arrived."

Monroe wiped his face on his shirt and followed Tommy out. I stood there and prayed.

Dear Lord, I come boldly asking for Your divine safety and protection of my plan. Lord, I commit all things in Your hands.

Guide us to what you have promised, Lord. Amen.

CHAPTER 39

Sick and Tired

I stood next to the spigot behind the kitchen house while three girls cleaned off. One ran a little water through her hair while the other two washed their faces and hands. Elsie shuffled down the steps of the kitchen house, shifting the pot of fresh corn in her arms.

"Missus, the fugitive ain't eatin' nothin' I take. Smell worse 'n the jail. Conditions too much for him."

The shortest of the three girls ran water over her muddy feet, while the other two stood waiting. I wrung my hands, unsure of what to do. The Jailer still had me under lock and key. It had been weeks since I had snuck out to visit Essex. Twice I had tried, and both times I'd had to turn around because of the guards.

I motioned for the girls to follow me back to the sewing shed. My helper, Janice, had been returned to her master, so the responsibility of preparing the fancy girls fell again solely on me. I dressed the three ladies, collected their stories, prayed over them, and then released them to Clarence.

That evening, as I played the piano in the tavern the Jailer entertained two guests. Sissy had just served him his fourth drink and he seemed on the cusp of being inebriated. The two men who sat with him stood, shook his hand, and exited. Sissy cleared their glasses from the table and made her way to the bar. He gulped and then belched. I sauntered over to him and drew my finger along the back of his ear.

"Have a good night, love?" I took a seat across from him without waiting for permission.

"Those two men are looking to buy for a planter in Chesapeake."

"Might be a good opportunity to get rid of the fugitive."

"Eh?" He sucked on a chicken bone.

"Buck like that could be worth seven, eight hundred dollars. Unlike you to leave money on the table."

His eyes took me in. The one thing I could count on when it came to the Jailer was his hunger to consume, whether it be alcohol, food, women, money, power.

"You counting my purse?"

"Just thinking of the girls. We could use the money to take them on holiday to Philadelphia, like you promised them. Start looking into a school for Hester." I moved into his lap and stroked his ear again.

He squeezed me. "My sweet Pheby, smarter than most."

I pushed his hair away from his face. "Elsie said he stopped eating. Cannot make money off a sickly nigger." I leaned in and kissed him. His hands immediately moved down to my backside. "Clarence should go take a look."

The Jailer put his lips on mine. When he kissed me, it felt uncivilized. Then he pulled back and sighed.

"Clarence, go check on the fugitive. Make sure the nigger is still breathing. Sissy, bring me another drink."

I moved from his lap and he slapped me on the rump.

"Care for another song?" Before he could answer, I took my place and played something soft for his ears.

Clarence returned with his hands over his mouth. "Mr. Lapier. The fugitive barely breathing. Think we better move him. It is extremely hot up there."

The Jailer's green eyes revealed that he was not in the mood to deal with the matter. "Move him to the viewing room. I am not fetching a doctor. Pheby, go with him."

I cast my eyes down to the floor.

"And keep a close watch on my wench, Clarence. She got a soft spot for niggers." He belched. "Especially that one."

Sissy stood by his side and topped off his drink. He put his hand on her hip and seemed to forget about me for the moment. I stopped in the shed for my medicine bag and then followed Clarence up to the garret room. The stench reeked fouler than before. I choked, then coughed.

When I held up the lantern, I startled an army of white maggots that were marching under his head and over to the feces in the corner. In the middle of the floor, Essex curled in a ball. The clothing I had stitched for him dripped in filth. Insects nipped at his ankles and feet. He did not swat them away.

"Unshackle him so that he can walk."

"No."

"Then you must be prepared to carry him in all his waste."

I flashed the light on Essex's infection and soiled spots. Clarence removed the key from his pocket and unclasped his foot fetters, then the chains on his wrists. We each lent Essex a hand and pulled him to his feet. He lurched, unsteady, and then found his footing.

"Hold this." I thrust the lantern at Clarence and took a small broom from my bag and dusted the bugs away.

"Move it," Clarence commanded.

Essex tried obeying orders, but his knees wobbled and he collapsed toward the floor. Clarence reached out and caught him before his head hit the wall. With one arm on Essex's waist, he half dragged him down the steps. I led the way to the side door of the tavern. The Jailer's hearty laugh reached my ears as I opened the door to the viewing room. It was nothing more than a closet used for buyers to sexually sample their female slaves prior to purchasing them. The space held a single chair and an old blanket, which I opened and placed on the floor. Clarence let Essex drift to it.

First I rubbed his clothing down with a basil, lemon, and vinegar oil mixture to kill the insects and any eggs that had nested on him. Then I brushed at him again, dusting the oil through his hair and overgrown beard.

"He needs a bath."

"Just give him the medicine so we can be on our way," Clarence replied from the chair. He looked bored and could not stop wiping his hands on his pants.

I tipped the brown jar to Essex's lips. He looked me in the eye but had the good sense not to say my name.

"He needs food."

"Fetch it."

I eased Essex's head down and then rose to my feet. In the kitchen house, I spooned broth into a cup and took a piece of bread. When I returned, Clarence was chewing on his cuticles while I fed Essex. I placed a small dish with an onion by his head in hopes that it would draw out the fever, then covered him with the remaining edge of the blanket.

Clarence moved to reattach the shackles.

"The man can barely stand, let alone run. Give him the night to heal. There are no windows in here. Lock the door."

Clarence thought about it for a second, and then walked out of the room.

◆

Fridays tended to be the busiest day for moving fancy girls. Well before dawn I went to the shed, took inventory, and made sure we were prepared for the day. I thought I was the only one moving before the rooster crowed, and nearly let loose my bladder when Elsie walked through the door carrying a pile of burlap shirts.

"Just been over moppin' out the tavern. Fugitive ain't keep down none of him food. Don't look like his fever break neither."

"Anyone over there?"

She shook her head. "He asked for you."

I ran my fingers over my dress. "What did he say?"

"Where the yella wife wit' the medicine."

My stomach quieted down. He had not betrayed our connection. Elsie placed the laundered shirts on the table and then headed out of the shed. Instead of carrying my whole medicine bag to Essex, I thought it best to hide a few things in my pockets. The brown jar; a balm I'd made with black elder, peppermint, and ginger for when the girls came down with fever; sliced onion; and some bread. I knew his feet were still swollen, so I tucked a piece of white willow bark in my pocket and made my way.

When I opened the door, Essex was tossing around on the floor, moaning. I rushed to his side.

"It is the yellow wife."

He smiled through his pain.

"Clever."

"Knew that if I called you by name, it would give away my affection for you." His eyes were teary.

"You are going to be okay." I took the balm and rubbed it across his forehead, over his chest, under his arms, and into the soles of his feet.

"Drink this." I tipped the jar. Then sprinkled turmeric on his tongue. "This should help with the swelling."

"The letter."

"Shh. I am taking care of everything. You rest and get your strength up."

He squeezed my hand and I kissed his forehead. "Do not ask for me again. Just be ready when I come."

CHAPTER 40

Fattened for Slaughter

The Virginia State Fair was a good sign that autumn had arrived in Richmond. Families came from both near and far for the excitement of horse races, taste of fresh-squeezed lemonade, and games with prizes for the children. Farmers competed for the biggest grown watermelon, and mistresses showed off their cooks' flaky-crusted pies. New crop machinery and agricultural equipment were on display, along with stalls of the latest fashions for women. In the very back of the fair was the saloon, where cordials flowed and cigars were smoked, and the highest quality of slaves were available for purchase. It was from eavesdropping in the tavern that I learned that the Jailer had come to his senses and planned to sell Essex on opening night, just a week away.

To prepare Essex for the sale, the Jailer had let him remain in the room at the back of the tavern where the temperature stayed cooler. Elsie's job was to beef him up by serving him three meals per day, instead of the one meal of spoiled mush that had been left for him when he was in the garret room. The Jailer had me make him root tea to restore his strength, but Elsie administered my healings. Aside from the night he had been moved to the viewing room, and the morning I crept to him, contact with him remained forbidden. I still had not been permitted to go to the market with Abbie. My only reprieve was church on Sundays, which he did begin to permit.

With the approach of the state fair, business had picked up, and the Jailer insisted that I spend every waking hour in the shed preparing girl after girl for sale. Sissy worked around the clock managing his guests at the tavern, while Abbie managed the shopping and the house. With the lot of us so busy, I convinced the Jailer to let the girls stay at Grace Marshall's home for the week so that we could prepare for the fair with no distractions. Since the girls adored their tutor, he agreed.

On the eve of opening night, the Jailer had his colleagues over for a pre-fair celebration. I entertained for what felt like hours before the group was intoxicated enough to disperse. When the Jailer and I reached the house, his eyes were bloodshot and glassy. He pulled at my dress, and his rough hands fumbled beneath for my bloomers.

"Not in here, what if Abbie comes?"

My words fell on deaf ears. He held my waist and took me against the piano, breathing hard and moaning into my neck. When he was finished, he slapped my rear end.

"You never disappoint."

Humiliated even with no witnesses, I fumbled with my skirts. The Jailer leaned his weight on the piano, his trousers still around his knees. "Do you love me?"

My fingers went to the pins in my hair.

"Of course I do, honey."

"Say it." He suddenly appeared sober and solemn. "Say that you love me."

I reached for his hands and looked into his eyes. "I love you, and the life you have made for our family."

He smiled.

"Nightcap?"

"That would be lovely."

I went to the drink cart and poured him a liberal shot, slipping in the sleep aid that I had concealed in my sleeve.

"Let us go up. Big day tomorrow."

He gulped down his drink and staggered up the stairs. In his bedroom, I helped him out of his clothing and tucked him into bed.

"Where are you going?" He grabbed my wrist.

"For my sleeping gown. I will return directly." I kissed his cheek.

In my bedroom, I stood by the door and waited. Ten whole minutes passed, and then I heard him breathe heavily. Quick and quiet, I crept down the stairs. Abbie stood at the back door with a small satchel strapped across her shoulders. Her look was no longer skittish but stern. She was still small in stature, but her spirit had grown in the past few weeks of concealing our secrets. She looked ready.

"You know what to do?"

She nodded and hobbled out the back door, dragging her lame foot behind her. I crept over to the stables. Monroe was asleep on a pile of hay and I had to nudge him, then cover his mouth with my hand to keep him from calling out.

"No time to waste, stay silent at all cost. Move."

Tommy popped his head up. "Me too," he pleaded.

I did not have plans for him.

"Please, Miss Pheby. He will kill me when he knows I aided you."

I motioned for him to follow, feeling protective over him, like I was his mother too. Abbie was behind the stables holding the kerosene lantern. She motioned to the boys to spread out the hay so that she could start the fire.

"I will meet you at the spot," I mouthed, then lifted my skirts and rushed over to the tavern. When I entered, I listened for movement. There was no sound, and I hoped that the girl I had paid to keep Clarence distracted was doing her job. The key to the viewing room was hanging on the hook. When I unlatched the door, Essex sat upright in the chair and smiled at me. It was the same grin he had given me when I had snuck into the stables to meet him back home, and it made my throat catch. The steady meals had done him good. His color had returned, and just that morning Tommy had shaved him and cut his hair to prepare him for sale. But I had other plans.

"Hurry."

He grabbed my face and kissed me. If his life had not been on the line, his lips could have undone my resolve. I pulled away, breathless, and ushered him out of the small room. On our way out, I grabbed the hat that I had stashed by the piano along with a waistcoat and shoes. Both were too big but I told Essex to slip them on. Because of the public flogging and the newspapers, folks knew what Essex looked like. He would need a disguise if we were going to get him out of Richmond undetected.

Adrenaline coursed through me so quickly that it was hard to think. From my pocket, I pulled a pair of reading spectacles, a fishing knife, and a small purse.

"Fasten these to the inside pocket of your trousers."

When we got outside, a fire of hay, papers, and debris was kicking up a fuss. I led Essex past the stables and around to the back entrance of the jail. I tied a white scarf around my mouth and nose to protect my stomach from the smell of decaying flesh. It had been months since the guards buried those who died in the jail, and bodies were everywhere. We had to step and then climb over a pile of corpses to reach Abbie and the boys along the back gate.

For the past few weeks, Abbie and Tommy had come out at night and pried at a hole in a weak link in the fence. They had dug out the dirt below and hidden their work by covering the spot with rubbish. We moved the garbage and wood planks aside. The boys and Abbie crawled through. Essex had broad shoulders and I could see them getting stuck.

He had read my mind, and at once Essex started pulling and kicked at the fence. Tommy and Monroe removed more dirt until the space widened so that Essex could slither through. We heard the dogs barking in the distance; then Clarence's voice shouted out, "Hamp, fire! All hands on deck."

"Move!"

We were all on the street side, but already I could hear the alarm go off, signaling to the neighbors that help was needed with a fire. Soon they would all be storming to the jail with buckets of water and slabs of wood to help beat back the blaze.

"This way," I ordered, but Abbie hobbled next to me and yanked me to the left.

"Faster way."

We ran, and I had my hand around Abbie's to help her limp quicker. Halfway down the road, I realized it was the same route that I had taken seven years ago when I arrived in Richmond. We had to cross the open area of the Mayo Bridge; there was no other way to make it to the river. But there was no cover. We would be exposed in the open space. Running would draw attention to us, so I kept Monroe's hand in mine and walked as swiftly as possible. When we reached the lip of the bridge, I heard the rattling of chains, then a white man calling out orders. If the man saw us, he would question my intentions, and no doubt return us to the Jailer at gunpoint. The man was coming from the left, so we went right and planted ourselves behind the thickness of twin bushes.

We squatted down in the dirt until all fell quiet. When I felt sure that no one was around, we trekked down the well-worn dirt path toward the river, keeping to it until we came to another wide bush where we could take cover with the water view in front of us. I pulled Monroe to me.

"What is the plan?" Essex scooted closer to me.

"We need to wait for word."

The gravity of what we had just pulled off hit me all at once. The longer we waited, the more antsy I became. Where was the boat? Too much time had passed. Someone was bound to realize that we were gone.

"Abbie, you sure they are coming?"

"Certain."

I had had to rely solely on Abbie to make the arrangements through the bakery. I had not realized that Abbie had known the owner of the bakery since she was a girl, and after several notes from me to him, and pleading with Corrina at Sunday's church services, they had agreed to arrange for passage. Monroe's eyes found mine, big with worry. Getting my son to freedom had become my life's mission, and now that we were so close, it dawned on me that I might never see him again. I held him in my arms and prayed over his life and safety. I cradled his face in my hands and kissed his cheek.

"You might not understand it, but everything that I have done is because of my love for you. Always remember that."

Essex touched my shoulder, and that was when I realized what I had forgotten to do.

"Monty, this is your father, Essex Henry."

"The prisoner?"

"Yes."

"How do you do?" Monroe said formally. Essex pulled him to his chest. Then I heard a swish in the water.

"Wait here." I climbed down through the muck. My heart soared at the sight of the boat pulling toward the dock. I stood in the light of the moon and waved the white handkerchief as instructed. The captain slowed the vessel and dropped the anchor.

"Friend of a friend sent me."

"Cargo needs to move quick. You got the money?"

I whistled for the others to come out of hiding. Essex had Monroe's hand, and Tommy walked behind Abbie.

I handed the captain the last of the purse that I had been collecting and hiding over the years. "We have four."

"You arranged for three."

I took the pearl necklace from around my neck and passed it to him. "Please."

He looked at it and waved his hand for them to board. A tall black man was at the back of the boat and reached out his hand. Abbie was the first to step on, and when her hand touched his, she jumped into his arms. I peered closer. The man was Basil. He had returned for her. He waved and smiled at me.

I hugged Monroe again. "Go on, baby."

"Mama, you not coming?"

"I have to stay behind. But you, son, are meant to see freedom. Go with your father and live the life you have been promised. I will find you soon enough."

I had already sewn a pouch of protection inside his pants. Monroe's eyes filled with tears and he threw his arms around my waist again. I kissed the top of his head and then motioned for Tommy to take his hand. Basil hurried them both down below.

"I am not leaving without you again, Pheby." Essex's shoulders bunched around his ears, the way they did when he dug his heels in.

"You must."

"I can't. Not again."

The captain called down, "We have to go. Do they have their papers?"

I held them up for the captain to see, and then handed the pile to Essex. I wrote passes giving them passage to Baltimore. Essex folded them into his pocket. I removed the necklace he had made for me from around my neck and tied it around his.

"You have our son to consider, and I cannot abandon my daughters."

He shook his head. I kissed his lips.

"Someone has to stay behind and be the lamb."

"Last call!" shouted the captain.

"Please do not risk this second chance. Go. I have memorized your friend's address in Boston. I will find you again."

I did not wait for Essex to climb on board. Instead I turned and walked back up the worn path. My temples pulsed as I contemplated that I had yet again come close to freedom only to have the opportunity slip from my grasp. Still, for the sake of my son and daughters, I knew that this was the right choice. The one that Mama would have made for me.

I strolled back toward the Lapier jail as another coffle was led across the bridge. They came the same way I had come. The same way it would always be, until enough hearts had the courage to change. As long as there was breath, there was hope.

Epilogue

—— · ——

My beloved Hester,

I apologize, dear daughter, for the length of time it has taken me to reply.
You can imagine how harried our world has been since the end of the war
between the States. Richmond is unrecognizable. When the Confederate
commanders realized the war had been lost, they ordered soldiers to set fire
to our bridges, tobacco factories, and weapons caches, to deny them to the
federal troops. The fire quickly blazed out of control and countless people lost
their homes. The entire business district burned to the ground. However, the
gutting of the city could not dampen the jubilation of the people being set free.
If only my mother could have witnessed the emancipation with her own eyes.

The newly freed men, women, and children cheered on the Union
troops as they entered the city, and then paraded in their finest attire
down to the State Capitol to celebrate this most blessed victory. Oh, how I
wanted to march alongside them.

As I am sure you can imagine, the slaves' freedom caused distress and
chaos for most owners. Your father became desperate to keep his source of
wealth and tried to flee with a coffle of fifty people. When he got to Danville
depot he was denied entry onto an already crowded train heading south, and
was forced to free his captives on the spot. He never recovered from the loss.

And so, sweet daughter, it is with a heavy heart that I inform you
that your father passed away on October 25, 1866. Officially, he died of
an attack of cholera, which held on to him for ten days. Though I think
he died of heartbreak, as a result of the war. The Richmond Examiner
was very kind in his obituary, describing him as "an honest man." I have
included the clipping for you.

Darling, do you remember Reverend Nathaniel Colver, who would come down from Boston to speak at the Free African Church? He has returned to Richmond to establish a school to educate and train the freed men for the Baptist ministry. Your father, in his will, left the Lapier jail and what little remained of his fortune to me. And so I leased the property to Reverend Colver for three years. I needed to do something redemptive with the property where so many had suffered. The irons and cuffs from the floor have been removed and replaced with desks and chairs. The jail has shed its awful nickname Devil's Half Acre and is now called God's Half Acre. Praise be!

My dear Hester, always know that I am very proud of you and your sisters, and my heart is comforted by the fact that the three of you are safe in Massachusetts, getting the education my mother so longed for me to get and that I so wanted for myself, even if it entails you passing as white women to do so. Know that every decision that I have made has been for the betterment of my children, and I regret nothing. Remember you are free. Free to choose. Free to live. Free to love. And your freedom will be even more expansive if you continue in your new world without looking back. Your lineage of being born to a mulatto mother and a father who owned and operated a jail is of no consequence for the life you are living, so carry these secrets to your grave. Renaming you with my father's surname, Bell, will continue to provide distance, and I trust that you, Isabel, and Joan will do well because of it. Birdie, on the other hand, has declared that she will never join you in Massachusetts, never join you and your sisters in turning her back on her history. At ten years old, she has become quite active in teaching freed children how to read. Such a wise girl already with an incredible heart, she says it is her mission from God to educate those who have suffered under the irons of slavery. Even though she has not responded to any of your letters, please keep her in your prayers as she sets about to right the world.

My mother could not even imagine the life you are living, so please do not risk it with your sentiments. Burn this letter after you have read it. It is for your safety. You do not need proof of me for I am always in your heart.

With love and affection,
Pheby Delores Brown

February 2, 1874
Ipswich, Massachusetts

Dear Mother,

Thank you so much for sending the purse. My wedding was extraordinary and beautiful in every way. I kept to the story that you were much too ill to travel. It was a lovely day, and I wish that circumstances were different so that you could have experienced it with me, but I understand the gravity of what is at stake. My John is a fine husband, and has taken care of me in every way. There is nothing that I want for, and he is extremely kindhearted and generous. Isabel and Joan have grown into utter beauties, though Joan keeps reminding me that she wants to be known for her brains, not her beauty. She has become quite the writer and is teaching at a nearby school. Isabel is being courted by a very well-off lad in his final year of law school. They seem to be a suitable match, and every day we await his proposal.

I have enclosed my wedding announcement that ran in the newspaper. You will not believe this, but a few days after the announcement ran, I saw Monroe on the street. Yes, our Monty! We pretended to be strangers meeting at a vegetable stand. He managed to slip me a note asking me to meet him at a church on the edge of town the following morning. I went under the disguise of helping Joan with her students, and it warmed my heart to see him. Mother, you would not recognize him. Tall and extremely handsome. He told me things that I did not know. Even though we both grew up on the Half Acre, our experiences were very different, and I apologized for the beating I caused him over that silly hide-the-puppet game. Monroe, still good-natured, laughed it off. He has taken a wife and they have two children, Robert and Mary. Mother, I did not know that the fugitive, Essex Henry, who lived on top of the jail was Monroe's father and your great love. The secrets you keep! And I never knew that it was you who freed them all. What I do remember is you falling ill for weeks after the fire at the jail, and fearing you would not recover. It was because of our faithful prayers that your health was restored. Glory be!

Mother, I also regret to be the bearer of bad news, but according to Monroe, Essex Henry died in Canada of tuberculosis. Monroe said he only had a few years with his father, but they were good years. First in Ohio and then settling in St. Catharine's, Ontario, where Monroe resides now. Speaking of lost, I think of July every single day. Still no word from her?

Now that I have married and moved into my husband's home, I agree that our correspondences are even more dangerous. I have not taken your advice and burned your previous letters, as they are all I have of you. Like you with your mother's recipes, I will hide them, along with the extra purse, as you have instructed, for an emergency. I send all my love, and please tell Birdie that we miss her dearly. Even though she refuses to forgive us for living as white women, nor responds to our letters, we each pray for her daily. I wish she was not so stubborn about giving up her identity and joining us in Ipswich, but I do understand that it is her choice to remain by your side. Please know that you are both in my heart always, and that I pray for your good health and happiness daily. Isabel and Joan send their love.

Yours truly,
Mrs. Hester Francine Bell Dillingham

Author's Note

This book is a work of fiction and all the characters are from my imagination, intuition, and alignment with Spirit. It was inspired by the story of Mary Lumpkin and Lumpkin's jail in Richmond, Virginia. I first discovered Mary Lumpkin in the spring of 2016 by accident. My family had just moved to the Richmond area less than a year prior. Close family friends came for a visit, and in looking for an activity that both the kids and adults could enjoy, my husband suggested we take a walk along the Richmond Slave Trail. The trail, unveiled in 2011, had seventeen markers running nearly three miles from the Manchester Docks to Lumpkin's slave jail. We started along the James River, giving the children a chance to read the markers aloud. While listening to them read the marker for Lumpkin's jail, I found myself drawn to the story of Robert Lumpkin, who lived on a half acre of land with his wife and five children, where enslaved people were held, bought, beaten, and sold, in a complex that was said to reek of the most offensive odors. I live on three-fourths of an acre, and could not stop wondering what the conditions were like for his wife raising children. As we continued along the trail, I discovered that Robert Lumpkin's wife was a former slave named Mary. Knowing that interracial marriages were illegal in the 1800s, I assumed that Robert was black. My mind started racing. How could a black man be the biggest slave trader in Richmond?

The kids grew tired of walking along the river so we got back into the car and skipped ahead on the trail, driving to the original site of Lumpkin's jail and African burial ground. The energy around the jail was both eerie and surreal; I felt the presence of souls wanting their voices to be heard. It was like the ancestors had latched their spirits into my skin and followed me home. I spent the next three days reading everything I could find on the jail. I learned that Robert Lumpkin was, in fact, a white man and that Lumpkin's jail was a notorious holding pen and "breaking" center for more than three hundred thousand enslaved people from 1844 until 1865. Lumpkin was so well known for his cruelty to blacks that the jail was known as the Devil's Half Acre and he as the Bully Trader.

My curiosity led me to Anthony Burns, the most publicized prisoner ever detained at Lumpkin's jail, who had escaped from a plantation in Virginia to freedom in Boston. Burns was recaptured in 1854 under the federal Fugitive Slave Act and kept at Lumpkin's jail for 120 days, very similarly to the way I wrote it in the story. His one relief was a hymnal, secretly given to him by Lumpkin's slave concubine/wife, Mary, who had taken pity on Burns.

After stumbling upon this piece of history, I could not stop thinking about Mary. What was life like for her and her children? How did she live on the Half Acre, both witnessing and assisting in the business that profited from fellow enslaved people? Did she actually love Robert and adapt easily to being mistress of the property, or had she operated simply from a place of survival?

In my research, Mary was described as an enslaved mixed-race woman who had arrived at the jail as a child. She would birth five of Lumpkin's children. It was said that he treated her and her children as family. He formally emancipated Mary after the Civil War, married her, and sent two of their daughters to a finishing school in Ipswich, Massachusetts, where they passed for white. In Lumpkin's will, he left all of his property and money to his "yellow wife." She, in turn, leased the land to Dr. Nathaniel Colver, who used it as a seminary school for the freed slaves. This school would later become the historically black college Virginia Union University.

Online, I scoured plantation ledgers for the names that I used in the book as my way of paying homage to the ancestors. I also used real people who were operating in the slave trade in Richmond during that time, including Silas Omohundro, Hector Davis, and David Pulliam, who were all major in the Richmond slave trade along with their mulatto wives, Helen, Anne, and of course Corrina Hinton, who dazzled me with her beauty, charm, and head for business from the start of my research.

I studied pictures on websites and visited several plantations, including Green Hill plantation, Greenway plantation, Shirley plantation,

Prestwould plantation, and Burroughs plantation in Virginia. I read several books in preparation for writing *Yellow Wife*, including *Money over Mastery, Family over Freedom* by Calvin Schermerhorn; *Back of the Big House* by John Michael Vlach; *Incidents in the Life of a Slave Girl* by Harriet Jacobs; *Within the Plantation Household: Black and White Women of the Old South* by Elizabeth Fox-Genovese; *A History of the Richmond's Theological Seminary, with Reminiscences of Thirty Years' Work Among the Colored People of the South* by Charles Henry Corey; *Narrative of the Life of Frederick Douglass: An American Slave* by Frederick Douglass; *Fifty Years in Chains, or, The Life of an American Slave* by Charles Ball, which lent me the whipping scene of Essex with the hot pepper bath and the recounting of the fancy girl telling Pheby about "the punishment of the pump." I also read *The Known World* by Edward P. Jones; *Slaves Waiting for Sale: Abolitionist Art and the American Slave Trade* by Maurie D. McInnis; *The Richmond Slave Trade: The Economic Backbone of the Old Dominion* by Jack Trammell and Alphine W. Jefferson; and many online periodicals.

Acknowledgments

It is by the Grace of God that I moved to Virginia on His word and discovered the story of Mary Lumpkin. I am grateful for every step of this journey. Imani, Monique, Kaya, and Xola Moody, thank you for embarking upon the Richmond Slave Trail with us where the nugget of this story was planted. To my lovely family and friends, I appreciate you all. My father, Tyrone Murray, for reading every page with gusto and pride. My mother, Nancy Murray, for your unwavering love, and Francine Murray for your support. My wonderful in-laws, Paula Johnson, Glenn Johnson Sr., and Pacita Perera for lovingly cheering me on. My favorite sibs: Tauja, Nadiyah, and Talib Murray for always having my back, and my cousin Elisa Garbett for sharing Vinnie Brown with me along with our family tree. To all the Belles, with a special thanks to Claudia and Anne for being my guiding light, and Ashkira for allowing me to return the favor. To my early readers who urged me to keep writing this story: Mary Patterson of the Little Bookshop; Robin Farmer, Samantha Willis, and Toni Bonita. To Kimbilio and all my fellows. All the book clubs and readers who still love good fiction and spread the word for authors like me.

My A-team: Wendy Sherman for never giving up on me, and Cherise Fisher for being my backbone. I could not imagine writing without you. Editor extraordinaire Dawn Davis: I'm in awe of your magic and working with you has been a dream come true. Thanks also to the wonderful team at Simon & Schuster for having my best interest at heart: Leila Siddiqui, Brianna Scharfenberg, Carly Loman, Chelcee Johns, Lashanda Anakwah, Chonise Bass—you remind me of a younger me, and to everyone who has worked tirelessly behind the scenes to lift this book up. Shelby Sinclair, thanks for your keen eye and vast knowledge of our history. My children, Miles, Zora, and Lena Johnson: everything I do is for you. And my beloved husband, Glenn, who on that beautiful fall day pushed me to visualize my machine, and here we are. Thank you for being my rock, and my first pair of ears when my novels are just a sensation in my gut. After twenty-five years, we are just getting started.

Lastly, but certainly not least, thank you, dear reader, for picking up this novel and trusting me to feed your soul with what I hope is a good story. Your unwavering support fuels me to show up on the page.

About the Author

Sadeqa Johnson is the award-winning author of four novels. Her accolades include the National Book Club Award, the Phillis Wheatley Book Award, and the USA Best Book Award for Best Fiction. She is a Kimbilio Fellow, former board member of the James River Writers, and a Tall Poppy Writer. Originally from Philadelphia, she currently lives near Richmond, Virginia, with her husband and three children.